Witches Get Stuff Done

MOLLY HARPER

sourcebooks
casablanca

Published by Sourcebooks Casablanca, an imprint of Sourcebooks
P.O. Box 4410, Naperville, Illinois 60567-4410
(630) 961-3900
sourcebooks.com

Originally published in 2022 as an audiobook by Audible Originals.

Cataloging-in-Publication data is on file with the Library of Congress.

Printed and bound in the United States of America.
VP 11 10 9 8 7 6 5 4 3 2

To my family, you're my magic.

Chapter 1
Riley

RILEY EVERETT WISHED SHE HAD the internal fortitude to admire Starfall Point as it rose in the watery distance. Unfortunately, she'd thrown up everything in her body over the rail of the island's midmorning ferry. She had no fortitude left, internal or external.

The Loyal Retriever cut through the choppy blue waters of Lake Huron with a surgical grace that should have been reassuring. Instead, Riley was anxiety-sweating through the newly purchased cargo jacket necessary to protect her from the brisk early May wind.

Brisk. Wind. In. *May.*

Her Floridian brain simply couldn't comprehend those words being strung together.

Maybe it was only brisk to Riley? Maybe she was cold because she was used to the soul-melting heat of Orlando? Maybe it didn't matter because she felt like she was going to throw up again.

Wisps from her chin-length cap of dark gold hair clung to her clammy cheeks as her stomach attempted to turn itself inside out like a possessed balloon animal. And the worst part was there was nowhere to hide. She'd dashed for the ferry's bathrooms just after the *Retriever* left the dock, only to find one marked with an OUT OF ORDER sign and the other locked tight. She'd had to hang over the railing to be sick, much to the gleeful horror of the school group standing nearby.

It might have been easier if she'd been able to sit inside, away from the sight of the churning waves, but all the seats inside the ferry cabin were taken by semi-elderly tourists in some sort of discount group. It seemed early in the season to brave the chill and the wind, even if the island was considered one of the most picturesque spots in Michigan. She supposed that's why there was a discount.

Riley was left to sit on a peeling blue bench built into the exterior of the main cabin, which seemed to magnify every pitch and roll of the boat by the power of ten. And it was very difficult not to resent the group of eight-to-ten-year-olds standing at what Riley considered to be an ill-advised distance from the railing in their bright yellow Sunnyside Day Camp windbreakers. They were whooping and screaming with every dip of the hull like they were riding some epic roller coaster headed straight to Hades. Oh, to be young and not have the taste of regurgitated breakfast burrito coating one's mouth.

"Is she gonna do it again?" one kid asked, shoving handfuls of rainbow fruit snacks in his face. His obvious half-agonizing, half-hopeful state, made Riley think of untold Jane Austen adaptations involving evil zombie children.

"It's another ten minutes to the island. I'll bet she'll go one more time, at least," the boy's little buddy, all ferret features and spiky auburn hair, said as he eyed Riley intently.

Were all "up north" kids so morbidly interested in public pukers, or was Riley a special case?

She had never been this nauseated in all her thirty-three years. Hell, she'd worked as a cocktail waitress on a half-derelict cruise ship during the hurricane-plagued off-season and had never been this sick. Maybe her motion sickness was lake-specific? Or could her "boat anxiety" just be regular anxiety? She *was* traveling to meet her heretofore unknown, long-lost elderly aunt after a lifetime without any relatives besides her parents. Riley couldn't help but feel she was sailing into some sort of trap. Didn't half of the women featured on true crime podcasts end up murdered because they answered messages from strangers? Hell, she was pretty sure this was how a lot of 1970s horror movies started.

Maybe she should just forget this whole thing. She could open her phone for the first time all day and email her aunt, who hadn't responded to any of her messages in the previous few days, and tell her, "Sorry, I came down with a sudden case of 'not wanting to die in your clearly demon-based world domination plot,'" and run back to Florida like her ass was on fire. Elderly people rarely checked their emails, right? She could get as far as Tennessee before Aunt Nora figured out Riley had ditched her.

Of course, an abrupt turnaround would mean she'd have to get back on the boat almost immediately after landing on Starfall, and Riley wasn't sure she would survive that.

Much like her emotional state, the *Retriever* pitched wildly into the waves, throwing Riley's weight against the cabin wall. Her stomach gave another watery twist. Riley groaned, clapping her hand over her mouth.

A desperate and awful pressure rippled up her throat, like some sort of digestive earthquake. With the schoolkids milling around between Riley and the nearest trash can, she had no alternative but to run to the railing again. She wrapped her arms around the rust-roughened metal, lest she get thrown headfirst into the water while she gagged. The schoolkids' excited noises changed very quickly to a chorus of disgusted *"ew!"*s in stereo.

"She's gonna barf again!" Fruit Snacks yelled.

"Nope, she's thrown up so much that she can't throw up anymore!" Ferret Face hooted. "My uncle Max calls it the 'dry heaves.' Mom says that's why I'm not allowed to drink anything from his fridge."

Riley's realized Fruit Snacks was holding up his cell phone as if he was recording her. Oh, shit. She was going to end up on some sort of horrible "Best Boat Barf Fails" compilation video.

In a day filled with emotional punches to the chin, this was the final indignity.

Riley breathed deep and immediately regretted it as the smell of exhaust and dead-fish-slash-lake water filled her nostrils. Right. If she'd learned anything over the years, it was when to strategically retreat. Relinquishing her hold on the rail, Riley stumbled towards the little alcove containing the bathroom doors. She rattled the knob, which was still locked and immobile.

"Oh, come on!" she yelled, feeling her stomach lurch again. She banged her fist on the door, every impact with the sturdy metal biting her chilled skin. "There are *other people* out here who need the bathroom! *Wrap it up!*"

"Won't do you any good," a tall, willowy woman with a bright shock of strawberry-blond hair sighed to Riley's left. Hunkered against the OUT OF ORDER door, the redhead was dressed in a prim dove-gray suit that made her fair skin look slightly sallow and didn't quite look up to the task of protecting her from the cold. Riley was pretty certain there was a tinge of blue under the woman's work-appropriate nude lip gloss. Her eyes narrowed at the closed bathroom door. "I've been locked out of the bathroom for most of the ride, and the situation is too damn close to desperate." She flinched, as if she'd just heard the words coming out of her mouth. "Please, pardon my language. I'm Alice Seastairs."

"Riley Everett," she said, nodding to Alice, who seemed genuinely distressed by her use of a fairly minor curse word. To lower the social stakes, Riley offered, "My mom used to tell me that some people think that they're the center of the universe. And then she would rattle on about 'mainlander assholes' and end up ignoring me for the rest of the day."

Alice snorted and then blanched again, covering her mouth with a slim, elegant hand. Now that Riley had cursed at a higher level, she seemed to relax a bit. "Well, your mother sounds like an interesting person."

"She was," Riley nodded as she felt another prickle of cold sweat flush her cheeks. She groaned, leaning against the wall behind her. Though she wasn't looking up at Alice, Riley could pinpoint the moment that her new acquaintance started feeling sorry for her. Riley's mother, Ellen, had died a few months before. Riley touched on the subject so rarely that she hadn't quite grasped the art of not dropping it on people like that.

Hank Everett felt the loss of his beloved wife so deeply, he was rarely able to talk about her, not even with Riley. That was why his insistence that she accept Nora's invitation had shocked her—particularly after his response to Nora's message was, "Well, your mom always said she was an only child, and an orphan. But maybe you should look into it."

Riley had been living with Hank for *months*, helping him cope with the loss, and suddenly, he was strong enough—hell, *eager*—to send her away? Didn't most fathers make it their goal in life to keep their daughters off *Dateline*? Then again, maybe Hank thought Riley would use up all her questions and conversations about Ellen with this over-helpful stranger, and he would never have to relive those painful memories.

Leaning against the wall and bracing her hands on her knees, Riley felt Alice pat her shoulder. When a thrum of electric discomfort shot through her, ricocheting into her chest, she thought maybe it came from the act of discussing her mother with a stranger. She wondered what Ellen Everett would think of Riley traveling all the way to the Upper Peninsula of Michigan to meet her aunt Nora. Probably not much, considering Ellen had never told Riley that Nora or Starfall Point even existed. Maybe that was contributing to Riley's sense of unease? Knowing that her mother hadn't wanted her to know about this part of Ellen's life, her history?

Riley's relationship with her mother had always been distant, something she'd attributed to her parents having Riley later in life and not being used to her generation's insistent communication. Now, she wondered if Ellen just didn't trust her to handle the family history.

Could it really be so bad? Starfall Point had looked so

charming in the photos—aggressively quaint houses, fudge shops, and island-wide garden shows. Riley had found one website claiming the town had a negative crime rate, as in the good deeds done there outstripped the bad, but Riley couldn't confirm such a thing existed.

Riley realized she'd been silent for so long, Alice probably thought she was either going to throw up again or start crying. She wasn't sure which Alice would consider preferable. She looked up to find Alice holding out a can of ginger ale. "Try this. I don't normally take the ferry myself, so I never know how I'm going to handle the motion. I always get one at the dock, just in case... Not to be indelicate, but I didn't want to put more pressure on my bladder."

"Thanks," Riley sighed. Cracking it open, she drank down the cold, sugary bubbles and was grateful. She noticed Alice squirm in discomfort as Riley glugged down most of the can and realized the other woman was probably thinking of the inevitable consequences of consuming liquids.

"Hey, there are people out here, waiting!" Riley yelled, pounding her fist on the bathroom door again, her hand stinging at the repeated angry impact. But her bravado seemed to drop through the bottom of her stomach as the boat tipped over a particularly high swell. She braced her arm against the wall and clutched her middle. "Sorry, Alice, the bathroom hog seems impervious."

"Oh, I think I like you very much," Alice told her. "I also think I might be slightly afraid of you."

"That seems like a reasonable response," she whimpered in return.

"They say staring at the horizon helps," Alice told her gently. "Look, there's Starfall."

Slowly, Riley poked her head out of the alcove to see a coastal postcard come to life. Storybook houses formed a sort of wall at the front of the island's craggy stone hills with tiers of similar buildings rising behind them. Dabs of bold color dotted the houses' front porches in the form of hanging flower baskets. But her eye was drawn high on the point where Shaddow House stood, as if the rest of the island was meant to sit at its feet. The house where Aunt Nora had lived and worked for decades looked metastasized, like it was originally built as a quaint Victorian family home with a turret tower and rather theatrical front porch, then grew unbidden into its current disarray of random additions and chimneys. The robin's-egg-blue siding stood out from the pale grays and yellows typical of the other houses. The dreamy color seemed at odds with its somewhat ominous name.

For just a moment, a strange dark gray mist seemed to shroud the house between blinks of the eye. Riley shook her head, fluttering her eyelashes rapidly and downing the rest of her soda. Maybe she was sicker than she thought?

"I've lived here for most of my life, and I'll never get used to the way it just seems to rise out of the water like that," Alice sighed, smiling gently. "Like some friendly sea creature."

"Oh, you grew up here?" Another strange thrum bolted through Riley, a bit of sadness. She'd thought maybe Alice was an outsider too, and that they would both approach the island as strangers to it. But now she was alone again.

Alice nodded, her smile faltering a bit. "I moved here when

I was nine. I spent a lot of time roaming around unsupervised, until my grandparents decided it was time for me to work in the family antiques store. I probably know every inch of the island, except Shaddow House, of course. It's never been open to anyone, tourists or locals, for that matter. The family prefers their privacy. They don't want a bunch of fudgies traipsing through their rooms. And honestly, I can't blame them. Sorry, I tend to overshare when I feel that my internal organs are in danger of bursting."

Riley hummed in sympathy. She couldn't imagine what her aunt Nora did at Shaddow House if she wasn't organizing tours. Maybe she was something like an estate manager or a housekeeper? That seemed like a lot of work for a woman who was sixty-eight years old. Also, she was very curious as to what a "fudgie" could be, but she was afraid to ask.

Alice shrugged. "People tend to act like public places are disposable when they're on vacation. Or if they start to take a privilege for granted. Or if it's a day ending in Y."

For the first time in a while, Riley grinned. She hadn't connected with another person in so long; she didn't want this peculiar kinship to be over so soon. Maybe if she asked her aunt nicely, Riley could sneak Alice in on a special *private* tour of Shaddow House? But she didn't want to make any promises or set Alice up for disappointment. For all she knew, Aunt Nora was going to hand Riley a box of Ellen's old CDs and softball trophies, then boot her back onto the ferry.

And then Riley realized that she'd neglected to mention that she was Nora's niece, and now it felt like the moment had passed. It would be weird to bring it up now, right? After Alice had made comments about Riley's family, wouldn't that make Alice feel uncomfortable? Great. She used to be a lot better at this, the "talking to people" thing. Hell, she used to work as a telemarketer. People hated to talk to telemarketers, but somehow, she'd managed to make a living at it even while *she* hated it.

"Starfall Point, docking in five minutes," a cheerful recorded voice announced over the PA system. "Feel free to gather your belongings, but please don't stand near the gangways. You'll be enjoying our beautiful island before you know it. Thank you for choosing *The Loyal Retriever* on the Perkins Ferry Line, the *finest and oldest* family-run ferry service operating on Starfall Point."

"Maybe I can get off this boat without having to relieve myself off the side," Alice muttered, making Riley snort. She liked Alice's strangely formal way of speaking and wondered if it was a result of living on the island. She raised her hand to beat on the door, hollering again in Alice's defense, when suddenly, the door opened. A slumped form appeared in the doorway, and Riley's fist froze in midair.

All yelling stopped. Riley was stunned silent by what was possibly the most beautiful man she'd ever seen. He had black hair cut short around a long, angular face and eyes so dark blue, they rivaled the waters around them. His jawline was so ridiculously sharp, she was afraid to touch it—not that she thought he would be open to any such thing, anyway. But he was as pale as she was, possibly paler, with a sickly gray ring standing pale around his mouth.

"Could you please stop banging on the door?" he rasped, his lips going somehow even more ghostly.

In that moment, Riley was sorry, incredibly sorry for screaming at this man and harassing him while he suffered whatever
horrors were happening in that bathroom. This was something
beyond physical discomfort. This man was *in agony*. Having just
watched her father cycle through devastating loss, it was clear to
Riley that this man was going through *something*, and she was
only making it worse.

And then, Alice slipped past the man with discreet but urgent
speed. She closed the door behind her, reminding Riley of how
miserable she'd been for the past half hour, not to mention Alice's
bladder distress—which couldn't be healthy at any age. And true
to form, Riley got angry all over again.

"What is *wrong* with you!" Riley thundered, the effort making
her throat almost buckle. "Have you really been locked in there
this whole time? There are other people on this boat!"

The ferry pitched again, throwing her face into his wrinkled
gray suit coat. While he was rumpled, he smelled pleasantly of
smoky cedar and…old paper? The enveloping warmth of it made
her mouth water, but she'd always been weirdly content in used
bookstores. The man grasped her upper arms in his hands and
pushed her away gently. The ginger ale felt like it was boiling
in her belly, sickly sweet, and she could feel that awful pressure
building just under her chest.

"I have my reasons." His voice was almost as shaky as hers,
but she could hear the disdain in his voice. She'd heard it often
enough during her brief and regrettable engagement. Just thinking
about how that ended, the condescension, her own disappointment, the demands for Riley to "be reasonable" when she was the

one who had been wronged, made the burp bubble crawl painfully up her throat.

As it rose, she realized it wasn't just a burp bubble. Eyes wide, she bent at the waist and deposited half a can of ginger ale on his shiny black loafers. She barely registered his squawk of protest over the children's horrified and triumphant yells.

"I-I can't believe you did that," he stammered as she rose, his expression somewhere between shock and dismay. She wiped the back of her hand across her mouth, glaring right back. At this point, she was just glad she missed her own sensible red Keds by a mile.

"Maybe if you hadn't declared yourself king of the public toilet, I wouldn't have had to," she snapped back before swallowing thickly.

For a moment, he looked past her, terror glazing those dark blue eyes, and she was sorry all over again. This certainly wasn't the way she wanted to start her time on Starfall Point, a roaring vomit-monster who frightened schoolchildren. But then her stomach shuddered again, and her remorse was replaced with desperation. Fortunately, Alice had pulled the door open and ushered her into the restroom. Her elfin new friend even held Riley's hair back as she tossed up the remnants of the ginger ale.

When Riley finally emerged from the bathroom, with Alice supporting her elbow, the ferry had docked and the (unreasonably gorgeous) bathroom hog had disappeared. Even as she felt relief, she was oddly bereft. She had made the worst possible impression on that guy, and his shoes. Even though he had deserved it... Yeah, she wasn't sure how to finish that thought. She was caught between the urge to find him to apologize and the equivalent need to further defile his footwear.

The Loyal Retriever had docked between ferries that were nearly identical to itself, other than *The Ruby Slipper*, which was painted in a red theme to match its name, and *The Starshine II* with a paint job in a nearly eye-gouging shade of mustard. Riley assumed these were the other "newer" models of the family-owned line mentioned on the PA.

"Is someone coming to pick you up, Riley?" Alice asked.

Riley grimaced. She wasn't sure who was picking her up. When Aunt Nora had first contacted her by direct message, Riley ignored what she thought was a catfish. *Sure*, a long-lost relative her mother had never mentioned, luring her to a faraway and isolated location where no one would hear her scream for help, *blah blah blah*.

Eventually, Clark Graves messaged Riley, asking her to search for him online and call his law office, apparently understanding Riley's need for Google confirmation. Nora's longtime lawyer informed her that Aunt Nora's health had been failing for a while, and she was desperate to meet Ellen's child. Nora had only recently learned that her sister passed when she saw Ellen's obituary posted online. Riley didn't understand that. How had Ellen abandoned a sister who had missed her enough to regularly search for Ellen's name online? Then Clark had emailed her plane ticket and ferry information just as Riley was "let go" from her position at a social media marketing firm in Pensacola—if the phrase "let go" was sufficient to cover having your whimsical word art and carefully cultivated succulents tossed in a box and then tossed *after* you while you and three dozen of your cubicle colleagues were herded from the industrial park.

Contrary to what her ex said, Riley was not prone to impulsive decisions. After her firing, she had methodically packed her bag, actively avoiding her phone and the commiserating group texts and emails from her coworkers, believing she was doing the healthiest thing for her. When she'd stepped onto the ferry, it had felt like Riley was fated to return to her mother's hometown. Now, it was starting to feel like she was making a huge mistake.

Clark had promised to meet her at the dock for that afternoon's ferry. His picture hadn't been included on the site for Tanner, Moscovitz, and Graves, Attorneys at Law. And his social media presence was nonexistent—which, honestly, Riley understood. As a client, she wouldn't want her lawyer posting drunken selfies with his buddies.

But suddenly, a thought occurred to her. What if she and Clark didn't recognize each other? She looked just like everybody else on this boat, if a little greener. What if he didn't know her and she just walked past him on the dock? Would she have to lug her stuff all around the island trying to locate his office? Starfall didn't allow motor vehicles anywhere near the pristinely historical tourist areas like the Main Square. Also, she'd packed heavy, having no idea how to dress for weather other than hot and humid.

"Riley, do you have someone meeting you?" Alice asked again.

And then, an even worse thought occurred to her—what if she'd already met Clark? What if Clark *was* the bathroom hog? He could have taken the ferry for some sort of errand that day with plans to meet her on the dock. What if she'd vomited on the one person who could ease her arrival on Starfall Point?

"He's a family friend, sort of," Riley told Alice. "Clark Graves?"

"Oh, Clark? He's…a terribly nice fellow, but he's not here now," she said with a pause that left Riley wondering. Surely, Alice would have mentioned if Clark was the bathroom hog. So that was one potential error averted. Now, Riley could concentrate on her aunt Nora and her purpose for just a second, instead of worry and nausea.

Alice claimed one of Riley's larger duffle bags without asking. To Riley's shock, the slight woman didn't buckle under the weight. "He might be stuck at the office. I could take you there, but honestly, I think you need a bit of a pick-me-up before you meet any more strangers."

Riley's rational traveler limits quailed at the idea of going somewhere with Alice, whom for all she knew, was trying to recruit her to *another* pyramid scheme. But the idea of being able to clean up a little before facing her aunt was very appealing.

Riley's feet made contact with Starfall for the first time, sending a bolt of lightning sizzling through her system. She felt ill all over again, and it took all her concentration to stay upright and in control of her limbs as a strange energy rippled from the ground to the top of her head.

Alice's eyes went wide and she stumbled a bit, nearly tumbling left under the weight of the bag. Riley sniffed, grabbing her arm and righting her. "Are you all right?"

"Sure." Alice nodded shakily. "Just getting my legs back under me. Would you like to stop and get a coffee or some water? Maybe something to get some sugar back into your system?"

Riley sighed, "Yes, please."

Still not quite steady on her feet, Riley followed Alice to Starfall Grounds, a spot of modern in the middle of a row of shops intentionally engineered to look quaint and historic. The blue shake exterior was a calm contrast to the energy of the chalk-board style logo on the window, declaring, CAFFEINATED SERVICE, SWEET TREATS. PETRA GILINSKY-FLANDERS, PROPRIETRESS.

Opening the door was like walking into a cloud scented with cocoa, coffee, cinnamon, and unabashed gluttonous sin. A display case that ran the length of the store showed whole cakes, cookies, brownies, cupcakes, tarts, and some stuff she didn't even recognize. Riley's mouth watered, and she was reminded all over again that she'd thrown up what little she'd eaten that day and was suddenly *starving*. She was going to do some serious carb-based damage in this place.

A blond woman with broad shoulders and a rosy-cheeked, no-nonsense sort of face waved them in. A man of equally broad proportions and improbably high cheekbones was grinning as if he'd just said something clever, while the woman called, "Welcome to Starfall Grounds! How can we fuel you today?"

The woman's name tag read PETRA, so Riley assumed she was the owner of this establishment. Her masculine doppelganger didn't have a name tag, so Riley wasn't sure what that meant. As Riley and Alice approached, Petra ignored the man but spoke in low tones to a grumpy-looking, curvy brunette slumped against the muffin display case. The shorter woman seemed to be inhaling her caffeine through her nose, but given the dark circles shadow-ing the pale skin under her wide whiskey-brown eyes, Riley was going to guess she was a bartender.

Riley remembered that warily exhausted expression greeting her in the mirror every morning after her graveyard shifts at the just-off-campus sports bar her senior year. There was a special sort of tired that came from dealing with drunk people for hours at a time. She felt a strange affinity to this stranger.

"Would 'one of everything' be too ambitious?" Riley asked, keeping her question short because she didn't want drool leaking down her chin.

"Well, 'one of everything' might be a little much for one weekend," Petra replied, chuckling. "Maybe we can narrow it down to just one pastry group? Alice, your usual?"

Alice nodded, keeping her lips pressed together before saying, "Yes, please, Petra. Good morning, Caroline."

The little brunette inclined her head, but kept her face attached to her coffee cup. Riley noted that Alice was *also* ignoring the large blond man. What was that about?

"Oh, come on, Alice, you can't still be mad about one little bowl," the man said, dipping his bearded chin almost to his chest and making his bright blue eyes seem bottomless. "I did say I was sorry."

Alice seethed, "Do not attempt to give me the baby doll eyes, Igor Gilinsky. That was *not* 'one little bowl' as you called it. That was rare porcelain and part of a washstand set, which is even rarer. And it no longer exists because that dog of yours refuses to stay out of my store!"

"Iggy," Petra groaned. "I've warned you about that dog."

"Mimi is a free spirit," the blond man protested. "She goes wherever she decides she belongs. And on that day, she decided that she belonged in your store, instead of that very pretty pitcher and bowl."

"Which is now worth nothing, because Mimi rammed herself into the washstand and knocked it off," Alice snipped at him. "Shattering it into tiny, yet expensive pieces."

"Technically, it's still worth whatever the pitcher is worth, because it got a pretty good bounce and wasn't damaged that much," Iggy said, making a face that he probably thought was persuasive. "Which I am happy to pay, if it will put a smile back on your lovely face."

Alice continued to glare at Iggy, unmoved.

"Just think of the impression you're making on this nice weekender, being all unforgiving and holding a grudge against an innocent dog," he said, nodding at Riley and leveling a devastating smile at her. "Hi, there. Welcome to Starfall."

Riley raised a hand in greeting, while Alice plucked what looked like a very official invoice from her shoulder bag. She handed it to Iggy. "I accept cash or credit, no checks."

"You just had an invoice ready in your purse—" Iggy's brows rose. "Two hundred and seventy-five dollars for a *bowl*?"

"And the pitcher," Alice told him.

"That's insane!" Iggy cried. "I'm not paying it!"

Alice replied, "Then keep your canine companion indoors!"

"Mimi won't even wag her tail at you anymore! I'll tell you that much," Iggy told her, striding across the café.

"Hurtful, but I think I can live with that," Alice retorted.

"You know you're paying that right, Ig?" Petra called before Iggy reached the exit.

"Yeah, I know," Iggy grumbled, jerking the door open and slamming it behind him.

"My brother is going to pay you extra for your trouble," Petra assured her. "Without being a jerk about it."

"I know. He's a good person under the bluster," Alice sighed. "And a certain amount of breakage is expected, especially when tourists let their children rampage unsupervised through the store. But honestly, that dog is unnerving in its insistence on being inside my store. It's not as if I store bacon in the cabinets."

"You're not wrong," Petra replied. "And Mimi is just a little more stubborn than most dogs. And people."

"And I'm not a weekender. I'm a new local, Riley Everett." She reached over the counter to shake Petra's large, long-fingered hand. Riley gestured to the display case. "I'm just going to sign over all of my money to you now, because you're going to have it eventually anyway."

"Oh, I didn't realize," Alice whispered almost inaudibly, making Riley regret not bringing up her aunt on the ferry. Alice had seemed so confident and pleased for just a moment, and now Riley had taken that back from her.

"I'll try to just take a little of your money at a time," Petra said with a grin. "Nice to meet you. And breakfast is on the house for new locals."

"New blood?" the small brunette commented, her lips twitching. "Don't be offended when the boys at the bar open a pool on how long you'll stay."

Riley's brows rose. "A pool? Meaning a betting pool?"

"Be nice," Petra warned Caroline. "And it's nothing personal. A lot of people come here, thinking it's going to be something out of one of those made-for-cable 'woman relocates to an isolated but charming location, opens a pottery-studio-slash-private-detective-agency-slash-bakeshop and finds-herself-slash-empowerment' movies?"

"And then winter hits and they leave just as fast," Caroline muttered. "Also, don't open a bakeshop, because Petra and her rugalach will destroy you."

"Be *nice*," Petra said again. "I won't have your bitch-itude chasing away customers just because you worked a double shift yesterday."

Petra turned her cool blue eyes on Riley. "But also, she's right, my rugalach will destroy you and your hypothetical bakeshop."

Riley nodded, snickering. "Understood."

"And as usual, Petra's right. I'm being bitchy. Caroline Wilton," Caroline said, jerking her narrow shoulders. "And I just worked a double at our island's most beloved historical tavern, The Wilted Rose, because someone's cousin hasn't quite processed yet that 'I would rather go to the beach with a hottie who goes to State' isn't an excused absence for work."

Caroline's voice rang with a quiet love, tinged with resentment, that frankly, made a shiver run up Riley's spine. Growing up, she'd heard the same tone from local kids who worked at their parents' tiny tourist traps—Putt-Putt golf courses, corn dog restaurants, and pirate museums located about two hundred miles from any known pirate sightings. The pride, mixed with a longing to be free, to have the room to do anything else with their lives, was heartbreaking.

"I have a lot of cousins," Petra shot back. "That could be anyone."

"It's Milla," Caroline told Petra as she boxed up a small selection of pastries for Riley to try, earning her undying loyalty.

"Yeah, Milla has difficulty focusing when it comes to boys from State. Or girls from State. She doesn't like limits or labels. How do you like your coffee, Riley? I try to remember all the locals' preferences. I've got to keep up with Caroline and her magical mystery cocktails."

"I just give drunk people what they ask for," Caroline said dismissively, though she smiled into her coffee.

"Hey, I've done that job," Riley protested. "Sometimes interpreting what drunk people are saying takes damn near clairvoyance."

Caroline snorted. "That's true enough."

"Riley Everett." She extended her hand, pleased when Caroline reached out to take it. She cast an apologetic glance at Alice. "I'm here to meet my aunt, Nora Denton."

Alice's hand was light on Riley's arm. "Oh, no, Riley, after all that I said about the fudgies!"

Petra's hands fell to her sides. "Oh, Riley. I'm so sorry."

Riley was distracted from the strangely familiar tone of this apology by Caroline's hand hanging midair in front of her.

"So, the prodigal niece returns?" Caroline asked.

"I never knew I was missing," Riley said, turning her head to Alice. "And I should have said something earlier, but

I couldn't figure out a way to do it without making things more awkward."

Alice squeezed Riley's bicep gently. "Understood."

The moment Caroline's hand touched Riley's, a number of things happened at once. A rush of warm, pleasant energy echoed from Alice and Caroline's hands towards her heart, pulsating out and restoring a bit of the equilibrium she'd lost since stepping on the ferry. The bulbs in three old-fashioned hanging lamps overhead popped with a snap of ozone, drawing a shriek from a nearby customer browsing coffee mugs for sale. A strong wind, scented with coffee and candle smoke, blew the shop door open. The wind tipped over several potted hyacinths that lent warmth and charm to the little bistro tables, sending a shower of soil to the floor. Steam whistled out of the espresso machine like a freight train, making Petra gasp, "My baby!" and run to its rescue.

"What the hell?" Riley whispered, eyes wide, as the comic symphony of disasters unfolded. Her hand was still clutched in Caroline's warm, steady grasp.

Alice clung to Riley's arm, almost shaking. "Oh, my word."

"Well, that's new," Caroline muttered, going behind the counter without prompting to grab a broom and sweep up the dirt. Alice ran for the electrical panel and switched off the broken lights. She crossed to the supply closet to fetch new bulbs. Following their leads, Riley went behind the counter to help Petra get the espresso machine under control. Petra had invested in a top-of-the-line Italian model that was far beyond Riley's three months of barista experience, but she could help vent the building steam, clean up the over-frothed milk, and tote soiled paper cups to the garbage. And given the grateful smile Petra flashed her, it had been the kind *and* judicious thing to do.

"It's like trying to unearth the Rose after Superbowl Sunday," Caroline huffed.

"I have been there," Riley assured her. "I once had a tray of mimosas crash at my feet during a Mother's Day brunch on a glass-bottom boat outside the Keys. One of the other servers got distracted by synchronized swimmers in mermaid costumes and took me out. It was a whole thing."

Caroline's lush coral mouth quirked. "I get the feeling you've lived, Riley Denton."

"Everett." Riley corrected her. "And you're not wrong."

Within a few minutes, the four of them got the shop back to rights.

Petra put her hand on Riley's shoulder, but without the strange pyrotechnics of the moments before. "Riley, we need to talk about your aunt Nora."

The bells over the shop door rang with tinny insistence. Riley turned to find a sandy-haired, besuited man, watching the chaos unfold. He was holding a sign that read RILEY DENTON-EVERETT like a particularly dapper airport limo driver. He was tall and lean, with a pleasant expression on what looked to be a blandly handsome face.

Could this be the elusive Clark? He looked like a lawyer, polished and poised, but there was something off about him, something about his expression that didn't quite match the rest of him. She'd seen that look before, but couldn't quite place it. It was the overall arrangement of his perfectly symmetrical features, an intentional attempt to hide his feelings. She didn't know why, but it made her chest tight with dread.

Alice's voice sounded oddly strained as she said, "Clark?"

Her entire body seemed to recall all at once why Clark's mien was making her uneasy. She'd seen it before, standing in a hospital waiting room, watching the face of her mother's surgeon as he made the long walk down the hall towards her family.

Clark Graves had bad news to deliver.

Chapter 2
Edison

EDISON HELD SAT IN HIS tiny office in the Starfall Point Public-Library-Slash-Post-Office-Slash-Public-Works, and repeatedly smacked his forehead against his equally tiny desk.

His shoes, freshly rinsed, sat drying on a brass rack near the long-defunct fireplace, proof that the events of that morning actually happened. Why had he gotten on the ferry? He'd had every opportunity to jump off the boat, even as it pulled away from the dock. Why had he just let himself be taken? He had vacation savings. He could have chartered a helicopter. Why had he tempted fate?

Edison whimpered as water dripped from his soggy shoes to the worn-shiny brickwork. Maybe this was his karma catching up to him? He considered himself a good person, kind to strangers, a cheerful supporter of several nonprofits, head-patter for random domesticated animals of all types. But he was willing to go full-on *Hunger Games* when it came to surviving the ferry ride.

There was a knock on his creaky office door, and an equally creaky voice called softly, "Eddie, sweetie? Are you all right? You've been hiding in there for about an hour."

Edison groaned into the surface of his turn-of-the-century walnut desk. After six years on this island, Margaret Flanders was the only person on the island that continued to call him "Eddie." Grasping that he just wasn't the "Eddie" type had been the keystone of his gradual, hard-won acceptance amongst the locals. Margaret was the only holdout on the Eddie front, but Edison suspected that had something to do with Margaret wanting the position as head (and only) librarian for herself for the better part of four decades. Margaret got her own back in her own way.

And they'd had multiple discussions about the inappropriate nature of her calling Edison "sweetie," "honey," or any diminutive endearment, even if he *was* younger than Margaret's children.

"I knew this trip to Lansing was a bad idea," she huffed, setting a proper silver tea tray on the desk—one of many household artifacts left behind when the Van Deever family decided to donate the building to the island community. The Van Deever furniture business had suddenly expanded in Grand Rapids in a post-Industrial, pre-Depression boom so quickly that the family couldn't travel up north to properly enjoy their tidy little summer mansion anymore. Given the lack of real estate on the island, it had seemed like good sense to house multiple public offices in one place. The courthouse-slash-police department-slash-jail was just across the street.

Margaret poured steaming hot water into a delicate Limoges teacup, another Van Deever throwback. "You should have just attended that conference remotely or something. They do that all the time nowadays with the webcams and such."

"I was giving a speech," Edison groaned, sitting up and suffering the indignity of a bright pink Post-it note stuck to his forehead. "The keynote speech for the Midwest Librarians Association's annual conference on running public facilities in nontraditional spaces, a research topic on which I am the MLA's committee chair, with pass-around visual aids. I've put off attending the conference for years, and this was the closest they've ever held it to my location. The association president herself informed me that I had officially run out of excuses. I *couldn't* do it remotely."

"I could have done it for you!" Margaret cried, putting her hands on her hips. "And don't start your jawing about wanting plain old Earl Grey. You need peppermint to settle your stomach. No sugar."

Edison ignored her fussing. He'd become used to her "mothering" over the years, combined with her proprietary attitude towards this cramped little space that used to be the workspace for the lady of the house. It was better to just let her feel useful and undo the damage later...because Margaret's husband sat on the library board. "I'm the head librarian, and the only paid staff member. It would look pretty bad for me to let my volunteer do my job for me."

"*Senior* volunteer," she corrected him.

"In terms of my continuing employment, it would look pretty bad for me to let a volunteer, no matter how *senior*, do my job for me," he countered.

Margaret shook her head. "I only say that I don't see why you had to put yourself through that ferry ride when you don't have to. You know what it does to you."

Edison sipped his tea as Margaret bustled around the room, sliding files back into their proper place and grabbing books from the "repaired" stack to reshelve. While her back was turned, he used the little silver tongs to drop two sugar cubes from the bowl into his cup and stirred quickly. He had his reasons for staying in the innermost room of the boat, huddled against the wall, clutching his laptop bag to his chest like a newborn's security blanket. Normally, this didn't cause problems. Edison rarely rode the ferry, and when he did, Captain Perkins knew to put an OUT OF ORDER sign on the bathroom he was using to prevent little scenes like the mutual meltdown this morning.

Edison wasn't a complete asshole, no matter what that hauntingly lovely lunatic may have thought. He *hated* that he occupied one of two available closeable small spaces on the boat, when there were so many people aboard, and eventually, some of them were going to need the facilities. But it was the only place on the boat he felt safe. As long as he couldn't see the water, he could pretend it wasn't there. It was the same with the island. He lived as far inland as one could possibly go, in a charming little bungalow surrounded by trees. It made his house considerably cheaper, compared to most real estate on the island. There was no view.

He should have known something would go wrong with this particular voyage when he heard the door opposite banging over and over, as the day camp kids dashed in and out of the other bathroom. After his shoes were defiled, Edison noted the OUT OF ORDER sign was taped on the other bathroom door. He supposed he had the camp kids to thank for that.

Normally, he didn't leave the safety of his sanctuary until the lines were secured and the gangplank was extended, but halfway through the voyage, some...person started screaming at a highly distressing pitch while hammering at the door like a deranged blacksmith. That didn't exactly help his stress levels.

When he finally opened the door, he was fully prepared to verbally take down the harridan. But when he looked at her, she seemed so sad in a way that was all too familiar. Angry, but sad. Lost, but also sad. There were deep shadowed crescents under those fathomless gray eyes, even while they were flashing with unholy fury, and he was seized by the urge to wrap her in his arms and hold her there until that look went away. And that had nothing to do with the scent of gardenia and ocean air wafting from her collar. It was the common human desire to comfort someone who seemed at her lowest. But—given the compelling little line forming between her brows—he was pretty sure she would have smacked him if he'd followed through with those hair-sniffing aspirations.

Said aspirations had made him feel even more guilty for his facility-hoarding, but then she'd opened her mouth. *After* she opened her mouth, he still felt bad, but the impulse to hug her or smell her seaward flowery hair was definitely—significantly—reduced.

"Well, you got through it, and that's all that matters. You don't have to do it again for months," Margaret said, stacking some disordered papers in his inbox. "Now, on to new business—"

Edison snorted. Trust his highly organized, geriatric right hand to run a conversation like a meeting agenda. Margaret registered the snort but didn't respond. "According to the Nana Grapevine, Nora Denton's long-lost niece is supposed to meet with Clark this morning to talk about…something to do with Shaddow House. Norma wasn't allowed to look at the paperwork. Then again, I haven't been able to get her on the phone all morning, so I could be missing out on whatever she's found out, even as we speak."

Edison snorted again but had the presence of mind to hide it with a cough. The Nana Grapevine was Starfall's social media before such a thing existed—an invisible network of well-meaning-yet-competitive grandmothers who shared everything they knew via actual landlines in a constantly escalating news cycle. Norma Oviette had been the legal secretary for more than twenty years at Tanner, Moscovitz, and Graves, Attorneys at Law, not to mention one of the keystone members of the Nana Grapevine. So, if the Nana Grapevine reported that Nora Denton's niece had arrived on Starfall, it was practically gospel, and it had happened hours ago. He was already a step behind.

"You need to make a move if you want to be part of the unofficial greeting committee. So, toodle on over," she said, with an unintentionally—maybe?—dismissive wave of the hand. "Maybe take some flowers. Make a good impression. She'll appreciate it. Get in good with her before she hears about how you got along with her aunt, and the Shaddows' lawyers close in."

"I'm a grown man with multiple advanced degrees," Edison replied. "I don't *toodle*. Anywhere."

"No man should be too proud to toodle, Eddie," she told him solemnly.

Ignoring the *absolutely intentional* dismissiveness, Edison shook his head. "Wouldn't it be better if I went to the house and welcomed her? Otherwise, she's just carrying a bunch of flowers all over the island, which can be annoying," he said, not even trying to deny that he was trying to put off social interactions with strangers. It had simply not worked out for him that day.

Margaret gave him a wink before reaching into the bottom drawer of the filing cabinet and pulling out his backup dress shoes, neatly tucked under his backup shirt and tie, and backup pants. "No time like the present, given the circumstances."

"You know, technically, as a volunteer, no matter how senior, I'm your boss," Edison reminded her.

"Well, technically, as a member of the library board, I'm your boss," she retorted, backing towards the door.

"Your *husband* is on the board. The governing powers are not transitory."

Margaret shrugged. "I'll just have to call Burt and tell him to give me a proxy vote."

"Your husband doesn't take your calls until his lunch break, which he doesn't take for another hour," he said. "So, I guess that puts us at an impasse."

Margaret's forget-me-not blue eyes narrowed as she backed towards his door, surprising Edison by letting him have the last word. "There's no way she's going to let that stand," he murmured as the door clicked shut.

From the other side of the door, he heard her call, "I guess it does!"

"There we go." Edison nodded, pointing absently in her general direction. "Wait, given *what* circumstances?"

When she didn't answer, he tilted his back to rest on the worn leather club chair. Of all the things that stuck in his craw about his day so far, it was that knowing that Margaret was right. He did need to touch base with the mysterious Denton niece. Maybe, unlike her aunt, this woman was a reasonable, rational human being and could persuade her aunt to allow him inside Shaddow House. He imagined some middle-aged woman, probably in her forties, given Nora Denton's age. And given Nora's aloof, sometimes downright cantankerous nature, he imagined she would be difficult to approach, even more difficult to "toodle" toward.

Miss Denton had never appreciated the flowers he'd tried to give her, telling him she didn't appreciate his thinking she needed help with her garden. When he'd tried five pounds of Waterstone's Wonderous Fudge, widely regarded as the best fudge on the island—she scoffed at him, asked him if he thought she'd never explored the main street of her own town. And then slammed the door in his face. And Edison was pretty sure that he heard her laughing at him with other people. But he couldn't figure out who those people might be, because no one that he'd met on the island so far had been allowed in Shaddow House.

It was just a house, an old, uniquely designed home. A little odd, yes, in its near-constant state of renovation, but nothing to get obsessed over. Until you considered the horde of rare antiques rumored to be contained within. The stories of how the Shaddows had amassed those treasures over the years—Faustian bargains, pawn brokers to the rich and doomed during the French Revolution, really, *really* fancy garage sales—were as numerous as the ghost stories on the island. But given what he'd seen through the doorway, on the rare occasions that he got Nora to answer the door, he could believe those stories. He'd glimpsed medieval armor, the sort of decorative brassware bits the Médicis used to commission for fun, a massive Swiss-made grandfather clock he'd only seen in the high-end private auction catalog his parents loved to pore over. The Shaddows were the most fascinating island institution that no one seemed to know anything *real* about—yes, everybody knew the stories about the ways they'd made their money, how they built their house, but no one seemed to know any specific information about any members of the family who had lived on Starfall. No one seemed to know how they'd lived there, how they'd contributed to the community, why they'd left. The Shaddows had somehow managed to keep those secrets trapped inside their walls, and no one seemed to care.

It was so bizarre to him, for a town so devoted to its history to allow such a large part of that history to be locked away from them, hidden from the public. The locals just accepted the Shaddows' right to privacy, despite nearly every other home of its caliber being open to daily public tours during the high season. It was just common knowledge that Shaddow House was a sort of blank space in the landscape of the island. And that Nora Denton hated fudge, which would have been handy information to have before he tried to buy her off with it.

Also, what sort of human being hated fudge?

Maybe his mother was right. Just because someone refused to tell him something, didn't mean he had to chase that information down like a dog.

No, that couldn't be it.

With dry shoes in place, Edison stepped out of his office into what was technically the Van Deevers' former parlor. The airy space, with its narrow floor-to-ceiling windows and winter sky–colored walls, was home to the nonfiction section, which had always struck Edison as counterintuitive. The children's section was housed in the former nursery, which was more intuitive. Margaret had probably disappeared into the floor-to-ceiling stacks of the fiction sections upstairs in the family wing. The house's former library housed the DVD and audiobook sections, which again, struck Edison as an odd choice, but it had been made clear to him when he moved cross-country to beg for the opportunity to work in this tiny town, that he was not there to reinvent the wheel. He was merely meant to carry on what was a pretty solid legacy his predecessor established, all things considered.

As usual, Edison was struck by the way the town council had managed to keep the ornate gravity of the Van Deever's mansion— all dark, heavy wood and stained glass and ornate tilework where it wasn't needed—with the utility of the services provided there. He waved to the local postmistress, Judith Kim, a short, sturdy Korean-American woman whose unflappable manner and carefully styled salt-and-pepper bob intimidated Edison on several levels. She stood behind the mail counter, sorting the town's limited post into small piles. The post office was just off the dining room, in the former butler's pantry, with the locking silver closet used as storage for locals' packages. The former dining room held a bank of shiny new post office boxes.

As a partial federal facility, it was barely grandfathered in under historical consideration, but someday, Postmistress Kim had told Edison, the town would have to build something new. He could see it in the resigned way she waved back, like she knew her time in the cozy, quirky cubby, just under the public works office (housed upstairs in the former guest wing) was limited. Edison wondered if Judith resented that the library never suffered the same uncertainty.

If anything, the library stood to expand if the post office relocated. Unlike some small towns, which were seeing a decline in library use, the Starfall Point Public Library saw a bustling business. There was only one bookstore on the island, and it focused more on tourist interests like local history. Ebooks and streaming services hadn't quite taken off for the aging part of the island's population, who favored "something they could hold."

As difficult as it was to work in this hodgepodge of spaces that didn't quite suit their purpose, this building certainly fit Starfall Point, a place that was like no other. Edison had barely invested any thought into moving here when the opportunity presented itself. He realized now the online posting had only been made public because the law required that outside applicants be considered. He'd needed the solace he could find here, craved it desperately when he'd stumbled off the ferry under a haze of anti-anxiety meds. And he could do the work he loved here, the work his family barely understood.

As Edison emerged into the bright light of a dwindling afternoon, he took a deep breath, imagining that he could smell the lilacs that were soon to come. Springs in Michigan were enough to make you forget the brutal snow. And the light here felt cleaner somehow, washed by the proximity to water he pretended didn't exist.

It would get more crowded, the closer they crept to Memorial Day, and he would have to adjust to the thunder of thousands of feet on these charming but worn cobblestone streets. He tried not to resent the annual intrusion of tourists onto this little rock. He knew the money they brought to the island was an important part of keeping them all afloat throughout the rest of the year. But like most locals, by the time Labor Day rolled around, he was ready for the rentals to empty, the streets to quiet and life to get back to normal. But he supposed as he took in the scene of blooming green life and quaint chocolate box houses, he couldn't blame people for wanting to take a little piece of this place to tuck into their pockets and take home.

He moved past the multitude of souvenir shops where those crowds could do just that and decided against buying flowers at Starfall Point Blooms. He'd learned very little from his father, having largely avoided anything to do with the Held family business empire. But he knew that offering too much to someone you were trying to approach for a deal automatically put you at a disadvantage. So he simply crossed towards Lilac Street, ironically bloomless, trying to assemble something like an opening gambit for this unnamed niece.

A few steps later, he thought maybe he saw Ilsa Lundgren glaring at him from the patio of Starfall Grounds. Frowning, he craned his neck around, his steps slowing. Ilsa was one of the founding members of the ladies' reading circle. She had been the one to motion for his rehiring the previous year at the library board meeting. He had to be imagining things.

He raised a hand to greet Betty Cortez, who ran Starfall Point Pages, the history-focused bookshop. She raised a sable brow and turned on her heel without returning the greeting.

Well, that was weird. Usually, he was one of Betty's favorite customers. Even when he didn't find something to take home with him, she'd find some title he hadn't thought of reading yet.

But today, she'd just turned away. Maybe she hadn't recognized him? That seemed unlikely. Living amongst a constantly changing crowd, locals eventually developed an aptitude for lightning-fast facial recognition. It had gotten Edison out of (and sometimes into) a lot of awkward situations over the years.

Normally, his interactions with the older ladies went more along the lines of his working relationship with Margaret—friendly, purpose-driven, occasionally snarky. The only lady he hadn't shared that dynamic with had been Nora Denton. She could keep him on his toes when it came to verbal sparring, and he'd respected that. But she'd always held him at a not-quite-polite distance, even farther than she'd held everybody else around her. Now, it seemed like Nora's sour attitude towards him was spreading.

Maybe Edison was imagining things.

With one foot off the curb, he turned back toward Starfall Point Pages to see if maybe Betty had come back out—maybe she'd realized she'd accidentally snubbed him? And with that one moment of inattention, Edison damn near got run over by what was essentially a thirteen-person tandem bike.

"Jeez!" he shouted, stumbling back onto the sidewalk. Mitt Sherzinger, the burly bike tour captain who boasted the thickest thighs in town, lumbered by with three rows of fairly fit tourists helping him move the behemoth that was Mitt's Mega-PedalCart, patent pending. Because Mitt had basically welded the thing together with no plan and a lot of ambition. Edison had no idea how the man steered the thing. It probably had something to do with his thigh muscles.

"Folks, one of the pleasures of living in such a small community is how often you *run into* your neighbors," Mitt announced over the little bike helmet-mounted mic, which he funneled banter into constantly over the course of his ninety-minute island tour. Mitt was known for his plethora of "dad jokes" to keep his customers entertained during this limited money-making window. At least, Mitt liked to believe that, and no one had the heart to tell him otherwise.

"Good thing our esteemed librarian Edison here is so light on his feet," Mitt added, giving a jaunty wave over his shoulder. "Sorry about that, Edison!"

Edison waved him off, a frozen grin pasted on his face, to avoid offending the tourist bystanders. Starfall Point had leaned into its walkable nature with a decades-old ban on cars in the more historic parts of town. And as a result, the lack of traffic and pollution became part of the island's charming tourist draw.

Owning a car on the island was honestly too troublesome to be worth driving the short distances. Many islanders sustained themselves with bicycle power alone. Trips that couldn't be accomplished on foot were done with the help of pedicabs, which meant Mitt's services were always in high demand.

What had Edison been thinking of before he was almost mowed down by Mitt and his oversized thigh muscles?

Right, how to approach Nora Denton's (most likely) halfway-to-elderly and (even more likely) embittered niece. He supposed that *Hi, I tried over and over to get your aunt to let me into the Shaddows' family home, but she takes her responsibilities far too seriously and now I'm hoping you'll help me find a way into the house, maybe behind her back* would also be tipping his hand.

He stopped within sight of the law offices of Tanner,

Moscovitz, and Graves and straightened his tie. The raised-hair sensation of being watched struck him right in the back of the neck, making him turn toward the large display window of the Starfall Point Snow Globe Emporium. Was it his imagination or was Gerda Henderson glaring at him from behind a row of tiny glittered Starfall Ferry globes? That seemed unlikely. For the last two years, Gerda made him thumbprint cookies with homemade jam harvested from the blueberry bushes in her backyard. Because he said he liked them *once* at a Friends of the Library meeting.

But the look she was giving him was decidedly frosty. His access to the cookies could be in danger. Even more confused, Edison climbed the front stairs, gripping the old brass doorknob to the law office with trepidation. Maybe he wasn't ready to talk to Ms. Denton's niece. Clearly, he was not capable of predicting the behavior of the women who were already in his life—much less the ones he didn't know yet.

But the decision seemed to have been made for him when Norma Oviette jerked the door open, crossing her arms across her chest. "You should be ashamed of yourself, deeply and profoundly ashamed."

Edison's breath caught in his chest, and he forced himself to inhale deeply. Norma couldn't possibly mean that the way it sounded. She didn't know his reasons for coming to Starfall. She couldn't know how much fear it struck in his heart to hear those words, or how right she was. He cleared his throat as she wrapped her bony, yet not at all frail, brown fingers around his wrist and dragged him into the law office's elegant waiting room.

"Can I ask what I did?" Edison inquired, which he supposed

was one of those questions that annoyed people. Also, he clearly wasn't imagining things. Those ladies definitely had been glaring at him. Norma was also *currently* glaring at him.

"What did I do?" he asked again.

"You locked that poor girl out of the bathroom when she was so desperately ill—and *distraught*. Edison Held, my heart just broke when I saw how green she was. How could you do that to such a nice young lady? And what were you doing on the ferry anyway?"

Relief and confusion went to war in his head. How would the Nana Grapevine get wind of his ferry activities? The only people on the deck were those schoolkids and Alice Seastairs, who really didn't talk to locals much. Unless...

Oh, no.

The door to Clark's office opened, a pair of small red Keds—clad feet stepped out onto the beige carpeting, and a feeling of doom settled over him.

Norma knew about his ferry activities because she got word of them directly from the awful, but fetching, mouth itself; the mouth that managed to produce a remarkable degree of vitriol, even while "so desperately ill." Clearly, Norma had used the time Edison spent hiding in his office to activate the Nana Grapevine, resulting in the glares.

"You!" the shoe violator growled. She looked decidedly less miserable than the last time he'd seen her. And she was even more beautiful without the deathly pallor and the shadows under those gray eyes, heaven help him. She was definitely *not* middle-aged, but...more than halfway to embittered, given the hard-set line of that generous mouth.

"You," he groaned. "*You're* Nora Denton's niece?"

"Apparently," she intoned.

"Um, is everything all right?" Clark asked, coming out of his office behind Norma and looking back and forth between the two of them like a lost tennis fan. "Edison, this is Riley Denton-Everett, the late Nora Denton's niece. Riley, this is the head of our local library, Edison Held."

Edison's hand stilled at his side. Nora Denton was dead? That couldn't be true. Nora was a force of nature, too tough and too smart to be outdone by something as trifling as time or mortality. A new sort of shame, hot and dull, washed through him. He'd never been on good terms with Nora, and he would never get the chance. She'd been a curious, complex woman, and Edison was sorry that she was gone. He was even sorrier that he'd started off on such a bad note with Nora's niece. How was he was going to fix this? Why didn't Margaret say anything? Or had he misheard Clark? "Excuse me...did you just say...?"

"What is happening here?" Clark asked, the confused expression still wrinkling his brow. "Do you two know each other?"

"We've met," Riley said dryly. "On the ferry. And he didn't make a great impression."

Edison shook his head, murmuring, "No, I did not."

"Wait, hold on, Ed, *you* rode on the ferry?" Clark exclaimed.

Still at a loss for words, Edison realized that the least he could do was offer his condolences. "I'm very sorry to hear about your aunt. She was an interesting woman. The island will be a lesser place without her."

"Thank you," she said, but the response didn't reach her eyes.

"And I'm sorry for the unfortunate incident on the ferry as well." And just when her expression started to soften, his stupid mouth took over and he added, "I have a condition that um... makes the ferry ride difficult."

"Do you suffer an anaphylactic reaction to selfish jackasses?" she asked. "I have a similar condition. It can make life so difficult."

Oh, no, he was in so much trouble. She was not only achingly beautiful in that otherworldly way that made him think of boyhood days reading Tolkien, but she was smart. The kind of smart that would keep his interest long after he'd forgotten how damn pretty she was—if that was even possible.

"Forgive me," Edison said, "I think we've gotten off on the wrong foot—"

The color returned to her cheeks in a violent bloom. Unfortunately, it was angry color—bright, virulent red. "The wrong *foot*? What? Is this about the shoes? Maybe if you hadn't just stood in my way, your fancy footwear wouldn't have suffered."

Edison's jaw dropped. "Not at all! It's just, if we were in each other's shoes...or if the shoe were on the other foot...Oh my god."

"Look, I don't have time to deal with your twisted foot-related humor. And I definitely don't have the money to replace those designer loafers...so good luck with that. Just please, stay away from me while I'm here. I think it would be best for both of us," she said, smiling with an acidic false sweetness that made him step back. Then she added, "Watch yourself," as Clark rolled her suitcase toward the door.

Over his shoulder, Clark mouthed the words, "What the hell, Edison?" at him before slipping out the door behind her.

"She's not *that* nice," Edison muttered.

"I beg your pardon?" Norma said, arching her iron gray eyebrows. "I think she was restrained, all things considered."

Edison sighed, knowing Norma was right. Riley could have gone at him a lot harder. She clearly had the vocabulary for it. "So, she's going to stay?"

Norma shrugged. "We don't know yet. She's just suffered a loss, and I think it's hit her pretty hard, even if she didn't know Nora all that well. But it won't help if you go around poking at her. Just leave her alone for a bit, Edison. Maybe she'll be able to talk to you without thrashing you verbally after a few days."

"I'll apologize better next time," he sighed, slumping toward the door, knowing when he was well and truly defeated.

"And some flowers wouldn't hurt!" Mrs. Oviette called after him.

Edison stopped just outside the office, his chin dropping to his chest. He would never tell Margaret she was right.

Chapter 3
Riley

NORA DENTON WAS DEAD.

The last of the Dentons, her mother's only relative, lost consciousness while walking to the post office and never woke up. Nora had been declared dead about twenty hours before Riley even arrived on Starfall—while Riley had been ignoring her phone notifications. Dr. Toller, the island's only doctor, believed that the heart troubles that had been plaguing Nora for years had finally taken her.

Riley should have known better. She was not the sort of person for whom life presented special "miracle" loopholes. Why would the universe hand her the opportunity to finally know her mother? Clark's stream of conversation seemed to flow over her while she sank deep into the realization that the last connection to her mother on this earth had been severed. And then the word *funeral* snagged on her ear, and her attention focused on Clark.

This all seemed like a bad omen to Riley.

Clark Graves was, as she suspected, a perfectly pleasant person, kind in his delivery and earnest in helping her cart her luggage from his office to Shaddow House. But still, she felt like bad things were on the way. She hoped it was just a result of all the unsettling surprises mixed with a post-nausea haze.

The legal language he'd tried to impart was painfully tedious. In fact, she'd sort of zoned out as Clark read the bits about "sound mind" and "bequeathing." She wasn't even sure *bequeathing* was a word in real life. But then Clark began to read the list of items Nora had left to her, and her mouth dropped open in shock.

"I'm sorry. Did you just say, 'Stewardship of Shaddow House'?" she'd asked, squinting at him.

Clark had swallowed, eyeing her carefully. "Yes, I did. The job comes with a generous salary, benefits, lodgings within Shaddow House, and use of any of the house's contents. Plus, you will inherit Nora's complete financial portfolio, which is considerable. She hardly had any expenses, so she had time to save quite a bit."

He slid a form across the desk listing an amount that made Riley's eyes go the size of saucers. Was this money...Riley's now? She would have more money in her checking account than the few hundred dollars that covered her immediate needs? Riley had never lived beyond paycheck to paycheck before, and the very idea of that sort of freedom felt like a weight being pried loose from her chest. Goodbye, student loans. Goodbye, car payment. Goodbye, lingering debt to that yoga gear sales thing that turned out to be a pyramid scheme.

Still, this "too good to be true" offer set off some of those familiar red flags.

"So this seems...illegal?" Riley suggested. "My aunt couldn't really leave me a *job* in a will, right? That has to violate a lot of employment laws. And wouldn't the Shaddow family have something to say about her appointing her successor? They don't even know me. Why would they want a stranger living in their very old, very *expensive* house?"

"There's documentation from the Shaddow Family Trust giving blanket approval to whomever Nora appointed, 'with our full endorsement and heartfelt gratitude.'" He'd handed her a sheaf of very official-looking paperwork, welcoming Nora's nameless appointee and outlining her salary and benefits package.

And still, she felt the need to ask, "What happens if I don't take the job?"

"You get nothing, except for the letter and the trip to Starfall," Clark said. "No inheritance and no salary."

"Wait, when did she make these changes to her will?" Riley asked. "I was under the impression that she only recently found me through social media."

Clark checked the papers. "She made these changes about eight months ago."

Eight months ago. Her mother had only died *six* months ago. Clark told Riley that Nora only found Ellen because of her recent obituary. Was that a lie? Had Nora been in communication with Ellen before she'd died? Ellen certainly hadn't said anything to Riley about it, not that she would have anyway.

"It might help if you read the letter," he suggested gently.

"Which says I have to do that on the steps of the house," Riley had said, showing him neat handwritten instructions on the outside of the envelope. "Any idea why?"

Clark had shrugged. "I don't know. I've never been inside Shaddow House."

Riley had hoped that getting off the damned ferry would quell the emotions storming through her middle, but it only seemed to get worse the higher they climbed up the hill towards Shaddow House. Confusion, grief, regret were all churning through her so fiercely, she'd barely registered the cheerfully painted buildings lining Main Street or the heavenly smell of melting butter and sugar wafting out of the storefronts. Her instinct was to turn around and go right back home. The whole point of visiting the island was to meet Nora. What was left for her to do now? But going home would mean getting back on the ferry. And she didn't think her body would be up for that challenge for at least a few days.

Could she swim back to the mainland? Maybe she would be less seasick if she crafted a vessel out of her luggage?

Poor Clark. It wasn't his fault that the chief emotion rising in her belly to blow away all the rest was *disappointment*. Disappointment that she'd arrived too late. Disappointment in herself for believing that for just a moment, she was going to get the answers she'd been looking for all her life, a way to fill in the blank spots her mother left in their shared history. And disappointment that Clark had witnessed her second encounter with the bathroom hog.

In the back of her mind, Riley had really hoped that the next time she saw that miserable man, he wouldn't be nearly as attractive. She'd hoped that being miserably sick had somehow caused a glitch between her eyes and her brain. She'd hoped that, when she saw him again, she would see that in reality he only had one eyebrow or some unfortunate dermatological fungus.

But no, if anything, the comfort of being on land just brought out the oceanic blue of Edison Held's eyes and the surprisingly sensitive curve of his bottom lip. She wanted to stay angry, especially after his sarcastic commentary earlier, but she couldn't resist wondering what it would feel like to reach up and run her fingers through that thick dark hair. Which was just…inconvenient. She hadn't had anything resembling those intense, compelling feelings since her ex, Ted.

Nope, not the right time to think of Ted. No time was the right time to think of Ted.

Now, as they carted her bags up the hill to the Shaddow House, Clark was rattling off what sounded like a brochure version of the home's history. The Shaddows had come to the island with the first European settlers in the late 1700s. Franklin Shaddow, the second son of an ancient, wealthy English family line, was heavy on gold but short on real estate. He saw opportunity on this tiny plot of land resting between what would become two slices of Michigan. Franklin brought his wife and children to help build an empire on salted fish, fur, iron, copper, and whatever else he could, well, take to cement his place as a robber baron. The family eventually built an enormous mansion to put all other fancy houses on the island to shame, and then just kept rebuilding it until it attained its current elegant quasi-Victorian façade.

As the island leaned more towards a genteel tourist spot, the house simply sat as the town grew around it. In the early days, Shaddow brought over his faithful retainer, Edward Denton, as his steward, establishing a role that would last for the Dentons long after the Shaddows' legendary wealth took them to larger cities.

Clark was describing Nora Denton's final years as the last Denton to take care of the house and the treasures hidden away inside, when he suddenly paused.

"I'm so sorry that your first hours on the island have been so, uh, eventful, Riley," he said, expertly dragging her suitcase on a crowded sidewalk. "I really regret that it's been so chaotic, and I should have gotten you before your flight took off. I did try calling, but every time I thought about it, some other crisis or phone call came up. Between handling the details of your aunt's memorial service and keeping the office going, I forgot you were coming until this morning, when the reminder popped up on my phone."

"*You're* planning her memorial service?" Riley asked.

"Planned it, past tense." Clark nodded, his expression sad. "Well, technically she planned it herself. It was my job to make sure her final wishes were honored. For years, Nora wasn't sure if she would have anyone in her life to do that for her, so she left a pretty comprehensive funeral plan. She didn't want a viewing or any sort of 'fuss for the lemon bar set,' as she called it. Her cremation was scheduled this morning. We'll scatter the ashes privately when it's convenient for you, though your aunt asked that it be scheduled within the week. She didn't like the idea of lingering."

Riley frowned. "Cremation?"

"It was what she wanted." Clark's lips tilted into a wry, reluctant smile that crinkled his warm brown eyes. "I'm sure she had her reasons. Maybe she'll explain them in this letter."

The closer they came to Shaddow House, the less appropriate it seemed to talk. He handed her a fancy linen envelope stamped with a blue crest, a large curlicued S placed inside the outline of an elaborate Victorian house. Her full name, with the strange hyphenation that she'd never used in her life, was perfectly centered on the front in a careful hand. The envelope was sealed with blue wax bearing the same image. Over the lip of the envelope, the same precise hand had written, Only to be opened on the steps of Shaddow House.

"I don't go by Denton-Everett, by the way," she noted. "It's just Everett."

"Not here," he replied. "The Denton name carries a lot of weight on this island, and you'd be wise to put it to good use."

Riley shrugged. "Fair enough. And it's Riley, please. Once you've seen me in this state, I think we're automatically on a first-name basis."

"Fair enough," he agreed. "But I think we should go ahead, get up to the house, and read the letter now," he said, and then he suddenly blanched, as if he realized mid-sentence that he'd made a faux pas.

"I get that you want to get to this letter opening as soon as possible, but…" Riley pursed her lips. She'd come all this way for a *letter?* It seemed like such a letdown, even with the unprecedented amount of money she was being offered—which, again, sounded suspiciously like a plot from one of those 1970s horror movies she'd worried about before. She was losing her nerve, frankly, but she wasn't about to admit that to Clark. "Maybe I can just run over to my hotel and change into fresh clothes so I feel human first?"

Wash off the anxiety sweats, her brain suggested. *Maybe brush my teeth so my mouth doesn't taste like it housed a dead rodent?*

Clark shook his head. "I was under the impression you planned to stay at Shaddow House with your aunt."

"Well, I was under the impression that was a little too much closeness with a relative I barely know," she retorted. "She said something about a Duchess Hotel?"

"The Duchess is still running on winter rates, meaning reduced availability." Clark said. "And the early fudgies have it filled up, plus all the B and Bs and rentals."

Riley stopped in her tracks, practically dropping her bag. The Duchess was the only large hotel on the island. There's no way Nora hadn't known when it would open for the summer tourist season. Had she been hoodwinked by a septuagenarian?

Also, there was that weird word again. *Fudgies.* Was *she* a fudgie? Was it an insult?

"I think that reading the letter would answer a lot of questions for you," Clark told her. "And some for me, if I'm going to be honest about it. I worked with Nora for, oh, more than ten years now, and I can't say I knew her well. Or at all. No one did, really."

"But I thought you said the Denton name carried a lot of weight on Starfall," she replied.

"It does. Because the Dentons have lived on Starfall Point since before anyone around here can remember. People here respect that, even if your aunt wasn't particularly well-liked." He held up a hand when her mouth opened in shock. "I don't mean to speak ill of the dead. When I say she wasn't well-known, it was because no one could get close to her. She mostly kept to herself, up in that big house, all alone. Most of us tried to reach out. When you live in a place this small, this isolated, you try to be one big family. It makes life here a little easier. But she held us all at a distance. She was nice enough, but it was sort of...on the surface, you know? Like the conversation you'd have with an acquaintance at the grocery store when you're trying to end it as quickly as possible so you can go on with the rest of your errands."

She nodded, her own lips quirking. It was sort of comforting, knowing that Aunt Nora was as reticent as her mother. Maybe it was a Denton family trait? And were there other family traits Riley didn't know about? Nora had promised she would explain everything once Riley reached the island.

It has to be face-to-face, none of this text-timing and videoing all you young people can't seem to live without, Nora had told her in their one all-too-brief phone call. *You're a Denton, and you belong on Starfall Point. Once you're here, I'll tell you everything you need to know.*

Only that wasn't going to happen now, because Nora was gone. The letter in her hand felt distressingly thin, like the polite one-page form refusal you'd get from your dream college. Riley sincerely doubted it contained the answers she wanted, not even a tenth of them. All she wanted was a shower and a bed and enough sleep to chase away this miserable feeling. But what was the point of waiting? It's not as if she wanted to stay on the island long. She'd only set aside two weeks for her visit, anyway. She might as well get it over with and get back home, try to find another job, get back to her life.

"It wasn't personal," Clark assured Riley, then pausing to talk to a middle-aged man in a dark green Starfall Playhouse collared shirt. He was clearly a client, and Riley didn't begrudge him Clark's attention. It gave Riley a moment to glance around Side Street, a classic collection of quaint attached storefronts aimed at residents rather than tourists. The law office, the newspaper, a theater advertising the SUMMER MUSICAL REVUE showing daily in June.

In contrast to the bustle on the Main Square, this area was relatively calm. Riley saw a slender young woman in pale blue minidress with a long, pointed white collar, standing ever so still as she peered into the window of Martin & Martin Realtors. Probably because it was the one business on the island that didn't include the word *Starfall* in the title. Frankly, Riley was shocked by that, and she'd only been here a few hours.

Maybe she was transfixed by her own reflection? It was a pretty amazing dress. Riley had always wanted to wear something like it, but baby-doll styles tended to make her look short waisted. The woman stood in front of Martin & Martin Realtors, perusing a display of listings. It was the sort of listless thing you did when you didn't have any dreaded errands hanging over your head, nothing pending.

In that moment, Riley desperately wanted to be her.

Clark reappeared at her elbow and was mid-sentence. Riley wondered if he'd been conversing "with" her for some time and just hadn't noticed that she wasn't listening. She really needed a nap or another seltzer or something, because she was drifting into all-out rudeness here.

"Nora never allowed visitors, unless it was the workmen completing the various construction projects," Clark was saying as they started up the zigzagging path to the hulking mansion. "She said the Shaddows wouldn't want strangers in the house. But the Shaddows also didn't hire locals, not even for minor repairs. They always hired firms from off-island."

"That must have caused some hurt feelings," Riley noted, pleased that she was only huffing and puffing half as much as Clark was. She'd kept up a regular exercise routine since her ill-fated stint as a professional croquet player, for which she was grateful as they approached the house.

"Eh, more curiosity than anything else," he said. "Over the years, a few teenagers have tried to sneak in, just to get a look inside, but the Dentons have always found ways to discourage it."

"Am I about to walk into a house full of booby traps?" she asked. "Because I think you're legally obligated to tell me if I am."

"It's just a house, Riley," he assured her. "Nothing to be afraid of."

Up close, Shaddow House loomed infinitely larger than it had when she was on the boat. It sprawled out grandly on either side of the entrance, and her eyes struggled to keep up with all the details. The house was a sea of unexpected angles and hidden eaves, all adorned with gingerbread trim painted in different shades of blue and aqua and gray. But beyond the elegant façade, something made the hairs on Riley's arms stand up. Something wasn't right here.

"Have you ever met a member of the Shaddow family?" she asked as they approached the enormous double door with potted palms on either side and an elaborate S etched on oval beveled glass.

Clark thought about that for a second. "Now that I think about it...no. No one has. I don't think they've visited the island once in my time here, but they're supposed to be these jet-setting millionaires with homes all over the world. The locals say they made their money in mining or railroads or something probably not altruistic. It sort of makes sense they wouldn't want to summer with the fudgies."

Riley stopped short on the steps. "OK, there's that word again. What the hell is a fudgie?"

"It's a local term for tourist. Something about traveling close to the Upper Peninsula makes them crave fudge," he told her. "At any given tourist spot, you will find a far above average number of fudge shops, doors propped wide open, pumping the smell of melting chocolate out into the street."

She laughed. "I'll have to watch for that next time."

"Well, this is it," he said, dangling a nondescript, completely modern stainless-steel key in front of her. Riley was a little disappointed. She was expecting an antique skeleton key with a potion bottle attached or something. Then when she slid the key into the lock, it refused to turn. She jiggled the door handle from a few different angles, but it just wouldn't budge.

Clark's brow furrowed, but he didn't look particularly surprised by the door's not functioning properly. "I could call a locksmith."

"I worked for a locksmith for a few months," she told him. "I think I can get it."

"Really?"

"I've had a rich and colorful work history," she replied, propping her sunglasses on top of her head as she peered down at the lever handle. The lock appeared to be in working order, no rust or random objects jammed inside the cylinder. Maybe Clark had the wrong key?

If all else failed, she could always get proper tools from the island hardware store to work the lock open.

While the brass construction was pretty typical for the make and model, there was a strange circular depression at the top of the deadbolt. It seemed more than decorative. It looked like it was essential to the workings of the door. Otherwise, why would it be placed on top of the handle with the lock mechanism? The depression was shaped exactly like the seal on her envelope, a twisted S sheltered within the front outline of Shaddow House.

Pulling the envelope from her shoulder bag, she stared at the seal and the handwriting over it instructing her to only open the letter on the steps of the house. She snapped the wax seal, and to her surprise, underneath the seal was a wafer-thin metal disc replica of that same image. She shook the disc into her hand and saw a tiny hole in the middle of it, the diameter of a thumbtack. Etched on the other side of the coin was an even stranger symbol, a trio of loops centering around the hole. It sort of looked like an empty nuclear symbol, not exactly in keeping with the aesthetics of the rest of the house.

Weird.

Clark's brows rose. "Well, that's strange. You'd think I would have noticed the weight."

A curious line between his brows, Clark attempted to take the disc from her hand, but she was already moving toward the doorknob. She placed it into the depression and pressed it down like a "start" button. A circlet of metal closed around the disc, trapping it in place. Riley yelped as a tiny pin sprang through the disc and punctured her thumb. She yanked her hand back, blood welling from the little wound and covering the metal image of Shaddow House. The mechanisms inside the knob clicked. Hissing, she flipped the steel key, which now turned easily.

"Are you all right?" he asked, frowning deeply at the blood dripping from her injured thumb. She nodded, pulling a small first aid kit from her bag and wiping her thumb with a prepackaged alcohol wipe.

Clark pursed his lips. "This is a question I've never had to ask a client before, but are you up to date on all your shots?"

"I'm at no risk of tetanus," she assured him. "I had to keep up with all my shots when I worked as a dog groomer a while back."

"You were a dog groomer?" he asked. "*After* you were a locksmith?"

"Rich and colorful work history," she said again, pressing the disc on the lock and popping it loose, avoiding the poke-y center. She dropped the disc into her pants pocket as her eyes adjusted to the dim interior light.

A bell chimed somewhere inside the house, or was it in her head? All the nerves and residual nausea she'd felt since the ferry faded away and she felt...at peace. How was that possible in the creepy, thumb-stabby house? The first impression she had was the smell of lemon and beeswax, with the faint undertone of vinegar. It was the same smell that hung in the air on cleaning days at her childhood home. She'd asked her mom why they used such old-fashioned methods instead of the convenient cleaning products available *right there* at the grocery store. Her mom had only shrugged and told her sometimes the old methods were best. Since Nora didn't allow local workmen, did that mean that she'd cleaned this place herself? Would Riley be required to clean all this herself? If so, the inheritance money and benefit package might not be worth it.

Suddenly, a thought occurred to her. If the Dentons had always taken care of Shaddow House, did that mean Nora had lived here all her life? Had Ellen grown up in this house too, cleaning the surfaces with beeswax and vinegar? How had her mother walked away from…well, a palace, to live in central Florida with her nice enough, but very ordinary father?

For his part, Clark's eyes darted around the foyer, like he was trying to take in every detail. And Riley couldn't blame him. There were plenty of details to take in—maple floors that shone like a mirror, bronze wall sconces, a long ornate red rug that ran from the entryway to the airy yet dignified parlor. Overhead, a tiered crystal chandelier threw splashes of rainbow light around the room. The walls were real plaster as opposed to drywall, painted a pale yellow that should have given the space a sunny feel. But it was cold, so cold that she rubbed her arms to warm them. Still, she wandered further into the house as if she was drawn forward by a magnet, eager to see more.

Every inch of this place seemed designed to intimidate and impress. And if Clark's face was any indication, it was working. He looked positively green as he moved further into the house, looking at the enormous brick fireplace that anchored the parlor. Wheezing, he stepped backwards, towards the sweeping staircase with its hand-carved wooden spindles. All the while, he rubbed his hand at his sternum.

"Are you OK?" she asked.

"Suddenly, I don't feel so well," Clark said, pulling at the collar of his shirt. A light sweat dotted his upper lip. Maybe Riley hadn't been seasick after all. Maybe she'd had some sort of stomach virus? Could she really have infected Clark that quickly?

"Maybe you should come inside and sit down," she offered. "I could get you something to drink."

Clark opened his mouth to answer, but his throat sort of jerked, and he clapped his hand over his mouth. He stumbled toward the door, his voice muffled. "I need to go. You have my card if you need anything. Call me."

Clark scrambled towards the door. Riley followed to close it behind him, but the moment he stepped through, the door slammed behind Clark as if caught in a sudden gust of wind. Her luggage toppled over with the force of it, and the sound echoed through the house in what felt like a threat.

Riley swallowed heavily.

How did a gust of wind come from *inside* the house?

Aunt Nora's letter weighed heavily in her hand. Riley opened the envelope and scanned her aunt's pin-neat handwriting.

Dearest Riley,

Sweet girl, if you are reading this letter, it means I am departed before we could meet. I regret that more than I can say. I wish I could be there to explain everything as I promised. The timing of your arrival was carefully planned, but sometimes, the chaos of life gets in the way of plans.

If you're standing inside Shaddow House, you have accepted the position as steward. And I am ashamed to say that was a bit of manipulation on my part. I knew that no child of Ellen would be able to resist a curiosity like this. And now that you've shed blood on the threshold of Shaddow House, its magic has accepted you and there is no turning back. There is no two weeks' notice. The position is lifelong. But I assure you, it is worth it.

There is magic in your blood, Riley Denton, magic older than you can even imagine. While most witches focus on the magic of nature and the living—which is a perfectly respectable vocation—ours is a completely different skill set. Our magic has always focused on the dead, building the bridges between this plane of existence and the next. We guide those who have passed and have become lost. We comfort those left behind. It is our privilege and our duty.

I'm sorry to burden you with this gift. I'm well aware that it's not what your mother wanted for you. We discussed it, fought over it, so many times. I'm sorry I'm not there to share our family's legacy with you, to teach you about the power in your veins. I'm sorry to tell you that from the moment you read this letter, you need to be very careful. You are not alone in this house. You never will be.

Once you are done being angry with me, rightfully so, explore my office. Everything you need to know is inside the house, waiting for you. There was simply too much information to share in a letter. Listen to Plover. He will know what needs to be done.

Also, please remember to clean your thumb with alcohol. Rule One of Stewardship: Safety first.

With Love,

Nora Riley Denton.

Riley dropped the single page and absently watched it drift to the floor. All the air seemed to have been sucked out of her lungs, leaving her hollowed out, bewildered. Magic? Never alone? No quitting? Plover? What in the Sam Elliott's mustache horror movie hell was happening here?

Riley had quit every job she'd ever had. Well, the ones she hadn't been fired from. How was she supposed to do a job like this? Alone on this tiny weird island she wasn't even sure she could tolerate? How in the hell was she supposed to fulfill a contract she hadn't even known existed?

Also, had she been named after her aunt?

For a panicked second, Riley wondered if the "magic" meant she wasn't able to leave the house at all. As at home as she might have felt in the last few minutes, she didn't want to be kept prisoner there.

Riley ran for the door, which swung open easily. She breathed in huge gulps of fresh air. In the distance, she could hear the waves hitting the shore of Starfall. She could see the crowds of people moving on the streets below, posing for pictures. Suddenly, Riley remembered that Nora died while walking to the post office, so...not a prisoner in the house, then. But what was Nora's letter talking about? Maybe Riley was being too literal. Maybe Nora meant metaphorical magic, like a feeling of being at home? Or maybe this whole thing was a colossal joke?

Riley stepped back inside the house to retrieve the letter from the floor. Why would someone go to all this trouble to pull this joke on her? Was she going to be featured on some horrible reality show about the extremely gullible?

She bent to pick up the fallen paper. A voice behind her, deep and cultured, made her jump as it announced, "All incoming post is left on the silver tray, Miss. Organization tends to make life's little tasks easier, particularly for the staff."

Riley shrieked, swinging her right arm back at throat level as she whipped around. In the corner of her eye, she made out the silvery form of a gaunt man in his fifties, silver-haired and distinguished. He was wearing a black suit, complete with a silver-on-black striped vest and bow tie, the sort of getup she'd seen the servants wear on Edwardian BBC dramas. He was standing so close that her fist *should* have made contact as she turned, but instead a mist rolled over her skin like cold sand. His body made way for her hand like a fog and then reformed, an imperious and annoyed expression on his face.

The man's upper lip curled back in annoyance. "Really, Miss. There's no need for theatrics. If you're this excitable, perhaps overseeing a house full of spirits is not a suitable position for you."

Riley stared at the goose bumps on her hand and then back at the ghost hovering in her foyer. "WHAT THE FUCK!"

Chapter 4
Riley

THERE WAS A GHOST, IN her foyer.

A ghost.

In her foyer.

Standing there dressed like an extra on *Downton Abbey*, as if it was perfectly normal.

And Riley's response was limited to a stream of curse words in her head and a screaming noise that she wasn't entirely sure was internal.

Nope, she was screaming out loud, because the ghost was holding up his transparent hands and shouting, "Please cease and desist at once, Miss!"

Riley's lower jaw clicked shut. The ghost's shoulders relaxed a bit. "Thank you. Now, I assume that you are Miss Riley Denton?"

"Everett," she said, though he didn't note the addition.

"My name is Plover," he said, inclining his head. "Miss Nora told me to expect you."

Riley gasped, "I'm sorry, what? What is happening right now?"

"As one of the more powerful spirits here, I act as an

intermediary between the stewards of Shaddow House and its, shall we say, residents." Plover attempted a smile, but it looked completely unnatural on his thin face.

"OK, OK NO," Riley shouted, holding up her finger. "I grew up in Florida, buddy, heart of Disney country. I've done the Haunted Mansion ride *hundreds* of times. You will not fool me with this amateur-hour bullshit."

Riley waved her hand through Plover's middle, her eyes tracking around the ceiling. "Where's the projector? Are you using water vapor or good old-fashioned angled mirrors?"

"If you please, Miss Riley, it's considered the height of rudeness to thrust one's hand through another's corporeal form without permission," Plover exclaimed. "No matter how intangible that form might be."

"Am I being recorded right now?" she demanded, still waving her hand though his chest. Her hand stung with a pins and needles sensation. "I will not sign the release form for whatever messed-up hidden-camera prank show this is! And screw you for using my family history against me! I knew I should have set my social media to private!"

"I assure you, Miss, this is not some scheme meant to trick you. I am, in fact, a manifestation—" Plover stopped his thoughtful explanation and exclaimed, "Young lady, would you please stop shoving your hand inside my rib cage? Just because I don't have a physical body doesn't mean I don't *feel* it!"

Plover's voice sounded genuinely pained. And while Riley was still convinced this whole thing was a special effects—based scam, the idea that she could be hurting someone was enough to make her yank her hand back. "I'm sorry."

Plover's indignant expression calmed. "Thank you. I will try to remember to make allowances. Unlike the rest of the Denton family, you have not been acquainted with the spirit world since birth, nor your magic. I'm sure this must be quite a shock."

The urge to start yelling questions and cuss words was strong, but Riley held it in. Plover motioned for her to follow him through a set of doors just beyond the parlor. She approached a large maple desk neatly arranged with little brass knickknacks and stacks of files. Riley didn't think any current technology would allow fake ghost imagery to travel from room to room, but she wasn't exactly an expert on the subject.

A stately blue cushioned chair, more like a throne, stood behind the desk. It was shoved back just a bit, as if Nora had risen suddenly to stride out to the post office on the day she died. Another fireplace, this time a white marble affair carved with elaborate gargoyles struggling with climbing roses, was behind the chair, waiting to warm the room. Tall stained glass windows to the left should have let light stream into the room, but it appeared there was another room on the other side of the glass.

"Miss Nora left detailed journals in this office for your perusal," Plover told her, gesturing to the largest gargoyle head carved in the center of the mantel. "Push the gargoyle's tongue back into his mouth."

Riley reached towards the grotesque, grinning head and saw the fresh wound on her thumb. She pulled her hand back. "Wait, is the gargoyle going to bite me?"

Plover shook his head. "I assure you that the blood contract with the doorknob is the only magic of its kind in this house."

"Blood contract with the doorknob' isn't even the weirdest phrase you've said today, is it?" she asked.

Plover pursed his silvery lips and thought about it for a moment, then told her, "No, Miss."

Riley reached for the gargoyle's tongue and gingerly pushed it back into the carved mouth. It slid easily. (Ew.) To the right of the mantel, a tiny drawer popped open from under a cluster of marble roses. Inside was a brass key, much more in line with what she expected for the front door.

"The key fits your aunt's desk drawer," Plover said, pointing at the shallow drawer in the center of the desk. He blinked rapidly for a few seconds, though it couldn't possibly have been necessary, biologically speaking—nor the breath he seemed to drag in for a few moments before adding, "Miss Nora preferred a mix of magic and practical defenses. 'Keep them guessing' is what she always said. She didn't want her journals to be easily accessible, should someone sneak past the house's safeguards."

"It's possible to get past the blood contract doorknob and the ghostly doorman?" she snorted, crossing to the desk.

"I am *not* a doorman, nor a footman. I'm the *head butler*, Miss. I have been the head butler in this household for nearly a century, as I was in life, to the most prominent families in the British Empire."

Riley slid the key into the desk drawer, which unlocked without blood sacrifice. Inside were several very fancy-looking journals bound in leather and blue linen. At the back, almost hidden by shadow, was a wooden box fashioned together in shiny strips of polished maple. She'd seen this sort of thing before, packing orders for a small-time carpenter who sold ring boxes online. It was a puzzle box, opened when the owner slid the strips outward in the right sequence. The first sliding strip was always easy to move, leading one to believe that the rest of the puzzle would be a breeze, but on this box nothing moved. It felt like it was nailed shut. Unfortunately, her experience working with the carpenter was limited to shipping. She was far more familiar with tiny metal lock components than tiny wooden puzzle components.

"Sure," she said absently. "Job titles are probably really important to wait, no, no, this is nuts. I'm not sitting here having a conversation with a ghost-butler about his qualifications while I search my long-lost aunt's secret journals instructing me on how to do some mysterious dead-people-related job *I'm* probably not qualified for. None of this is real."

She stood quickly, knocking the heavy wooden throne back. "I'm getting back on the death trap of a ferry and going to Florida, where things are normal. And that's a sentence I never thought I would say!"

Plover sputtered, "Miss Riley, please, I understand that this is difficult—"

"No, no. Having two half siblings who were so adamant on never seeing me that they refused Christmas presents for five years? That was difficult. Getting a bachelor's degree in general studies from an accredited university? That was difficult. Losing my mother to a car accident before I'd had the chance to have a single healthy, open conversation with her? That was difficult. This? *This is bullshit*!"

Riley, already out of the office, stumbled towards what she

thought was the foyer. But in her haste, she turned right instead of left, through an open pair of French doors that had probably served as the exit to the house's backyard at one point. Now, they opened on an atrium, centering on a stone fountain depicting Persephone, wearing a spring flower crown and kissing a skull cradled in her hand. The space was occupied by several statues in mismatched styles and surrounded by windows into other rooms. Lit from above by thick glass panels, it was probably an absolutely lovely room when you weren't in a blind panic.

Riley bumped into a metal garden chaise, her foot catching on the chair leg. Her arms windmilled comically, and she tumbled back. As the chilly water covered her face, she twisted, trying to sit up, but her legs were propped on the lip of the fountain. She was basically a clumsy turtle on its back. She opened her eyes, but instead of water surrounding her head, she found herself standing in the moonlit courtyard of an enormous French Renaissance country manor—because suddenly it was nighttime and she was outside, which made no sense. A strange, otherworldly feeling of being out of her own time, her own space, made her chest ache. She didn't belong here, but then again, she wasn't sure the young man in breeches and a puffy white shirt did either. This also wasn't his time or place. This was an echo of something he'd once done, quietly leading a horse towards the manor's stables.

Riley watched as a chestnut-haired woman in a dark red hood dashed out of the shadows. The lady giggled, kissing her lover as he took a heavy bag from her. They were so happy, so beautiful together in the moonlight that for a moment, Riley forgot about ghosts and mysterious blood contracts and the fact that she was probably, in reality, still under water.

What *was* this? A dream? A hallucination? It didn't feel *wrong* exactly, just something that she'd never experienced before—like driving a car for the first time. She didn't feel she was completely in control of what was happening, but she wasn't in danger.

The moonlit couple seemed to be eloping, from the way they were trying to load the lady's stuff on the horse as quickly and quietly as possible. Suddenly, a candle shone in one of the first-story windows of the manor, and the cloaked lady whimpered something in French.

The front door burst open, and a dark-haired man in breeches and an untucked shirt came running out, shouting all the way. Riley didn't understand much French, but it didn't sound anything at all like, *"I'm so happy with this life-altering decision you've made without my input! If anybody has a chance of making it work, it's you two crazy kids!"*

The woman cried out something that sounded like *"frère"* and Riley knew that meant "brother." The ardent lover tried to get the lady onto the horse, but she shook her head. The newcomer tackled his sister's betrothed, shoving him into the dirt. They both struggled to their feet as more candles lit the windows of the house. The men tussled, swinging toward the fountain, passing Riley as if she wasn't even there. The lady was caught in their momentum. The brother drew his fist back and elbowed the lady in the face.

As the brother shouted, "Eloise," the girl tumbled back, landing in the fountain. But unlike Riley, Eloise's temple hit the corner of the stone base at Persephone's feet. The sickening crunch of bone filled Riley's ears, and suddenly she was back in the water. The ill-fated woman was lying next to her, her dulled blue eyes open and staring into her own. Blood threaded through the water around them like poison, clouding Riley's vision.

Riley bolted up, her head breaking the surface of the water. She took a deep gulping breath, spluttering and coughing. Plover was standing at the edge of the fountain, staring down at Riley with a mix of disappointment and sympathy.

Riley coughed and pushed to her feet. This was real. Special effects couldn't make her see anything inside her own head, couldn't make her feel the sizzle of magic along her nerve endings. Riley didn't have a history of hallucinations or elaborate delusions. Ghosts were real, and she just witnessed one's origin story.

And it was possible Riley was a witch.

A grayscale version of the ghost lady, eyes deeply shadowed by death, was sitting next to Riley in the water, her fingers almost touching Riley's face. Riley yelped and none-too-gracefully lurched out of the fountain, her clothes dripping water all over the slate tiles.

"Mopping is outside of my housekeeping capabilities, Miss, so you're going to have to clean that yourself," Plover informed her.

Riley dropped her wet butt onto the garden chaise, watching as the ghost lady mournfully sank back into the water.

"That was..." Riley swallowed thickly and nodded.

"That was Mademoiselle Eloise Duchamps," Plover said. "Brought over to the New World in 1921 by your great-grandfather Jonathan Denton during the construction of the great atrium project. It took a crate the size of a carriage to transport her in one piece."

"The ghost or the fountain?" Riley asked.

"Both."

Plover did not appreciate Riley's leaving her wet clothes in a pile on the foyer rug, where she'd deposited them while searching for dry clothes in her suitcase. But he couldn't physically lift the pile, so he had to live with it. Or not, really. She supposed he had a choice.

Ghosts were *real*. Riley had never been one to dismiss the supernatural. She wasn't close-minded enough to believe this was the only plane of existence, that human life was all there was in the universe. But those thoughts had occurred to her at a philosophical, academic distance, before she'd gone for a swim in ghost water. Ghost water made everything very real.

For now, she was wrapped in her own bathrobe and her favorite pair of pajamas. She'd ventured into the cavernous kitchen to cobble together a cup of tea. Plover hovered anxiously behind Riley as if she could set fire to the kitchen any second. She supposed that was fair, considering the fountain episode.

The kitchen was all copper and brick elegance, heavy pots hanging from a rack over a monstrous cast iron stove. Workmanlike oak benches bracketed a long heavy table, the sort of thing Riley imagined her family eating messy informal breakfasts on, right in front of a rough stone fireplace big enough to roast an ox. There was an actual spit in there, if Riley felt like giving it a try. The one exception to this old-world splendor was a plain old white dry-erase board found at any office supply warehouse, hanging near the entrance of the walk-in butler's pantry. Riley thought it odd that Nora would use something so pedestrian to keep track of her grocery list, and was just about to say something when the dry-erase marker suddenly lifted from its little tray, as if suspended on wires, and scrawled out HI in block letters.

"Uhhhhh...Plover?" Riley whispered, moving away from the marble counter to watch the marker's progress across the surface. "What the fuck is that?"

"Is that particular profanity a favorite of yours?" he asked archly. "Must you use it in every sentence?"

"Correct my unpolished American manners later," she shot back, flinging her hand towards the whiteboard. "Is that my aunt Nora, trying to speak to me?"

For the breadth of a moment, an expression of longing crossed Plover's face, before he shook his head. "No, your aunt has truly moved beyond this world. As much as I might have liked her to stay with me, she'd been trapped in this place for far too long. It was her dream that her ashes be sprinkled at the head of the convergence of the Mississippi and Ohio Rivers, so she might circulate into the Gulf of Mexico and around the world."

It might be Riley's clearly overtaxed nerves, but did Plover sound *wistful,* talking about her aunt? Had Plover and Aunt Nora been a thing? Was that even possible?

"That is Miss Natalie."

"Wait. Who is Miss Natalie?" Riley demanded. "Is she another relative? How many ghosts are haunting this house?"

Plover said, "I believe the last count was one thousand, two hundred, and eighty-four spirits within these walls."

"Fuck." Riley gasped, making Plover wince. "Sorry. How

are there *that* many ghosts in one house? How many deaths have happened here? Is this like that H. H. Holmes murder castle?"

"The ghosts are not attached to the house, Miss, merely contained here," he told her. "They are attached to the many objects that the Denton family has collected over the generations. Generally speaking, the objects are either connected to the spirits' demise or represented great emotional attachment in life. They're placed in nearly every room in the house, save the bedrooms. The family believed that those rooms should remain a safe place of rest."

"So...these haunted objects are just scattered around the house, *unlabeled?*" she cried. "Because I didn't see any sort of plaque in front of the fountain that said, BEWARE OF SAD SOGGY LADY GHOST."

From the atrium, the fountain ghost made an offended gurgling sound.

"I'm sorry!" Riley called in response. "Unfiltered chatter is how I process!"

"Previous stewards believed it was dangerous to keep the items, labeled or otherwise, in one place within the house. If an interested party managed to break in, they would know which items to pilfer. So they are, as you said, scattered around the house, under the guise of everyday objects, unlabeled. For instance, there's a particularly irritable phantom attached to the toaster." Plover paused to nod towards an older Bakelite model from the 1950s, just behind her. "As long as the spirit doesn't have a history of injuring people, they are allowed to roam the house at will."

"You couldn't have mentioned this vicious haunted toaster while I was standing next to it?" she cried.

"Eventually, over time, you will develop a sense for which objects in the house are haunted and which are simply household items," Plover told her. "But if it makes you feel better, the toaster's ghost has never injured a living person."

"OK, but who the hell haunts a toaster?" she demanded as if he hadn't even spoken. "And, a final query, who the hell would *steal* a haunted toaster? What sort of messed-up alternate evil-appliance universe have I stumbled into here?"

"There have always been those who wished to put the dead to their own use," Plover said, his tone dark enough to make Riley clamp her mouth shut. "We ghosts are quite literally attached to our objects, emotionally and paranormally. For example, Natalie's most cherished days were spent at a Seattle-area office where she felt her purpose was fulfilled. She used this board while laboring on something called an 'app.' She and her coworkers scribbled ideas on it while scheming to help people find mates of their own age and interests through their telephones."

The dry-erase marker moved across the board to draw the icon of one of the most popular "mate finder" apps on the market. Or at least the logo they'd used several years before.

"It was profound for her, to have a place where she belonged, where she was understood by her coworkers, where she helped people," Plover said. "The cruel irony being that she never found soulmate connection of her own before she was struck down by a bubble tea truck while crossing the street."

Riley nodded. "Well, that's pretty terrible."

"Her persistent presence at the office was unnerving to her former colleagues, and she ended up here," Plover explained.

"Why can't I see her, like I see you?" Riley asked.

"She's choosing not to let you see her at the moment, an option available to any of the nonliving residents of the house. She says she's an introvert and prefers this method of communication with unfamiliar people."

"Makes sense," Riley said. "You do you, Natalie."

"You've probably seen spirits your entire life without realizing it, Miss," Plover said. "Your great-great-uncle Anthony interacted with the house's ghosts as a toddler, quite unaware that his 'gray friends' were anything but living."

"So, the men in the family can see ghosts too?" she asked. "That's pretty progressive."

"As one grows older, the lies we tell ourselves to deny the otherworldly grow stronger. If you'd never arrived here on the island, you might have gone your whole life without a single inter-action with the dead."

"Yeah, that would have been terrible," Riley muttered.

She reached for the kettle, and her hand froze midair.

Wait. The shower-curtain lady.

When Riley was little, her parents had moved into a lovely, spacious four-bedroom in one of the more desirable developments outside Orlando. In the competitive real estate market, it was an almost unheard of find that would allow Riley's half-siblings to have their own rooms, which they insisted they had to have in order to visit their father.

Riley had loved the house too, until the first night after the move, when she'd shuffled out of her carefully decorated butter-cup yellow bedroom to use the bathroom, using only her My Little

Pony nightlight to guide her. She had a distinct memory of reaching for the toilet paper, only to see another hand, blotchy purple and gnarled with dark blue veins over the knuckles, reaching from behind the closed shower curtain. Riley sat frozen as the those long bony fingers closed over the curtain, pulling it back with aching slowness until the silhouette of a twisted profile and stringy hair stood stark against the shadowed recesses of the tub. When that head had turned toward her, the curve of a hideous smile barely visible in the pinkish half-light, Riley had bolted out of the room, screaming for her parents.

Her mother had insisted that it was just a nightmare, nerves over the move, and starting a new school. But...they'd moved out of the house only a few weeks later. And it was so weird because Riley knew how excited her parents had been when they'd bought it. She remembered her parents having a huge argument about moving away. Or at least, her mother had argued. Riley couldn't remember her father saying anything...which wasn't unusual in their marriage.

What if that hadn't been her parents fighting? What if her mother had been trying to cast the bathtub ghost out of the house, but the spirit had been too strong to banish? What if they'd had to move out of the "dream house" for that squatty three-bedroom because they wouldn't have been able to cohabitate with a creepy bathtub ghost? Not without permanent emotional damage to Riley.

When she thought back over her childhood, there had been several sudden moves like that, moving into a house that her parents were excited about, only to suddenly change neighborhoods. Her mother had always attributed the moves to better schools or a shorter commute for her father. Were all of those moves because of ghosts in their houses? Her mother had clearly turned her nose up at magic, and Riley supposed that magic hadn't appreciated being tossed aside. No wonder her mother's magic hadn't been enough to cast out the bathtub ghost. And how was she supposed to teach Riley how to control it when she was pretending it didn't exist?

"Why wouldn't she tell me?" she asked, not talking to Plover in particular. The hurt, the pain she hadn't even realized was lurking there at the top of her throat hung between them like a stain on the air. "Why didn't she protect me?"

Plover shrugged his insubstantial shoulders. "From what I understand, your mother simply rejected her calling. And from what Miss Nora told me, magic doesn't tolerate disdain. A lone witch, without the support of her circle, who openly rejects her power? She wouldn't have much sway with the spirits."

Riley felt a flush of guilt. Her half-siblings had refused to set foot in the "dream house," or every house they'd owned after, because they insisted her parents never wanted them there in the first place.

There were other moments in her life that made a lot more sense now. The figure of a boy outside her cabin window at camp, who never got in trouble for being out on the girls' side after dark. That time she swore she saw a maid in 1930s garb at a super-modern boutique hotel in Charlottesville. The leisure suit–clad teacher at her middle school who never seemed to teach classes or talk to anyone. But that could have been a case of tenure gone wrong. What did she know?

A feeling of profound loneliness swept over Riley. She couldn't share this with anyone. Her father worked as an aerospace engineer. If she brought up ghosts to him, he would probably book a full psych evaluation for her. But instead of expressing that doubt, she changed the subject. "You're not going to explain the toaster ghost to me, are you?"

Plover snorted. "You're not ready to meet the toaster ghost, Miss."

"Is that statement weirder or less weird than 'blood contract with a doorknob'?" Riley wondered.

Plover seemed to pause to think it over, while his lips quirked up. She considered that a personal victory. "I'm not sure."

"Just to be clear, using the possibly evil toaster or any object random object in the house isn't going to leave me cursed or infected with some sort of magical rash or something is it?"

"The haunted objects' only power is their emotional significance to their respective ghosts," Plover assured her.

"And do I use the whiteboard to communicate with other reluctant ghosts in the house? Or is this a Ouija board situation? Because I have seen how this works out for the gullible blond girl in the horror movie, and that is a hard pass from me."

"Miss Natalie is the only ghost here able to physically interact with her board," he said dryly. "Even I cannot affect it physically. Like every ghost here, I can only manipulate my own attachment object."

Riley tried to prompt him. "And that would be...?"

"I don't know if it's in my best interest to tell you," Plover said, smirking. "It seems unfair to simply hand you the answers. You strike me as a young lady who needs a challenge."

"I could strike you as a young lady who starts stuffing random household objects into a trash compactor," she told him, her tone dry as dust.

"No!" he barked, making her brows rise. "That would be a costly mistake, Miss."

Riley grinned. So the ghosts didn't want anything to happen to their attachment objects. Interesting. Maybe she held more power here than she believed.

Plover cleared his throat. "Ouija boards are not necessary for a Denton. Your magic will allow you to communicate freely with the ghosts, once you acclimate and the ghosts choose to show themselves. You just have to open your mind to the possibilities, the power. Dentons who try to force it or resist it—they're the ones who suffer."

Dentons like her mother? Ellen had clearly rejected whatever this was—legacy, lunacy, whatever. She'd run as far away as humanly possible. Riley wondered how it was possible that Ellen had kept all of this from her. Had she really preferred distant isolation from Riley to sharing this weird-ass burden?

Probably.

Unwilling to explore that bit of emotional baggage in her current state, Riley sipped her tea. It was some fancy loose-leaf English brand Riley had never heard of, which required a tea ball to brew. The malty, slightly floral flavor settled her stomach like nothing else had that day. In fact, Aunt Nora's kitchen was stocked with all sorts of luxury food brands that required shipping from overseas—dark Belgian chocolates, British ginger biscuits, exotic Italian cheeses cased in wax.

"Well, I won't starve here, that's for sure," Riley muttered.

"Miss Nora rarely left the island, never for more than twenty-four hours. Her duties as steward required her constant presence, so she took her creature comforts where she could. She had a very good relationship with the family that runs the local general store," Plover said, standing on the right side of the fireplace, staring fondly at a small photo of Aunt Nora and Riley's mother on the mantel, which, according to the inscription, had been taken at a New Year's party in 1982, years before Ellen met Riley's dad.

Unlike most photos of the time, this silver-framed portrait lacked regrettable haircuts or neon clothes. Nora and Ellen were dressed in elegant, knee-length cocktail dresses in muted colors—Nora in a cheerful yellow and Ellen in a steely blue—their dark honey-colored hair twisted into matching chignons. Nora looked calm and confident, serenely smiling into the camera. Ellen looked...miserable, like she didn't trust whoever was holding the camera. And this was the photo Aunt Nora chose to display on her mantel? Why not some happy Christmas morning snapshot, or something taken during a family celebration? Riley wondered if it was the last photo that the sisters had taken together.

Riley noticed that Plover never sat down. She wasn't sure whether that was because he was dead or because of his training in life. She was not comfortable with how quickly she was adjusting to thinking this way.

Wait.

"Nora rarely left? Does that mean I'm not allowed to leave?" Riley demanded suddenly. "I can't even go off island for the weekend? Since the freaking doorknob tricked me into a blood contract?"

The frames on the mantel began to rattle. The thrill of fear down Riley's spine in response only made her angrier. She'd lost her mother. She'd lost the last link to the family her mother left behind. And she'd been tricked into some sort of blood pact with a haunted Scooby Doo storage warehouse. This was so much worse than cleaning private jets after charter flights full of entitled yummy mummies who left them a wasteland of discarded fashion magazines and spilled chardonnay. It wasn't as bad as the telemarketing, but still! Somehow, the angrier she got, the more frantically the frames danced across the rough-hewn surface.

"Please calm down, Miss Riley," Plover said, a guilty downward angle turning his mouth. "The items in this kitchen are quite old, not to mention expensive."

"That's me doing that?" she whispered, her fingertips tingling with a strange, creeping awareness.

"It's unskilled panicked magic, without purpose. It is the sort of thing an angry Denton child might accomplish in connection with haunted objects." She got the impression that Plover would have flushed guiltily if he had any blood circulating in his cheeks.

"Thanks for that," she muttered sulkily.

"I've seen many young Dentons experience something similar over the years," he assured her. "You *can leave* but it will be very uncomfortable, to the point where it's almost unbearable—at least, that's how Miss Nora described it. Your connection with your magic will grow stronger, the more time you spend in the house. And to answer your earlier question, no. I'm sure Miss Nora wouldn't have taken such measures if she hadn't been desperate. *You* are the last of the Dentons, for better or worse."

"Why couldn't someone else take the job?" she asked, trying desperately to keep the tired whine out of her tone. "Surely the Shaddow family could have tracked down some paranormal psychologist who would *love* the job as steward."

"The 'job' belongs to the Dentons. No one else. You may find helpmates, but the responsibility falls on *you*." Plover shook his head. "There was, as you might say, no backup plan. It is too dangerous to leave Shaddow House unattended."

All feelings of resentful claustrophobia made way to fear. "Too dangerous?"

Plover nodded. "There was a time when the entire family's energies were devoted to helping ghosts resolve their issues and move along to the next plane before they could do any harm to humans. But that was when the Denton family was two dozen strong."

"I thought ghosts couldn't hurt people," Riley said.

Plover sniffed. "Who told you that?"

Riley's lips curled back. "Pretty sure it was an old episode of *Charmed*..."

"Well, it was quite incorrect. We may not be able to affect inanimate objects, but living tissues?" Plover paused to shudder. "Nevertheless, the family shrank over the generations, until all that was left were your mother and your aunt."

"Why haven't you ever moved along to the next plane?"

"I simply have too much to do here," he told her airily. "That said, not all of the spirits in this house are as benevolent as me or

Mademoiselle Eloise. You will need to exercise extreme caution until you adjust to the environment. None of this gallivanting around the rooms willy-nilly."

"I wasn't gallivanting. I was fleeing in terror," she noted.

"Learn to flee at a more cautious pace," he replied.

"I'm assuming that these duties you keep referring to are related to feeding and watering the ghosts or something?" she asked, and Plover nodded slowly. "Also, why didn't a spirit from the family come to explain all of this to me? Why did they leave it to you?"

He sniffed. "You'll understand in due time, Miss. For now, I would advise you to locate the master list of objects, which the Denton family referred to as the Codex. It is stored somewhere in the house, again, to protect the objects from thieves. That is your first task as steward, using the information in Miss Nora's diaries and whatever may be contained in that puzzle box to locate the Codex."

"Can't I just wiggle my fingers and use magic to find it?" she asked. Riley reached into her pocket for the key-slash-coin. She unhooked the necklace around her throat and pulled the craft store finding—a chunk of citrine that reminded her of solidified sunshine—off the chain. She threaded it through the tiny hole in the Denton coin and slipped it over her head. It seemed too important to trust it to the vast ocean of debris at the bottom of her purse.

"Please consult your aunt's journals before you attempt any sort of magic," he told her.

"OK, am I allowed to ask for help? Contact the Shaddows? Where do they come in?" she asked.

"Your first instinct as steward is to *ask for help?*" Plover scoffed. "Perhaps you're correct. You may not be suited to this position."

"I was raised by a distant and withholding mother, Plover. Your reverse psychology won't work on me," she said, making him frown at her. "And it occurs to me that the space under that counter over there would be the perfect size for a trash compactor."

Plover stared at her for a long moment, as if he could see the wheels turning in her head. "I'm afraid I've exhausted my energy for the day. Good evening, Miss Riley. Sleep well."

Plover faded from sight without a word from Riley, which she was pretty sure was a violation of his butler etiquette. She supposed that didn't apply after death, though.

"Just so you know, if there are any evil haunted dolls in this house, they go in the trash compactor first!" she yelled after Plover.

After a moment, she added, "And that goes for any sort of toy that speaks a creepy nursery rhyme without its string being pulled—trash compactor! Any music box that plays off-key plinky-plunky music too slowly? Trash compactor! Any object that independently rolls down the hallway toward my bedroom door? Trash compactor!"

Riley slid onto the long table bench and reached for her teacup. Then, remembering that the cup could be haunted by some malevolent tea-flinging poltergeist, she dropped her head onto the table and thunked it against the surface. She hissed in pain. "This potentially haunted table is pretty solid. Ow."

Chapter 5
Edison

HOW HAD SO MUCH GONE so wrong so quickly?

How had he managed to take a situation that fate or irony or the universe's team of hateful comedy writers had made pretty awful and then just keep making it worse? He might have been able to salvage the "bathroom hogging" thing if he hadn't said the worst possible things to Riley Denton. Of course, she'd snapped back at him. She already seemed hurt, she'd just lost her aunt, and he'd managed to offer her no comforting words. And she was apparently staying in this strange place that was difficult to adjust to even when you weren't struggling with grief and guilt.

Maybe he was projecting a little bit there.

And *yes*, again, that little line between her brows when she was beautifully and brilliantly angry? Well, that was going to be a real problem.

How was she going to be able to stay on the island if the ferry made her so sick? What if her arrival made the Shaddows decide to sell off as so many descendants of the old families had done over the years? He'd failed not only Riley, but the residents of Starfall

Point, who could have finally had access to Shaddow house's rich history, *their* history...if he hadn't mucked it up so spectacularly.

He sat on the porch of his little house, facing quite intentionally away from the water, watching the sunlight filter green through the leaves. He forced his mind to focus on that verdant light, the peace inside it. He loved his little cottage, such a far cry from where he'd grown up near Balboa Island, the slick, contemporary mini mansions stretching the California real estate dollar to the breaking point.

It was quiet here, on the edge of the island's state park lands. No crowds. No noise. No traffic, certainly, unless you counted Dana, the eleven-year-old girl who delivered his paper. Damn near every morning, he saw deer shuffling through his backyard, as if he wasn't even there.

He took a long pull from his beer, smiling at the sound of long loping steps clomping up the driveway. He smiled. He'd heard so much about the intrusion of small-town interest on newcomers, but when he'd arrived, most everybody kept their distance. It was less respectful space and more backhanded rejection, but still, given his emotional state, it had worked for him.

But Edison had thrived in the impartiality of strangers here on Starfall. Part of the reason he came to the island was to get away from everybody he ever knew. Starfall was as far as he could get from California at the time. And he knew by surrounding himself in water, he would never leave. He wouldn't travel. He would stay in one place and give himself the small, limited life he'd believed he deserved. He'd needed the quiet, the space provided by the reluctance of the community to befriend a newcomer. He'd needed to mourn. His parents were concerned—not concerned enough to come visit, certainly, but concerned. They didn't understand his need to shut himself away on this tiny island where "no one who mattered" lived. Kyle Ashmark was one of those people who "didn't matter," one of the first people to actually visit him here at home.

Kyle folded his lanky, long-legged frame into his twin Adirondack chair. Edison wondered how he could stand the strain against his thin rounded shoulders that spoke more to his desire to appear shorter than a particular problem with his posture. Girls tended to get skittish around a guy that was six-foot-five, even if he was built like Jack Skellington. Kyle reached into the cooler between them and pulled out a beer bottle.

"Hey," Edison said, eyebrows arched. He picked a diet soda out of the cooler and handed it to Kyle, who was only nineteen and, therefore, under the legal drinking age. "Not at my place. I will not contribute to your delinquency."

"Fine," Kyle grumbled.

This dance around beer access was a ritual they did every time Kyle visited, something they'd done at least once a week since Kyle came home the previous spring, just shy of completing his sophomore year of college. That April, Kyle hadn't checked on his mother for a few days, instead catching up on his assignments and relishing the joy of being out in the big wide world. By the time the neighbors found her body, Susan Ashmark was long past saving. The guilt was just too much for Kyle to bear. He didn't have the energy to stay in school, to do anything but find a way to exist.

Edison knew how that felt. It was an awful thing to share with someone, but it bonded them just the same.

"So, I hear you had an eventful morning," Kyle said, grinning at him.

"Ugh." Edison groaned and let his head drop back against the wooden chair with a dull *thunk*.

"I heard she yelled at you *twice*," Kyle added.

"Nana Grapevine?" Edison asked as Kyle nodded, snickering into his soda.

"Yes. Agnes McBale, in particular. Did Ms. Denton really make you cry the second time?" Kyle asked.

"There's nothing wrong with a grown man crying," Edison told him, clearing his throat. "Not that I did."

"Even when she got the better of you verbally?" Kyle asked.

Edison grunted into his beer bottle.

"Did you really talk about being in each other's shoes after she vomited on yours?"

"Enough about me," Edison snapped. "What happened while I was out of town? How's work?"

Kyle shook his head, the setting sun turning his normally light-brown hair a shade of garish orange. "Same old, same old. Sitting in a security office all day at the Duchess, monitoring video feeds of exhausted tourists and fragile antique furnishings."

"What about that girl at the gift shop? Callie, right? You ask her out yet?" Edison asked.

Kyle made a sour face. "She thought *Call of the Wild* was the name of a perfume. My interest waned."

Edison shuddered. When Kyle wasn't working at the sprawling

Edwardian hotel, he volunteered at the library. He'd found he had more in common with Margaret and Edison than the kids his own age, which made Edison a little sad for him.

"How was the scheduled triweekly call with your parents? Was going off-island enough to get you out of it?" Kyle asked. Edison grimaced into his beer, making Kyle hoot, "Man, this is just not your *day*!"

"I'm supposed to call them later tonight. Remember, they're four hours behind. And 'Your mother appreciates her routines, son.'"

Kyle offered no sympathy, just grinning and asking, "Which lecture are you expecting this time? 'Academia is a fine pursuit, as long as you get the right job doing the right research at the right university' or 'Helds are lawyers, professors, philanthropists, pillars of the community, son. It's time for you to step up to the plate'?"

"Little bit of column A, with a smattering of column B, with a tiny soupçon of 'Helds are meant to hold public office, not *serve* the public.' Which tells you all you need to know about my family." He sipped his beer, remembering the disappointment that practically seeped through Amherst and Catherine Held's end of the line in a viscous sludge in every carefully scheduled call. It was why the calls didn't happen every *two* weeks.

"Well, how are they supposed to accept that you have a customer service job if you keep using words like *soupçon?*" Kyle asked.

Edison grumbled, prompting Kyle to add, "You never should have gotten the second doctorate degree. It gave them false hope."

"I got that degree before I even moved here," Edison told him.

His parents had assumed that his interest in majoring in library science had been a stepping stone towards something more dignified. Then when Edison doubled down, his father insisted it was some sort of extremely bookish rebellion. They'd dismissed him, ridiculed him, cut him from the support they'd offered so freely when they thought he was going to do what they expected of him.

But Edison couldn't live without the work that brought him joy. Since he was a child, Edison had loved how stories were like shoes, each person preferring their own style, their own fit. Sometimes, you had to help people try on story after story, letting the discarded ones pile up until they found the right one. As a librarian, he could be the one who helped people find their fit, particularly new readers who had the whole world of books ahead of them. But his parents didn't get that. Somehow they always translated this sentiment into "So now, you want to be a shoe salesman?"

If not for a generous trust from his maternal grandfather, he might not have been able to finish graduate school. His engagement to Erin had given them all a little breathing space, where his parents could pretend they weren't disappointed in his life choices as long as he married someone so obviously suitable. (Even if her more "qualifying" attributes had been that she was also smart, beautiful, funny, and relentlessly kind.) And then he'd lost Erin to stupid, senseless tragedy, and they had come through for him when it counted most. He couldn't let himself forget that. While his parents hadn't exactly "come around," they'd at least stopped trying to wrestle control of his life from him. They'd retreated to passive-aggressive guilting and a predictable arsenal of lectures.

"So I guess you managed to talk them out of visiting again, huh?" Kyle asked.

Edison rolled his eyes. "They put up a token protest as usual, but no, I don't think I'm in any danger. Unless the Duchess goes through a serious upgrade."

Kyle frowned. "They wouldn't stay with you?"

For the first time that day, Edison laughed wholeheartedly, at the very idea of his mother and father sleeping on his pullout couch. Kyle punched him lightly on the arm. "See? You're laughing. It can't be that bad."

"It *was* that bad," he assured Kyle.

"Any idea how to fix it?"

"Nope." Edison held up his hand. "And if you say flowers, I swear to God—"

Kyle burst out laughing. "I think you're going to need more than flowers."

Edison hung his head.

Kyle continued on, "I assume it's still your goal to get access to Shaddow House?"

"I've written to the Shaddow Family Trust at least a dozen times. They just ignore me. And Nora Denton called me a sanctimonious jackass. To my face."

Edison would be willing to admit that perhaps he had taken this whole quest for access into Shaddow House just a little too personally. Yes, the academic in him absolutely *itched* to get inside that place just to touch things. (While wearing acid-free white cotton archivist's gloves, of course.) But something about the way Nora Denton had completely rejected his overtures, without even considering what he asked, triggered the tenacious part of his personality.

"Maybe I should just let the whole thing drop," Edison mused. "She's grieving. We know how that feels."

"She also doesn't know anyone in this town, you realize that right?" Kyle told him. "She may not want as much distance from the town as her aunt did. Maybe she'll actually *want* to open up the house and get to know some of her neighbors."

Edison nodded. "I accept your premise, but that doesn't mean I'm in any position to ask."

"Yeah, it sounds like she wants your head on a platter," Kyle conceded. "Maybe portions of your buttocks, served sashimi-style."

"That's, uh, vivid."

Kyle snickered, "I was taking a creative writing class when I left school."

Edison shuddered. "Well, you're probably right about how she's feeling. It's got to be freaky to be a stranger in a new town with no family, living in that big old house by herself. And she's from Florida, so she's probably freezing. Maybe I could make amends by bringing her a pair of those cozy novelty fleece socks or something?"

"Making amends is a good idea, even if the sock thing is sort of weird, given your misguided accidental shoe puns," Kyle suggested.

Edison huffed out a breath, grateful that Kyle had helped him avoid yet another foot-related misstep. "Good point. No socks. Maybe a really nice fluffy blanket or something."

"You need to think a little bigger. What else can you give her that no one else can?" Kyle asked.

"A library card?" Edison suggested, feeling extremely lame, even as the words came out of his mouth.

"Exactly. See, now you're thinking! You can give her," he paused to make a grand hand gesture. "A connection to the community, a sense of belonging. Access to one of the premiere entertainment venues in town, without the hassle of paperwork."

"Is it possible that, as my friend, you're giving me a little too much moral support?" Edison asked. "'Access to one of the premiere entertainment venues in town'?"

"We don't have a movie theater. Blockbuster shut down before they could open a store here. The community theater only does those 'summertainment' musical shows for the tourists. The bookstore mostly sells local history and guidebooks." Kyle threw up his hands. "What would you call the library?"

"OK, you make a valid point. Though I don't think bringing her a library card is the right move here." Edison grimaced. "Or flowers. Or fudge."

Kyle nodded. "I'm not sure how you'll come back from what you did, but I support you entirely."

Chapter 6
Riley

IT WAS HARD TO EXPLAIN to one's father that "ghost problems" had prevented the expected call to assure him that she'd made it safely to her haunted destination. So Riley didn't even try.

"Dad, I'm sorry. I was so exhausted from the trip that I just fell into bed and passed out." She spoke into the cell phone, balanced on the edge of the massive four-poster bed, grateful for the morning light pouring in through her nearly floor-to-ceiling windows in the Cobalt Room. She cringed as she waited for her father's response. She'd never been good at lying to him, to her high school friends' frustration—but the story wasn't entirely untrue, she supposed.

She'd gotten lost twice on her route to the family wing. Nora had clearly occupied the Marigold Room, a sunny chamber decorated in varying shades of gold. A pair of sensible beige pumps were tossed beside Nora's enormous dresser. An ivory cardigan hung over the back of her vanity chair. Riley stood in the door, trying to glean something about her aunt's life, until Plover felt the need to reappear and point her in the right direction "for her own safety." And then he disappeared before she could ask any more questions, such as *Why does this door open to a brick wall?* or *Why does this stairway lead directly into the hallway ceiling?*

Plover's assurances that the bedrooms were spelled to be "ghost free" felt like cold comfort when her surroundings felt like a set piece from some Edgar Allen Poe story. Frankly, she'd been surprised to find modern conveniences like updated outlets and a healthy supply of hot water in her luxurious cavern of a bathroom. Not that she'd had enough nerve for more than a three-minute soap and rinse under the brass showerhead cast so the water poured out of Medusa's mouth. (Seriously, what the hell?) She had multiple flashbacks to every horror movie starlet murdered mid-shampooing and hopped out of the tub wielding her conditioner bottle like a blade.

She was grateful there were no ghosts around to see that.

She *hoped* there were no ghosts around to see that.

"It's not like you, not to call. I got worried." Her father's warm voice echoed across the room, bouncing off the cobalt-and-gold wallpaper.

The heavy oak bed was *built into* the wall. She'd never seen anything like it. Most of her life she'd slept on laminate furniture from catalog. She'd been distracted, staring at the ornately carved marble mantelpiece with hundreds of tiny symbols centered around the now-familiar "twisted S inside a house" motif. Her eyes would almost grasp the pattern of the shapes... Were those runes? But then she would blink and the image would fade. Riley huffed out a frustrated breath. She imagined she would have to learn how to light the damn fireplace eventually. A southern transplant like herself could only sleep under so many blankets.

Oh, good grief. Winter. In Michigan. *Northern* Michigan. She was doomed.

"Riley, are you there?"

"Sorry, Dad, just a little off-kilter."

"It's not like you don't have good reason," he scoffed. "I'm so sorry it's turned out like this for you. I should have known it wasn't a good idea, sending you to that island all by yourself. I *never* would have told you to go if I'd known your aunt Nora wouldn't be there to see you."

"Well, it's not like Aunt Nora abandoned me to a sudden urge to go to Vegas, Dad. She died."

"Still, maybe you bit off more than you can chew, family history–wise," he sighed.

Riley pinched the bridge of her nose. She'd *definitely* bit off more than she could chew, but she wasn't about to tell her father about any of it. There was no way that her father knew any of this. Hank Everett had never been the most demonstrative of fathers, but he wouldn't have let her walk into this unawares. He believed in preparation in all things, even if he'd preferred to sort of distance himself, formless, like a backdrop in an awkward family photo.

No. It was better for her dad to just stay at home in Florida, where the only threats were angry reptiles and the weather. And other Floridians.

"Even Katie and Junior are worried about you," he said.

Riley nearly dropped the phone, pulling it away from her face and pulling her chin towards her chest in disbelief. Her half-siblings didn't "worry" about her. They preferred to pretend she didn't exist, that her parents' marriage had just been a bad dream.

"Oh." Riley cleared her throat. "I didn't realize you were talking again."

Her father murmured, "Well, they've been calling, coming around more since…"

Since her mother died. Since Riley announced she was leaving. Now that the "problems" were gone, her half-brother and sister were willing to have a relationship with their father, something that they'd called "toxic" only a few months before, when they'd refused to come to Ellen's funeral.

She tried not to let it hurt, the disloyalty—that her father was so eager for a relationship with the people who had rejected her so thoroughly and viciously over the years that he was willing to let them just stroll back into his life as if nothing happened. As if they hadn't hurt Riley or her mother. She tried to focus on good things. Good intentions. That was what magic was supposed to be about, right?

At least, that's what she'd seen in movies and TV. Good intentions echoing back? So, she tried to focus on her father's happiness. Putting on her brightest tone of voice, Riley said, "I don't know. It's kind of nice here, quiet. And I'm learning a lot about Mom."

She could hear the pause on the other end of the line, hanging heavy like a lead weight. Riley couldn't believe she'd brought up the subject of her mother so casually, so thoughtlessly, especially in the same conversation about Ellen's death, after so many months of avoiding the subject like a faulty land mine. Hank cleared his throat, before rasping out, "Like what?"

"Oh, just stuff about Mom, the family, grandma and grandpa Denton and all that," she said, keeping her tone overtly vague. "Their neighbors have a lot of stories."

"Maybe you should come on home," her father said. "This is all too much for you, Riley, after everything you've been through in the last year."

Come home and derail the progress Dad was making with his other kids? He'd been waiting for them to "come home" for years. The minute she stepped foot in Florida again, they'd just leave him all over again. She swallowed thickly. "I think I'm going to stick it out."

"What do you mean, stick it out? How long are you planning to stay there?"

"I don't know," she lied. "It's not like I have a job to come back to. Unless you're planning on selling all my stuff at a yard sale, I think I'm pretty safe."

Riley's heart sank as she realized that the house's magic meant she wouldn't be able to visit her father for the foreseeable future. Would he be able to visit *her* safely, if he ever decided he could? What if the ghosts hurt him? What if they lashed out at Hank as the person who stole Ellen away?

He snorted. "Well, I guess you'll lose interest pretty soon and come on back. I know my girl."

Riley nearly objected, but then remembered that she'd had two jobs so far that year, and it was only mid-spring. "That's fair."

In the background of the call, she heard her dad's squeaky kitchen door groan open. Her sister's voice rang through the receiver. "Dad? Breakfast!"

It hurt more than Riley expected. It was the sort of casual drop-in visit her parents had always hoped for but had been impossible, with her half-siblings refusing to see Hank as long as Ellen and

Riley were home. Riley made excuses to get off the phone without commenting on Katie's presence. Her father didn't object and she was grateful for it.

Eager for distraction, Riley thumbed through the page of search results she'd found on Edison Held, PhD, the night before. Frankly, she was grateful that somehow the island had enough signal to support her apps. She hadn't *set out* to online stalk Edison. She really hadn't, but somehow, there she'd been at midnight, scrolling through his search results.

Edison's education itself was intimidating. He had *PhDs*, multiple. Riley had barely finished her bachelor's after switching majors twice. And that was only after her parents threatened to pull back what little financial support they gave her. Edison didn't have much of a social media presence—neither did Riley, because she didn't want to endanger her already shaky job prospects with posts an employer might find objectionable. But she found a wealth of impressive work under Edison's name, journal articles and chapters in books of historical research. He seemed to have an interest in the War of 1812 and the territory struggles along the border between Canada and the United States.

Suddenly, Edison's desire to see what was hidden inside Shaddow House made more sense. Portions of the house had been standing during the historical period that was his favorite, something he was obviously very passionate about. He probably thought there was some treasure trove of historical documents inside the house, and maybe there was.

Riley stretched as she hopped off the massive bed, sore and stiff. She'd stayed up all night, reading Aunt Nora's journals until she felt like her eyes might cross. She'd learned more about her family in a few hours than her mother had revealed in thirty-plus years.

Riley learned that the Dentons originally plied their craft as mediums in London, helping people communicate with lost loved ones and banishing troublesome ghosts attached to their former possessions. The Denton matriarch, Elizabeth, didn't want to destroy the spirits, but keep them from hurting people until she figured out a way to resolve their unfinished business and help them pass into the afterlife. Elizabeth and her husband, Oliver, designed special communication and containment spells to detect the haunted objects and keep the ghosts confined. The clients went on their merry un-haunted way, and the Dentons either helped the ghosts resolve the issues that kept them earthbound or, if the ghost was violent, *forced* them out of the earthly plane altogether. In return, clients allowed the Dentons to sell any objects that were no longer haunted, helping them amass a considerable fortune. They invested wisely, and that fortune grew.

The Dentons' magic appeared to be some sort of system of charmed herbs and salt, with runes they'd created themselves and drew in the air with one's hands. (Which was disappointing. Riley had been really excited about the potential for a wand.) The banishment efforts definitely looked more difficult than the whole "ghost counseling" thing.

By the time the Dentons moved to America, they'd also amassed a huge collection of haunted items and were seeking a place to safely store them. The family chose to settle on Starfall Point, an island that drew Elizabeth and their children with its energy, and eventually they decided to create the story of their employers, the Shaddow family, as a shiny distraction.

I still struggle to understand Ellen's decision to leave, Nora wrote in an entry dated ten years before. Shaddow House is a heavy burden. I won't pretend otherwise. But it is a sacred duty, not something our family can just toss aside. Ellen always spoke of her fear, of the cruelty of saddling her future children with a house full of nightmares. But to walk away, even if it meant losing her magic? That's a choice I could never make.

––––––––––

Riley awoke the next morning with her face still buried in the pages. She'd learned a great deal last night, but she'd seen no mention of the Codex. Plover had told her it was her first mission to find it, so perhaps she might search the house next. But how was she supposed to search this labyrinth of a house to find one specific book? What if the Codex wasn't even a book? What if Aunt Nora tried to get clever with the Codex and hid the record of all the haunted objects in a recipe box or something? And how was she was supposed to search the kitchen if all the appliances could potentially attack her?

She mused over it while unpacking her suitcase and slipping into her clothes. And after coming up with nothing, she decided to visit the real world for a bit to remember that it still existed. And for coffee.

As she was making her way out, Plover made an appearance near the kitchen. "Please, Miss, be careful. There are people on the island who will try to use your loneliness, your inexperience, to gain access to the house," he said, his brow creasing. "You cannot allow this to happen."

"Yeah, Clark mentioned something about rowdy teenagers and antiquers," she said. "Trust me, I don't want anybody in here. I can't afford a ghost-related lawsuit."

Plover's lips quirked, but he didn't smile. "Be sure that you don't. And that goes for Clark as well. It's not fitting that he cross this threshold again."

"Were you the reason he ran out of here yesterday?" she asked, laughing. "Did you make him sick?"

"I never liked that young man," Plover sniffed.

"Wait, did you make *me* sick, on the ferry yesterday?" she asked. "Are you able to do that at a distance?"

Plover stepped closer, his expression intense. "I would *never* do that, Miss Riley. I would never harm a Denton, no matter how I might clash with them. Your illness yesterday was a matter of your body processing magic for the first time. It's not surprising, really, but I doubt it will be a problem again."

Riley's mouth tugged back at the corners. "Yikes. OK, lot to absorb there. Don't think I didn't notice that you neglected to answer about Clark's sudden need to puke. I'll be back after coffee and breakfast. Keep an eye on the place for me."

She reached for the kitchen door and found that the knob felt...loose. There were tool marks around the outside doorknob, as if in desperation, someone tried to just pry the knob itself from the wood. Riley crouched to get a closer look and found that someone had taken a metal tool and tried to jam it into the inner workings of the knob.

The problem was that they didn't use the right size...file, maybe?...and they didn't know about the slide latch at eye level on the interior side of the door. Someone had tried to break in while she was sleeping. It was a chilling thought, but also insulting. Someone was trying to scare her, intrude on her space, make her feel unsafe. Who would want to do that?

She rose, her expression uncertain. "Plover, Edison Held wanted into this house pretty badly, right?"

"Yes, Miss."

"Do you think there's any chance that he could have tried to get in *without* permission?" she asked.

Plover frowned. "Well, he was quite insistent, but he didn't seem so ill-mannered as to burgle."

"The house is protected by like magical barriers and stuff, though, right?"

"I see we've devoted much of our time to study," Plover intoned.

"I'm still new at this," she pointed out. "Give me a break."

"The house is protected from magical interference from other families, but no, there is no otherworldly barrier to keep out common thieves."

"And I guess a security camera is out of the question?" she guessed.

"I don't think Miss Nora would have approved of video evidence of her family's work, no," Plover said dryly.

"And you didn't see anyone skulking around the kitchen door last night?"

"I am not omnipotent, Miss. But I can ask the others if they saw anything."

Riley gave him a wan smile. "Thanks."

Plover nodded sharply. "As ever, Miss."

Riley stepped out into the sunshine and breathed deeply. Again, the assurance that she could leave the house was like a balm to her frayed nerves. While her itchy feet told her to run—that she'd never stick around long enough to fulfill whatever tasks her aunt left to her—somehow, she wanted just as badly to stay. There was a rightness about Shaddow House that she'd never felt before, a bone-deep certainty that she belonged there. Was that what she'd been looking for in all her years of bouncing around between jobs?

As morning light stretched over the horizon, the earliest of the tourists were trickling over the cobblestone streets, taking pictures of the stately ice cream–colored homes while they bickered over which bike tour to take. She passed the same redheaded woman who'd been looking into the real estate office window the day before, staring with longing at the photo displays of homes available for sale. Riley couldn't blame her. If she could afford a non-haunted house here, she would have bought it in a second.

It felt good to be out amongst them, to remember that the life she knew just twenty-four hours before still existed, just not for her. People would leave the island, go to work, put their kids to bed. The world would keep on turning. Riley's part in it had just become a little stranger.

The shop was just as friendly and fragrant as it had been the day before—had it only been one day?—with Iggy still standing at the counter next to Caroline, who was inhaling yet another cup of coffee. Petra stood behind them taking inventory, her corn silk–blond hair in a messy topknot. Once again Riley was struck by the close resemblance between her and her brother, Iggy.

"Hey, here's the new local," Iggy called, grinning at her.

Iggy was just the sort of guy Riley would normally snap right up like the sweet treats in Petra's bakery case, all muscular simplicity and twinkling blue eyes. But all she could think of when she saw that beautiful smile was…Edison? The challenge of him, the way he made her brain fire in a dozen different directions. It was downright inconvenient—particularly when she considered the 'Ted of it all.' She wasn't ready to think of anybody in those terms, especially if those terms could endanger her access to Petra's pastries.

"Do you work here too?" Riley asked Iggy as she approached the counter.

"I make anything requiring pastry dough," Iggy said proudly.

"So the rugalach you threatened me and my hypothetical bakeshop with yesterday is technically *Iggy's* rugalach," Riley called out to Petra.

Iggy's smile ratcheted up a notch, as if Riley had just given him an idea. "She makes a good point, Sis."

"Quiet, you." It warmed Riley's heart when Petra pointed not only at her troublesome brother, but Riley too. She'd started connections here, however thin, but it felt incomplete somehow. Something told her to look inward, to figure out where that feeling was coming from, and all she could think of was Alice.

It felt wrong to be here with Caroline, specifically, without Alice, even though she barely knew either of them. Why did her connection to those two women feel more real than with any other person she'd met on the island in the last twenty-four hours? And when she tried to look deeper into the feeling, why did she feel like Caroline and Alice were supposed to be there with her at Shaddow House? It was possible she was experiencing some very serious delayed post-traumatic transference.

"So Clark got you tucked in all safe and sound, huh?" Caroline asked, her whiskey-colored eyes sparkling with mischief.

"Um, not in the way you're making it sound," Riley told her. "I mean, stable and apparently normal can be nice. I don't have much experience with it my myself, but if you two have a history—"

"Oh, no," Caroline scoffed. "I don't date locals."

"Caroline has a policy," Petra said, snickering as she brought the espresso machine roaring back to life.

"And that is where I leave you ladies, because I have heard about Caroline's policy before and"—Iggy paused to shudder—"that's something you only need to hear once from the girl you used to play Candyland with."

"You're also making the game of Candyland sound dirty, just so you know," Riley informed him.

Iggy recoiled. "Aw, man, I don't need another beautiful woman who's smarter than me, making fun of me every morning."

"I promise it won't be *every* morning," Riley said as Iggy kissed Petra's cheek. His sister tucked a coffee cup in one of his hands and a boxed pink-frosted cupcake in the other.

"So, Caroline's policy?" Riley asked.

"Tourists only, no connections, and even then, no more than twice in a summer," Petra said.

"It keeps thing simple," Caroline said, raising both hands. "I will not be shamed."

Petra raised her hands. "I'm not shaming you. I'm simply living vicariously through you, as someone who has been with the same man since tenth grade."

"What she's leaving out is that we all went to the same tiny school on-island since kindergarten," Caroline told Riley. "She got the one nice guy in our whole school. Literally. There were only twenty-three of us."

Riley's brain, educated at a school with two thousand other kids, had difficulty processing this information. She selected a cinnamon bun to nibble on while Petra broke away to help some tourists who wandered in.

Before long, the shared moment between them made Riley think of Alice again.

"Do you expect Alice to come by today?" she asked.

"Alice?" Caroline shrugged. "Who knows?"

Riley frowned. "Oh, I'd gotten the impression you were friends."

"Not really. I mean, she seems perfectly nice. I just don't know her very well, even though she moved here when she was a kid. Homeschooled because she's some sort of genius that was way too advanced for our tiny school. She never comes into the Rose. She's not judgmental about it. It's just not her thing. She just...holds herself apart. It kind of makes her unknowable."

Unknowable, Riley noted. The same way Clark had described her aunt Nora.

"At least for the person who spends all of her time behind

the bar," Petra added as she returned to her spot beside Caroline.

The three of them stopped talking as Edison Held walked past the shop window. To Riley's surprise, Edison didn't outright glare at her. He just stared for a moment through the glass and then walked away.

"What is his *deal?*" she muttered aloud.

"Oh, Edison's all right," Caroline said. "He never fails to find the perfect book for my weird and varied reading tastes."

"Caroline is the most voracious reader on the island," Petra told her. "We had one of those 'Read-a-Thon' fundraisers in middle school? She made the sponsors cry."

"I didn't finish college, so I'm filling in the gaps of my education," Caroline said, with a smile that felt a little empty to Riley.

"You ever heard of an e-reader?" Riley asked.

"I like the smell of old paper!" Caroline protested. "Anyway, Edison's a nice guy, quiet, keeps to himself."

"Isn't that what they normally say about serial killers after they find body parts in their deep freeze?" Riley noted.

Petra threw her head back and laughed. "He just gets a little prickly sometimes, and it's not surprising you didn't meet him at his best, if he was on the ferry. To my knowledge, he hasn't ridden it in, oh, three years now."

"Why is it such a big deal that he went on the ferry?" Riley demanded. "Don't most people who live on the island take the ferry pretty regularly?"

Petra shrugged. "Because Edison is terrified of boats."

As she walked back to the house, she pondered Petra's words. *Edison is terrified of boats.* Why? Well, that wasn't the question. After spending a morning on the ferry, she certainly got the "why." The question was, if he was terrified, why would he go on the ferry? Why live on the island in the first place? And why did he hide in a bathroom when he got scared? And why was Edison standing at her gate?

A solid chunk of indeterminate gray fluff sat on the sidewalk and appeared to be judging Edison and whatever was in his hands. Was this the fabled canine troublemaker Mimi? Riley could very easily see a dog that size knocking antiques off displays in Alice's store.

Edison was holding a gift basket, all decorated with a gauzy blue bow and overflowing with goodies. No interpersonal interaction beginning with a gift basket had ever gone well for Riley—new jobs, new apartment buildings, that yoga gear scam. This was bad.

She didn't know what to do here. Now that she'd cooled off, she really did feel terrible, knowing that she yelled at him when he was scared, cowering in the bathroom. Yeah, she'd been angry, but she wasn't a monster. How did you accept a gift basket from someone that you'd wronged so thoroughly? At least, she'd wronged his shoes pretty thoroughly.

Mimi fled the scene. Apparently, it was just a little too awkward for her. She could not have envied a dog more.

"This is for you," Edison said, handing her the hefty basket. It was full of books and…a fluffy navy-blue blanket?

"I think I owe you an apology," she said, just as he said, "I think I owe you an explanation."

"And an apology," he added. "The apology is the important part."

For the first time, she laughed in his presence, and it felt nice.

Riley took a deep breath. She wasn't angry at Edison anymore. She was just tired and curious, and eager to have a conversation with him that didn't make her feel or look like a crazy person. "I will accept your apology, but I just want to make sure—you're not going to play nice now and then try to talk to me into letting you into the house later, are you?"

"I wouldn't do that," he swore. "I mean, not unless you wanted to open it up, which you obviously don't...or maybe you do? I shouldn't go around making assumptions. But that's not the reason I came here, just so you know." As he rambled on, a flush of embarrassment pinked his cheeks. She wanted to put her hand on his skin to feel it warm under her palm.

"Look, I'm trying to restrain myself here, but you basically tortured me for an hour, and then you refused to apologize and now you're showing up with an actual basket of gifts," she said. "So I have to ask the question—what is it that you want? A tour? You want to post video on some sort of historians' social media for clout?"

"No, it's just the apology, I promise," he said, holding up one hand in mock surrender. "I am very sorry about the whole 'hour of torture' thing. I am sorry I made stupid, insensitive remarks while you were processing the news of your aunt's passing. I was agitated and panicked, and I said everything wrong. I'm very sorry."

She nodded, opening the gate and holding it open for him.

"I'm sorry I screamed at you. I was miserable and sick, and I took that out on you. I am very sorry."

Edison's smile was luminous, the release of tension from his face made her all the sorrier for what she'd put him through. It was all she could do not to reach out and take his hand. "Good. That means you can have this."

"Good grief." She stumbled a bit, under the weight of the basket, and laughed a bit. The slick, high-color covers of the books—*History of Starfall Point, Great Homes of the Midwest, Ghost Stories of Michigan*—winked up at her from under the crinkly cellophane wrapper.

"So, new start?" she offered.

"I would like that, thank you." He nodded. They moved together up the steps to the house. While she was ready to start over, she had to admit she had ulterior motives here. If Edison pushed to get inside the house, he might be the person who tried to jimmy open the kitchen door.

"I'm only going to walk you to the door, I promise. As a show of good faith, I won't even look inside," he said, bending behind one of the enormous potted petunias to retrieve a large flat cardboard box. "But I will hand you this package. Postmistress Kim is very conscientious about porch piracy."

Bobbling the basket and the box, Riley eyeballed the return label, which listed an antique shop in Missouri. She unlocked the door. To her relief, it did not demand blood sacrifice for her key to work. This time. "Thank you. Oof, It's heavy. This must be something my aunt ordered online, maybe?"

She watched Edison's response as she pushed the door open.

He studiously kept his eyes on her hands. The box seemed to vibrate against her fingertips, making her jump. There was a tiny hole at the seam of the box, as if something had tried to tunnel its way out.

"What the hell?" she whispered.

"Maybe you should put that down," Edison said, gently clasping his hands around her wrists. The sensation of his skin on hers somehow made the noise inside the box grow louder, sending a hot flush up her arms. Edison's eyes went even wider and his grip tightened.

Suddenly Plover appeared in the foyer, holding up his hands in a panic. "No, Miss! Don't!"

A silver-gray plume of energy burst out of the box, making Edison yelp. Riley stumbled into the house, dropping the box. It slid past Plover, who watched all this happening with a very confused expression. The package ghost, a middle-aged man in a dark cutaway coat and high collar, shrieked and gave Riley a look so accusing she felt it. In her soul.

Clearly, Riley had not worked for Shaddow House long enough to be suspicious of mysterious packages.

"How dare you, madam!" the man yelled. "Locking me away like some sort of prisoner! I have already lost my dearest wife to time immemorial. My darling Edith is beyond my reach forever! Isn't that punishment enough?"

"Oh good, another dramatic British ghost," Riley huffed.

"I beg your pardon, Miss!" Plover gasped, deeply offended. Riley cringed.

"What is that?" Edison whispered. "Riley, what is happening?"

"Hi," she said, stepping towards the package ghost with her hands raised. "Uh, welcome to Shaddow House. I'm your...host?"

Whirling on her, the man hissed, baring his uneven teeth at her. "You have no right to claim the honor of a hostess! This place is a hovel! Do you not possess sufficient staff to give even the barest sense of propriety?"

"I beg your pardon, sir!" Plover cried, even more deeply offended.

"And your *ankles*!" the man shrieked, covering his eyes with the back of his hand, as if he might swoon. "They are visible for all the world to see!"

Riley glanced down at the barest of gaps between her socks and the hem of her skinny jeans. "OK, no. I will not be ankle-shamed."

"What is this?" Edison wheezed. "How are you...? What...?"

Oh, right. Edison didn't know that ghosts exist. Shit.

Riley turned to Edison, struggling to find a way to explain something she wasn't even sure she was supposed to explain to the man described as a "sanctimonious jackass" in her aunt Nora's journals. "Um."

Eloquent as always.

It wouldn't have mattered how gracefully she'd described the ghost to Edison, because he passed out—just dead-dropped facedown on her polished floor with his feet where her welcome mat would have been if she had one. Well, that was one way for him to gain entry to the house, she supposed. But passing out also indicated that he hadn't expected to see a ghost, so he clearly wasn't trying to get into the house for the haunted objects.

"Well, hell," she mused.

"Such language!" their new guest gasped.

She looked up to Plover for advice, but he seemed just as horrified as she felt.

"Fine," she grumbled. She ripped open the shipping flat and found a dented, but ornate, painted wooden box, monogrammed with CM in flourished, swirling letters. Flipping the box open, she found a full silver service, made from heavy over-curlicued pieces. Clearly, this was the ghost's haunted object. She ran for the dining table and grabbed a large glass salt cellar. Putting the silver box on the floor, she poured a circle of table salt around it. According to Nora's journals, if Riley surrounded the attachment object with salt, the ghost would be contained to the object. And maybe he would stop shrieking.

"How is making a mess of the floor going to help this situation?" Plover demanded.

Riley shouted, "I'm improvising!"

Meanwhile, the ghost repeatedly hurled himself at the open front door, but his form was stopped every time, as if he was hitting a pane of glass. "Why may I not exit? Release me, hoyden! I shan't spend one more moment in this place! Oh, Edith, why would you leave me behind in such a world!"

She'd already tired of this man and his over-costumed drama. So far, the toaster ghost was her favorite. At least the toaster ghost was quiet.

Plover had recovered long enough to fix her with a disappointed glare. "Well, that was a decisive strike, Miss. The problem is that you have poured the containment circle around the haunted object while the ghost was outside of it, so instead of sealing the ghost inside, you've effectively locked him out."

"Dammit," she grunted, swiping the salt aside and opening up the circle. She closed her eyes, and around the noise of the ghost's tantrum, she tried to remember what she'd read the night before.

"Hey! Just be quiet!" she shouted in the same voice she'd used at closing time at one of the rougher bars she'd worked in outside Jacksonville. The ghost turned on his heel, all aghast astonishment, but before he could ask how she dared do something one more time, Riley made the "closing" hand motion she'd seen sketched in Nora's journal—the most rudimentary spell to attract a ghost back to its object. "You don't have to go home, but you can't stay in my damn foyer."

It was possible that her Jacksonville bar tone sounded an awful lot like her mother when Ellen was sending teenage Riley to her room. Taking a deep breath, she concentrated on the spirit getting drawn back into the silver box. She made the "closing" gesture again and the ghost turned to her, glaring.

"What is that?" the silverware ghost demanded, even as he glided across the floor towards the box. "This silly hand-waving? Is it to mean something to me? My dearest Edith would never behave in such a manner!"

"I know, I know!" she huffed, rolling her eyes as he disappeared into the lid of the box. She poured salt over the gap in the circle, sealing the ghost inside.

Without a giant dignified toddler fit filling the room with yelling, Riley could think again. She looked outside, where nice normal people continued to walk around in the daylight as if they had no idea that a hellacious ghostly meltdown had just happened just a few yards away. Because they probably didn't. She felt very alone in that moment. She supposed Plover counted, and then there was Edison.

Hmm. Edison. Even though he'd passed out from sheer terror, he did look sort of sweet, all peaceful and curled up on her floor. She'd never seen his face absent of stress before, and that made her sad. She was going to take this "fresh start" with Edison seriously. She needed friends on this island, if she was going to survive.

"Well, I guess this answers the question of whether I should let him in the house," she muttered, turning Edison over on his back.

"What are you doing?" Plover asked.

"Well, I can't just leave him passed out on my doorstep!" she cried.

"You could just nudge him out the door and then close it," Plover suggested, with the least dignity he'd exhibited since they'd met.

"Oh, this is a bad look," she grunted, dragging Edison's unconscious body into the house. "I should not have skipped *all* of the leg days."

With Edison settled against the wall and the door closed, Riley dropped to the floor beside him and picked up the discarded shipping box. "Who is James Timmons of St. Charles Antiques, and why is he sending me a box full of ghostly British tears?"

"I don't know him personally, but contacts all over the world knew to send Miss Nora haunted items for containment. You should expect more and exercise more caution while opening the post."

"I would just like to point out that you could have mentioned this yesterday," she snorted, tossing the box aside. She glanced at her unconscious floor-mate. "Plover, I don't think Edison was the one who tried to break into the house. Just based on the way he reacted when he saw a ghost, I don't think he's trying to get into the house to get access to you. I think he's honestly a big old history nerd."

"Well, that's good news, I suppose, Miss," Plover said. "I would have appreciated him giving your aunt Nora less grief while she was alive. Though, I suppose, in a way, she did enjoy the lively debate and coming up with various insults to his person."

"She planned them ahead of time, didn't she?" Riley asked.

"Sometimes I helped," Plover said, his lips quirking.

"OK, so Edison knows about the ghosts now, and he's been in the house," she said. "Is there any sort of Shaddow House precedent for this?"

He nodded. "Of course. Over the years, there have been friends of the Dentons that have been trustworthy enough to share their secrets with, but they have been few and far between. And in even rarer circumstances, the Denton magic would choose compatriots to help the family share its burden."

"So, non-Dentons were able to work Denton ghost magic?" she asked.

"With very close supervision from your family, yes."

"I thought you had to be a Denton for this to work," Riley protested. "That's why I had to bleed on a household article. Otherwise, I could have just stayed in Florida."

"There must be a Denton involved for the magic to work, but magic is its own living force. It does what it will. Their helpmates have always been sworn to absolute secrecy, with magical consequences if they broke their vow," he told her. "Miss Nora preferred solitude, so it made sense that her magic never chose anyone to help."

Exhausted, Riley sank against the wall, letting Edison's head loll against her shoulder.

"You could always try to persuade him that he imagined it all," Plover suggested as Edison's weight shifted, his body sliding across hers. She caught him as he turned, restless, cuddling against her.

Riley sucked a breath through her teeth, while nodding. "I'm going to owe him another apology. Yup."

Chapter 7
Edison

THERE WAS A GHOST IN her foyer.

A ghost. Standing in her foyer.

Edison woke up to Riley's voice, smooth and soft, and her small warm hand wrapped around his. Hmm. That felt nice. He wasn't quite ready to open his eyes yet. It was like he was huddled at the bottom of a well and hesitating to swim to the surface because, frankly, it was kind of nice down there. He kept his eyes closed, his head pillowed against something downy soft that smelled of sea air and gardenias. It was a scent that had haunted him since that morning on the ferry. It made Edison want to bury his face in the scent and live there.

"You probably need to make yourself scarce, Plover," Riley said carefully. "Wait, can he see you? I didn't even think to ask."

"Mr. Held could see me if I chose to show myself to him, but with the hostile silver spirit, I don't know whether that was choice or happenstance," another voice, cultured, older—British?—sounded nearby. He'd never met anyone on the island named "Plover," and the only British people he'd met were tourists. Riley definitely didn't seem like the type to let strangers into her house.

"Hehe, silver spirit," she chuckled, a musical sound that made him want to swim closer to the surface. "It sounds like something you would call a sexy older ghost."

"Please focus, Miss."

Whoever he was, Plover sounded grumpy.

She giggled. "Sorry, I think working intentional magic for the first time has made me a little loopy."

"I believe that's normal, Miss."

Wait. Magic?

Riley sighed, her warm breath feathering over his cheeks. That felt nice.

"If anyone saw me dragging Edison's lifeless body into my house, I am probably going to jail," she sighed.

"I understand that it's a quaint, charming jail, Miss."

"I'll bet." She was giggling again, but there was a bit of a sob at the end of it. Edison forced his eyes to open. He blinked against the late afternoon light streaming through the stained glass windows of the foyer. He was inside Shaddow House. To put a finer point on it, he was on the *floor* in Shaddow House. Riley was cradling him in her lap, her lovely face only inches away from his as she looked up at the source of the unknown voice. And he was snuggled against Riley's chest like a sleeping toddler, which was not terrible.

There were tears streaking down her cheeks. She didn't look hysterical, just tired and overwhelmed.

"It's going to be," he said, reaching up and touching her cheek, making her jump. She looked down and they were almost nose-to-nose. He could feel her breath on his lips. To his surprise, he wanted to lean closer, to press his mouth against hers. But he didn't think she would appreciate that.

"Whoa, whoa, slow down," she said as he sat up. "Plover?"

Edison turned toward Riley's focal point, blinking rapidly. Who was that and why could he see through him?

"What the fuck!" Edison cried.

"That's what I said," Riley replied, nodding.

"I weep for the English language," the British man—Plover—sighed, his eyes rolling skyward. Eyes that were silver and transparent because he was a ghost. Edison was looking at a ghost. A ghost that was annoyed with him for cursing.

"Yup, sitting up was a mistake," he said, slumping against her. Her arms closed around him so he wouldn't slide back to the floor. Again, it put his mouth dangerously close to hers. For the first time in recent memory, he felt the pressure of *want* coiling through his middle. He wanted Riley Denton-Everett in ways he couldn't even cobble together in his mind.

He reached up to brush his fingertips against her cheek. "You're pretty when you're not yelling deftly worded insults at me."

She laughed, making him grin. He felt a little lurch in his chest and realized he was very much in danger of feeling far too much for Riley Denton-Everett.

"So are you."

Ever so slowly, Edison pressed his mouth against hers. They were sharing breath and it was the most connected to life he'd felt since...in a long time. It was a bizarre thought to have when a ghost hovered nearby, but all he could think of was her mouth, which was warm and soft and tasted of blueberries. She moaned into him, her hands sliding under his shoulder and pulling him close. Her hair, smelling of rainy summer gardens, fell over his face. He melted against her, threading his fingers through it.

And while there was peace in her arms, he could only allow himself to enjoy it for a few moments. What must she be thinking of him? He'd yelled at her and made her uncomfortable, and here he was kissing her like he had a right to? With one last brush of his mouth against hers, he reluctantly pulled away from her.

When they parted, Plover the ghost butler had made himself scarce, which was possibly the weirdest thought he'd ever had.

"I'm sorry. My behavior is probably confusing, given how we started out," he said.

She pressed her lips together as she seemed to consider, and it made him want to kiss her lips all over again.

"I'm going to blame ghost-related blood sugar issues," he added. "We can still try to be friends, though."

She helped him sit up against the wall, which he might have found emasculating without the literal life-and-death issues hanging over their heads. "So, when you start over, you start *all* the way over. Do you pass out a lot?"

"Only when I realize the afterlife is real and there are invisible people wandering around," he said, nodding.

She snickered and she looked so tired. He slid his hands along her arms and let her slump against his side. To his surprise, she didn't pull away; she just let herself be tucked under his arm. It was a friendlier gesture more than any sort of romantic pass, but it was nice, feeling her safely folded against his side. "Well, sure."

"I get the impression this is new for you too," he ventured.

She explained her chaotic first few days in the house, discovering her aunt's legacy and her job as house manager to a host of ghostly tenants. As she did, a series of tumblers aligned in Edison's head. It made so much more sense now, that Nora had wanted to keep Edison out of the house. Nora had been trying to keep him *safe*, just like she'd been trying to keep so many other people safe, and the shame of what he'd thought of Nora—as being merely selfish—burned his gut. He made a mental note to put flowers at the location where Nora's ashes would be spread, by way of an apology. Now that he knew for sure there was an afterlife—that would take some time to process—he liked to think Nora would see that.

"If you stay there, I'll make us some tea," she said. "I would invite you into the kitchen with me, but you might touch the haunted toaster or something, and then where would we be?"

Despite her warning, he followed her to the kitchen saying, "The toaster is haunted?"

She nodded, fetching a tin of tea from the pantry. She busied herself with the kettle. Behind her, a dry erase marker rose and drew out a question mark on the whiteboard near the pantry.

"Natalie. This is Edison. Edison, this is Natalie," she said, as if that was a completely normal introduction. "She prefers to communicate through her dry-erase board, which I support entirely. I don't think it's much different than people who prefer text to calls."

Edison cleared his throat. "Um, nice to meet you, Natalie."

The marker squeaked across the surface, writing, JUST A HOOKUP? SOCIAL MEDIA OFFICIAL? MARRIAGE?

Edison had to admire her directness.

"Too soon for that discussion, Natalie," Riley replied. She turned to Edison. "So you really didn't know anything about the ghosts or any of that, huh? No nefarious interest in any of the haunted objects?"

"What? No! I'm not even sure what you're talking about!" he exclaimed. "I really just wanted to look around the house, see what sort of research materials you might have in here and try to persuade the Shaddows to add the house to a few tours."

"Because it's honestly that important to you that history should be shared with the public," she marveled.

"I may have told your aunt that it was criminal, in my opinion, to keep that much history to yourself," he said, closing one eye and cringing.

"That's kind of adorable," she told him, her nose scrunching into cute little lines.

"So how are you dealing with all this?" he asked, gesturing to the whiteboard.

"I don't think I have yet…" As she slid his carefully prepared mug of Earl Grey, she stopped to stare at his library name tag. DR. EDISON HELD, PHD. "So, you're a doctor?"

He sighed. "Not that kind of doctor—"

"I know what a PhD is," she snorted. "You should be proud of yourself."

He smiled. "I was, particularly the history degree. My master's is in library science, because I figured it was the best way to learn about the process of research. I was interviewing for a job at University of Illinois when…when I decided to move here."

"That explains your interest in bringing people into Shaddow House, I suppose. But why are you *here,* on the island?" she asked.

"I responded to the employment site post," he said. "I don't think they were expecting anybody to respond, because they tried to hire me without an interview. The hiring manager liked the idea of having a big-city PhD as the librarian. It also allowed her to thwart her archnemesis, Margaret, who was the other applicant. Looking back, I'm sure that was the whole point."

"Is it hard to get by as a small-town librarian? Asking as someone who's spent her whole life trying to get by."

Edison shrugged. "Money isn't everything. I have some family money and savings, and even with the cost of living on the island, I'm comfortable."

"Can I ask you something sort of sensitive? More sensitive than asking about your financial situation, which I realize now was sort of a dick move, but I still have all that ghost adrenaline running through my veins and have apparently abandoned all manners," she said, moving her hands in a whirlwind pattern.

He sipped his tea and reached across the counter to pat her hand. Sharing this experience, seeing a ghost rage around her foyer before she trapped it in a silverware box, had somehow broken down those barriers between them. And while he would definitely like to kiss her again at some point, he would be just as content to be able to sit like this at her haunted kitchen counter and talk over tea. "Given the amount of candor you've shown, I don't feel like I can say no."

"Why boats?" she asked. "Is it the ferry in particular that scares you so badly, or is it all boats?"

"It's all boats," he told her, clearing his throat.

"But you live on an island, which is only accessible by boat," she noted.

"As long as I don't look at the water, I'm fine."

"I don't know if that makes sense," she said, the corner of her mouth lifting.

He took a deep breath, squeezing her hand. She seemed to sense that he was trying to gather strength, and her face realigned into an expression far more serious. But her grip on his hand never faltered.

"My fiancée died years ago in a boating accident," he said, swallowing thickly.

Given the way her face fell, stricken, he wished he had said it some other way. He knew the look on someone's face when they were mentally reviewing everything they'd said before they knew what happened, and wondering how they'd inadvertently offended him. It was why he didn't talk about it very often.

Handling these conversations had been easier back home, right after the accident. Most people who lived in his coastal community had heard about the "*Sea Mist* tragedy." The news coverage had been respectful, considering that his mother's family owned a good portion of the local media outlets, but it had also been thorough. But the reporters could never manage to capture how senseless the whole thing was.

"I didn't want to sail that day," he said. "I'm not particularly good at it, much to my parents' embarrassment. They could get the *Sea Mist* underway in a few minutes between the two of them. Even as a kid, I'd rather be sitting in the shade of the galley, reading. Erin *loved* sailing, which was part of what helped her get so close with my parents.

"But that day, my parents swore we were just going out for a quick afternoon sail before dinner at the beach club. They said that we'd be back safely in harbor before the weather set in, just in time for cocktails. And they always knew what they were talking about with that sort of thing, so I trusted them. But then we were on the water and one of the lines failed, I don't even know which one, and we were sort of stuck out there. My parents were trying to get the sail put away so we could use the engine. And this freak storm just seemed to come out of nowhere, and everything just went *wrong*. Erin and my parents, I could see they were trying not to panic, but it was all going so wrong, so fast. Then the boat pitched on its side, and something hit my head."

It had felt like his temple was struck by the fist of God. The last thing he remembered was seeing stars and feeling the cold embrace of the ocean take him in.

"I woke up in the hospital, two days later," he said. "My parents were sitting by my bed, and I could see it in their eyes. Erin was gone. The boat just broke apart. She was trying to get to me. I was wearing a vest, but she still tried to get to me. That's just the sort of person she was... She was struck by some debris. I didn't even know that you could get pulled out of a vest, but... It just floated to the surface, and she got dragged under."

Erin's body had been found the next day, miles away from their accident site. He knew how it had looked, so sinister and awful. If his parents hadn't been there, if they hadn't followed all the proper procedures for immediately contacting the Coast

Guard, getting a search underway, Edison probably would have been suspected of killing Erin.

"How do you live through a loss like that?" she asked.

"One day at a time," he said. "Accepting that the life you thought you were going to have is gone forever and that trying to have any part of it back is just...pointless. So, starting over with something entirely different isn't just a good idea; it's necessary to your survival. After I lost Erin, I lived in a sort of fog, answering questions from the authorities, getting through the funeral with Erin's poor parents, explaining to my bosses why it was just too soon for me to go back to work. When that fog passed, I knew I had to get away, somewhere no one knew me or my family. I applied for the job here and moved without even questioning it. My parents just don't get it. They think I'm wasting my potential here and letting down the family."

"But you enjoy living on Starfall, right?"

"I wouldn't say *enjoy*, but I'm at least content. After the locals figured out I wasn't a medical doctor, they pretty much lost interest. I wouldn't say people ignored me, but they didn't exactly welcome me with open arms either."

"That really hasn't been my experience so far," she mused. "People seem pretty warm here. Then again, I've only talked to like, seven people. Well, living people."

"I was left alone, and that was what I hoped for," he said. "It took a season or two, and then the Nana Grapevine meddling began in earnest."

"Are you close with your parents, even though they don't get your choices?" she asked. "Also, what is the Nana Grapevine?"

"Trust me, you'll figure it out. And as for my parents?" Recalling their last phone call, Edison shook his head. "I think they're more dedicated to not getting my choices than they are to listening to me."

She squeezed his hand. "I know that's hard. I mean, I can't even bring up my mom in my phone calls with my dad without him completely shutting down. And I get that it's hard on him. He lost his wife. But I lost my mom. No one else really knew her, and I don't have anyone else to talk about her with."

"How long has it been?" he asked.

"A few months." She swallowed heavily. "A semitruck driver was texting and didn't see Mom stopped at an intersection. He rear-ended her and sent her car into oncoming traffic."

He recognized that quiver in her voice, the ripple of releasing one's story for the first time in a long while—one you weren't necessarily ready to share. He pulled her into his arms and tucked his chin over her head.

"We weren't ever close, you know?" she said into his shirt. "I didn't know much about her, which made any sort of outing or occasion or even buying her a gift an unnecessarily complicated *chore*. I would guess at her favorite foods, her favorite music, her favorite color. And I always guessed wrong, so I suppose I just...stopped. After all that, I don't know how much right I have to mourn her. My dad is devastated, but I'm just confused. My mother wasn't a bad person, but she wasn't a great mom, either. She was distant, difficult to know. It seems to be a dominant trait in my family."

He understood the lingering burn of loss more than she

could possibly know. But that was a little too much for "first-time" conversation, and they'd already covered some pretty serious trauma.

"Well, sure, but you also got superpowers, which is fun."

———————

Edison pushed the return cart through the library's true crime section, grateful for the sunlight streaming through the windows. Most of the titles on the cart were from Alice Seastairs, who had a secret penchant for murder stories. She seemed like a sweet lady, kind and unassuming, and so darn pretty that, if he'd been inclined to date, he would have definitely asked her out over the years. But the number of times she'd checked out books on forensic loopholes in murder investigations was enough to give him pause.

The idea of dating brought his mind back to Riley and the paradigm-shifting revelations she'd brought to his life just in the last week. Riley Denton-Everett was steward to a collection of haunted antiques and a regular communicator with the dead. And she was a really good kisser. He didn't know how to feel about the limbo they'd found themselves in after sharing profound spiritual experiences, followed by baring their grief. It felt too soon to do anything but be her friend, but he couldn't help but want much more. It was like a part of himself that he'd buried under concrete was cracking through. It hurt, but in a good way.

"You all right?" Kyle asked, his arms full of children's books that had been carelessly discarded by kids drawn in that morning for Saturday Storytime with Mother Goose. "You're kind of staring off into space with a weird look on your face, and given that you're basically holding an encyclopedia of violent crimes, you might want to reconsider that."

Edison glanced down at the lurid hardback in his hands. "Noted."

"So the Nana Grapevine reports that you and Riley Denton made up. There were even reports that you entered the inner sanctum."

Edison's lips pressed together in a flat line. The Nana Grapevine was definitely one of the drawbacks to living on Starfall. "Please tell me you understand that means her house."

"Well, I do now," Kyle said, smirking. "Though I am a little disappointed, in you and for you."

"Oh, give the boy a break, Kyle. I don't think you've been on a date in the better part of a year." Margaret was wearing her oversized Mother Goose hat and tiny silver pince-nez with a whimsical purple prairie dress. Her evident exhaustion wasn't a surprise, given the huge crowd of kids trooping out of the front entrance. Saturday Storytime was mostly for local kids, but during the summer, tourist parents were eager to find some wholesome, non-sugar-based entertainment.

"I have a girlfriend in the U.P.," Kyle protested.

"An Upper Peninsula girlfriend is the Michigan version of a girlfriend in Canada," Margaret deadpanned.

"I'm not going to take guff from Mother Goose," Kyle muttered, retreating into the children's section.

"My great-niece is single!" she yelled after him. "She makes a hell of a pierogi!"

"Bah!" Kyle yelled over his shoulder by way of a response.

"You shouldn't torture him when you're dressed as a nursery rhyme; you're going to give the kid a complex," Edison said.

Margaret tugged the pince-nez from her nose and rubbed at the reddened skin on the bridge. "He'll be fine. I'm glad he's volunteering here. It's good for him, to be out among people. He spent too much time alone after his mother passed."

Edison nodded. "You're only saying that because he cleans up the children's section after story time."

"You're not wrong." She leaned against the world religions section. "So, you and the Denton girl, what's happening there? Did you apologize properly this time?"

"Yes, and there were no flowers involved," he told her, preening just a little bit.

"I know. You gave her books. Or at least, access to books, which I can only describe as uninspired, giving her *your* favorite thing," she told him archly. "I thought I taught you better."

"She liked it—" Any further response he might have had was interrupted by Clark Graves walking into the library like he was running for office. "Edison! Good to see you! Love the hat, Margaret."

Edison blew a frustrated breath through his nose. What possible reason could Clark have to come by the library? Edison couldn't remember the last time he'd darkened the doors. And while he'd never wanted to discourage people from using his favorite public resource, he just didn't trust the man, who was too much of a dude bro for his liking.

"How can we help you, Clark?" Edison asked as Margaret made herself scarce. She had even less patience for Clark than Edison did.

"Haven't seen you around town since that, um, *memorable* meeting in my office," Clark said, smirking while he plucked books off the shelves at random and put them back out of order. There was not a more sinister microaggression towards a librarian.

Edison managed to keep the frown off his face, but it was a near thing. What did Clark want?

"I heard that you and Riley Denton have managed to patch things up after that rather unfortunate scene," Clark said, pulling his lips back into a sympathetic grimace.

Damn the Nana Grapevine.

"I don't think we have anything to talk about there, Clark," Edison said, all fake political politeness. "Besides, I heard you ran out of the house halfway to vomiting. You feeling better?"

"Oh, just a little sympathy nausea, maybe," Clark said, shrugging. "Riley was so sick, you know, from when you locked her out of the bathroom on the ferry? It must have rubbed off on me. I felt fine once I got back to the office. Besides, I feel a bit of responsibility to her, you know, since you did bring that awkward meeting into my place of business."

Edison took a deep breath to steady himself. He knew what Clark was doing, trying to provoke guilt for how he'd treated Riley, for the scene he'd caused at the law office. It was effective, particularly when Clark added, "And she is a client, sort of. She doesn't know anyone on the island. I just don't want whatever this *thing* is between you to keep her from wanting to stay, if it goes south."

Right, because Clark didn't know that Riley *couldn't* leave. But Edison wasn't about to tell him that.

"There isn't a thing between me and Riley," Edison insisted.

"But I bet you want there to be, right? She's not exactly hard to look at, is she?"

Something about the way Clark was smirking made Edison want to punch him directly in the face. The fierceness of it—the compulsion to smash his hand into Clark's stupid, handsome face—shook Edison.

"So, what was it like in the house?" Clark asked. "All those years working for Nora, and she never let me past the threshold. Is Riley settling in all right, or is it looking like she's living out of a suitcase in the parlor? She texts me every once in a while, but she doesn't really keep me updated."

Edison stared at Clark, focusing all his energy on restraining his face-punching impulses. Riley didn't owe this guy updates about where she was sleeping in the house. She didn't owe him text responses. Was Clark's interest in Riley more than professional? Wasn't there some sort of rule about lawyers dating their clients? Did that count when the client was technically Riley's dead aunt? Did any of this matter when Edison had clearly built a stronger connection with Riley than Clark's weird smirky implications? Was it terrible that Edison was even thinking in these unhealthy comparative terms?

"Just be gentle with her, OK? Maybe give her some space. You don't want to scare her off," Clark said, his voice a bit warmer. Edison tried to see it as a positive. Riley had someone else looking out for her. She had someone who wanted the best for her.

He was still a dude bro.

Chapter 8
Riley

RILEY SAT UP, BLINKING INTO the darkness. She could hear something downstairs. She supposed it was something she was going to have to get used to, living with dozens of dead roommates. But...this noise seemed to be coming from outside the house, like someone was tapping on a window.

Riley laid stock-still, listening, wondering if she was imagining the whole thing. She'd had trouble falling asleep, despite the downy comfort of the luxuriously fluffy blanket Edison had given her. Since her talk with Edison, she'd done a considerable amount of shame-scrolling on the one social media platform he bothered with—or at least he had bothered with at one point. His profile showed that he'd only posted sporadically starting six years before, when his feed was flooded with sympathy posts for Erin. A pinned memorial post showed the two of them posed perfectly together, showing off a—holy hell, that was a big rock.

Riley had shaken herself with a considerable amount of shame, checking out a dead woman's engagement ring.

Erin Bourne seemed like Edison's perfect match, one of those women whose hair never seemed to frizz, who never seemed to be making a dumb face when someone snapped a spontaneous pic. Her outfits looked effortlessly coordinated and tasteful. And she seemed...really and truly *good*, like the sort of woman who would risk her life when someone she cared about was in danger. And Edison had lost her.

Knowing what her father had just been through, Riley couldn't help but feel a flush of guilt for kissing Edison. At the time, she hadn't felt shame. But now? Who was she to try to take that lovely woman's place? What if Edison wasn't ready for anything resembling dating? What if she was never going to be ready after Ted?

Nope. There was definitely a tapping noise coming from downstairs. Even Ted-related thoughts couldn't block that out. Shit.

Crawling out of bed, Riley slipped into her bathrobe, creeping silently down the stairs. She followed the masking tape arrows she'd laid down on the carpet—to Plover's mighty protests—so she didn't get lost. She turned off the stairs, towards a newer wing she hadn't visited before, past the conservatory and the billiard room, into the library. She still couldn't believe she lived in a place with a conservatory. She wasn't even sure what that room was for. She opened a door expecting a powder room, but found a brick wall.

"When I'm not busy chasing down a possible home intruder, I'm going to draw a map." Riley rolled her eyes. She wasn't sure if it was the fatigue or her frayed nerves, but she swore she could see a dark shape moving along the library ceiling, oily and viscous. She could practically see finger shapes extending along the plaster before a head shape seemed to raise from the mass. She blinked and then it disappeared.

"What the fuck," she breathed.

She stopped, tilting her head, realizing she could hear the tapping noise again. What if she was imagining the whole intruder thing and this was a more violent flavor of ghost? She couldn't call 9-1-1 on a ghost. She'd end up the town joke.

Hands cold and shaking, Riley followed the sound. She passed the music room and paused. Outside, there was a pale hand pressing against the glass...but it wasn't ghostly pale. It was the color of white latex. Someone was standing outside her window, wearing a hooded sweatshirt and latex gloves, trying to find a way to pry the window open.

She waited for the terror to grip her, the way it would have when she was living alone in Florida. Seeing a dark figure lurking outside her window would have been her worst nightmare before she started seeing ghosts every day. Now, she was just angry. Fuck this guy and his stupid latex gloves.

"Oh, no, not today." Riley said, pulling her phone from her pocket. "I will not end up the title on a true crime podcast today."

She backed away from the window, watching the figure from the shadows while she dialed 9-1-1.

It only took a few minutes for the police to arrive from their Main Square housing by bicycle—which Riley found very comforting, really, considering they'd probably been in bed when she called. But by the time State Trooper Celia Tyree arrived in her uniform jacket with a gun belt buckled over U of M sweatpants, the prowler was long gone. The figure seemed to have heard

Riley hiss-whispering into the phone, his head popping up with something like wordless indignation, and then darted away.

Riley stood just outside her front door after Celia and her local backup, Lee Fenton, checked the perimeter of the house. She felt guilty for not inviting them in, but she didn't want to have to explain why they couldn't touch, stand near, or look at anything.

"It's probably just kids," Celia assured her. She was a slim woman, shorter than Riley had expected, with close-cropped dark hair and delicate features reddened by the sun. "A lot of people are curious about your house, locals and tourists alike. If you're going to be living here, you're going to have to get used to that sort of thing."

"Kids...wearing latex gloves?" Riley asked. "Trying to get a peek into my house by climbing through a window after midnight?"

"I didn't say that those kids make good or logical decisions. If you hear or see anything else, feel free to give me a call. Here's my number." She handed Riley a business card. "I'm happy to come by."

"Thanks," Riley said. "Nice to meet you."

"Just so you know, you might hear some comments about this from the locals," Celia told her. "There's not much for us to get up to, so listening to the police scanner is considered high entertainment."

"Oh...good," Riley said, waving at Officer Fenton as he loped towards her gate, hitching up his pajama pants as he went.

Riley closed and locked the front door behind her. Plover was standing there, a concerned expression on his face.

"Did you get a look at whoever it was?" Riley asked.

Plover shook his head. "Part of the point of construction was to keep us confused. As much time as I have spent here, I still struggle to find my way around the newer wings of the house."

"Doesn't it seem sort of cruel that my family continued unnecessary construction just to mess with you guys?" Riley asked him.

"I've never given it much thought, Miss."

"Well, there's no way I'm sleeping now," she muttered, settling into a squashy brocade chair just outside the atrium with one of Aunt Nora's journals. She waved to Eloise, the fountain ghost, who waved forlornly back from the water. "Can't sleep either, huh?"

The ghost shook her head. "Never."

Riley glanced toward Plover, to see if he would confirm that, but the butler had apparently found something else to do. It struck her as very sad, that ghosts never got real sleep. They just got... periods of inactivity?

"Anything I can do for you?" Riley asked, turning toward Eloise, only to find that she'd silently slipped back under the water. "Yeah, I wouldn't trust me, either."

It was at times like this that she would have really appreciated having a physical butler who could bring her a mug of hot cocoa. But she didn't think Plover would appreciate the request, and she was too damn tired to deal with the perils of her kitchen. Also, there was the whole guilt issue involving her ghost butler never getting any rest.

Riley's problems were not like other people's problems.

Speaking of which, under the heading of The Welling Problem, Aunt Nora had written...

On their journey north to what they were told was a particularly active spiritual destination, our ancestors met the Wellings. The family claimed to be witches of an ancient Scottish magical line, powerful mediums who planned to use the island's energy to help non-magical clients safely contact their benevolent, departed loved ones.

By the time they arrived on the island, the Wellings and the Dentons decided to join forces in this unknown New World. The families began construction on what became Shaddow House, with the Wellings planning a "ghostly communication center." The Dentons supported this effort but wanted to work more privately, resolving their collected ghosts' problems. As the wealthier family, the Dentons handled the design and most of the financing, while the Wellings took out loans to contribute to construction. Without telling the Dentons, the Wellings hid ritual objects of their own design at secret locations hidden around the footprint of the house, only known to them. The objects' magic, more powerful than the Dentons' somewhat outdated containment spells at the time, "locked" spirits to a particular location. But they served an even more sinister secondary purpose. The Wellings could use them to steal the will of nearby spirits, allow a magic user to control them.

The Wellings planned to use their so-called "ghost locks," combined with the location's energy to weaponize ghosts—starting with the spirits attached to the Dentons' collection—for contracted killings. They never wanted to help anyone, living or dead.

> The house was nearly complete with many of the
> haunted items moved inside and the locks' locations un-
> known. The Dentons had accidentally created a prison full
> of spirits increasingly agitated by the presence of the locks.

On the page, Nora had included a sketch of the ghost lock, but she hadn't been much of an artist. It looked like three squashed loops attached together around empty space. The drawing was one-dimensional and uneven but looked vaguely familiar. Under it, Nora had written, Multiple loops representing multiple magical uses?

Did that mean the locks could have other purposes the Dentons hadn't figured out yet? Riley shuddered. She did not want to be the one to figure that out.

Wait. Riley pulled the chain from around her neck, containing the key-slash-coin that had helped her unlock the door on her first day. On the opposite side of the Shaddow House insignia was the same three-looped symbol. Aunt Nora had left Riley a ghost lock inscribed on the item needed to unlock her front door, and Riley had been wearing it around her neck this whole time. It was an awfully big clue that Aunt Nora had left unlabeled, like all the haunted objects in the house.

"Augh, it's a big, overdecorated, multilevel metaphor." Riley ran a hand over her face. "Aunt Nora, you are the worst... Also, the whole locksmith part of my career path feels horribly ironic now."

She shook her head and continued reading.

> Casting against another witch family could have dire
> magical consequences, so the Dentons chose a more banal

route. While the Wellings had an abundance of malevolent magic, they didn't have much cash. The Dentons bought the Wellings' bank and called in their loans. (The laws of banking and magic are similarly binding.) Unable to pay the large sum, the Wellings were ruined financially and disappeared so their creditors couldn't find them. The Dentons resolved to be a lot less trusting and far more guarded. They faded from public life, spreading rumors about the mysterious Shaddow family that had taken ownership of the house.

Through their newly acquired bank, the "Shaddows" started giving out loans to encourage businesses to grow on the island, so the house wouldn't be isolated. This encouraged loyalty to the Shaddow family as the island's generous benefactors. The Dentons assumed stewardship of the house and told locals that the Shaddows were too busy traveling the world to take up permanent residence in Shaddow House. After a few generations, Starfall Point residents forgot the Dentons were anything but employees.

Our family learned much over the years, including developing more advanced containment magic. The Dentons discovered the ghosts could follow their objects out of the house if they concentrated their magic on a single spirit and allowed it. The Dentons could resolve their problems to send the spirits to the next plane. The Wellings had given us an unintentional gift. The locks made the house a more dangerous environment, but they also provided stability.

The family realized that construction confused the

spirits and confused any human intruders who managed to make it into the house, so construction continued
indefinitely. This problem compounded as their contacts in
Europe sent them more haunted items without prompting.
The safest option seemed to be helping the ghosts resolve
the unfinished business that kept them trapped, thus clearing space in the house.

While the family flourished for years, the work became
more difficult as the family diminished by the generations.
Fewer of us married, fewer had children. For a long time,
my parents helped me in our work, but when they passed
and Ellen left...the spirits seem to grow stronger and more
active with fewer Dentons to supervise them. I fear one day
they will be able to move more than their own attachment
objects. I fear they will able to break free on their own.

For decades, the Wellings were so diminished, our
family didn't consider it a threat. But they are out there,
somewhere, waiting for their chance to gain access to the
house. The longer we leave the locks out of our control,
the stronger the spirits within the house grow and the more
power the Welling heir will have if they find the locks first.

Riley blew out a long breath. "Well, dammit. How am I
supposed to fix all of this?"

When she looked up, she saw the faintest impression of a
dandelion yellow dress as a feminine shape darted around the
corner and into the hall. Riley waited a few moments, but the
running ghost didn't reappear. If this had occurred even one month

ago, Riley would have been horrified. But now she sat calmly and just let the ghost do her thing.

Aunt Nora's words certainly gave her food for thought. Even though she knew she'd had nothing to do with the decision, Riley felt such profound guilt that her mother left Nora behind to deal with all this. Ellen had abandoned her responsibilities, and for what? She'd never struck Riley as a particularly happy person. She always seemed torn. Was it guilt? Did Ellen spend years looking over her shoulder, wondering when the ghost Chernobyl she'd left behind would blow? Did Nora resent Ellen for that? Would either of them have handled things differently, if they'd known how suddenly they would die?

Wait.

"Did Aunt Nora have some sort of premonition that she was going to die?" Riley asked. "Is that part of our magic?"

"Premonitions were not part your aunt's many gifts," Plover said. "I'm sure she would have mentioned it to me. She would have wanted...she would have wanted to warn me, certainly. I can tell you that Miss Nora hoped that she would be here to induct you into this way of life. She spent months preparing the house for your arrival, just in case. But she kept me out of most of her plans. It was very frustrating, but she said it was dangerous for you to know everything all at once."

"And she didn't tell you about her plans? Maybe giving you like general outline?" Riley asked. "Maybe that would be a better plan than just trusting me to accidentally pick up on the hints."

Plover sniffed. "Your aunt didn't believe in hints."

"Right. Super helpful."

The next morning, the doorbell interrupted her attempts at making coffee, which was a surprise to Riley. She didn't realize she had a doorbell. She'd woken up to multiple texts from Clark, asking about the police presence at her house. Apparently, the news had spread all over the island after she'd finally fallen asleep. Clark was deeply concerned that someone might have broken in, which Riley supposed was nice. He even offered to come by and check her windows to make sure the first floor was secured.

She declined, and then he immediately offered to come by to talk about spreading Aunt Nora's ashes. Riley wasn't entirely sure how to handle that, so she just didn't respond. Plover's dislike of the lawyer had to mean *something*. She supposed ghosts could see more than the living, but did Plover have any real reason to be annoyed by Clark? Riley wondered if maybe he was just a little jealous of a man who could spend time with her aunt in the flesh.

Nope, not enough coffee yet to deal with the fact that Aunt Nora probably had an otherworldly boyfriend.

When the doorbell rang, she half expected to find Clark on her doorstep. Instead, it was Caroline, holding a cup of coffee, wearing a purple-rimmed pair of sunglasses that covered an unreasonable portion of her face. Her sable hair was styled to curve around her jawline, making Riley wince. She'd been to the "so tired it hurt to use a hair elastic" level of fatigue during her bartending days.

"Another double shift?" Riley asked.

Caroline took a long drink from her coffee while handing Riley a comically large latte from Starfall Grounds. "It's too early for me to answer stupid questions. I did enough of that this morning when I kicked that dentist from Wisconsin out of my bed."

Riley snorted out a laugh. "You are getting up on an awful lot of mornings this week."

Caroline pursed her lips. "I just felt like I needed to be here this morning; does that make sense?"

"Is it because of the break-in? Because I'm fine, really."

Caroline gasped, "What break-in? What the hell? I'm not allowed to keep the scanner on at the bar."

"It's a long story," Riley grumbled into her own coffee.

The southern politeness in Riley struggled with the idea that she couldn't invite Caroline into the house. It felt so rude to just stand there, not allowing her into her home, but it would have been ruder to subject Caroline to the terror that Edison had felt, seeing Plover for the first time. Fortunately, Caroline seemed to pick up on the awkwardness.

"You want to drink these out in the sunshine?" Caroline suggested, ever helpful. "Being a partial vampire, I try to get as much vitamin D as I can. Helps me avoid ye old-timey diseases."

How weird was her life that, for a second, Riley had to consider whether Caroline was serious about being a vampire? She sincerely hoped vampires weren't a real thing. She had her hands full enough with ghosts.

"Actually, I was thinking I might swing by Alice's antique shop to have her take a look at a box I found in Nora's desk. Want to join me?"

Honestly, she hadn't planned on going to Alice's shop that morning. But now that Caroline was on her porch, it just made sense in a way she could no more explain than her ghostly fountain tenant or the haunted toaster.

"Sure, that sounds like a nice quiet environment for me to nurse my lack of sleep. Freaking unreliable coworkers." Caroline held up a small linen-bound book. "And I've been meaning to return this. Your aunt Nora leant it to me."

It was a copy of Wilkie Collin's *The Moonstone*. Riley wondered if it was some sort of sign from her aunt. The funeral home had delivered Nora's ashes to the house the day before. Riley knew that her aunt had wanted to be sprinkled into a distant river so she could travel the world, but how the heck was Riley supposed to make that happen without leaving the island for more than a day or two? She didn't want to consult with Clark about the issue. How was she supposed to explain what Nora wanted? Maybe Caroline knew Nora well enough to give her some hints.

"Your aunt and I talked about books when she came into the Rose. She knew I was a fan of the lesser-known classics," Caroline said.

"Really?" Riley turned the book over in her hands, confused. This was the first time anyone had mentioned a positive social interaction with her aunt. It was the first time anyone had mentioned any kind of social interaction with her aunt.

Riley examined the book. It had been recovered at some point in a fine blue linen. It was sort of surprising, considering that the pages were in pretty good shape. She'd worked in a used bookshop for a few months, and the rare-find antique books she'd seen subjected to recovering were a last-ditch effort in preserving what little value was left of a battered volume.

As far as Riley could see, there was no reason to recover this. She turned it over in her hands. There was a tiny border of shapes along the top and bottom of the front cover, different from the tiny regular geometric shapes that she'd seen around the house. These looked like seashells. She knew she'd seen them before, but where? Where had she seen them before?

"So, she came into the bar?"

Caroline guzzled her coffee again. "Every few months or so, just to have a quiet drink. Never on game nights. The woman couldn't stand football. Loved curling, though."

Seeing Plover standing quietly in the recesses of the foyer, Riley jerked her head towards the door in what she hoped was a nonchalant gesture. He nodded. She grabbed her purse and the box, leaving the book, and carefully locked the front door. "Did she talk to people?"

Caroline shook her head as they descended the steps. "Not really, just sort of stared intensely at this antique painting we have behind the bar. I kept expecting her to offer to buy it or something, but she never did. Maybe she figured the house had all the antiques it needs."

Riley's brows rose, and she made a mental note that Caroline's painting was probably haunted. "Well, it's good to know that she had some friends."

"I don't know if I would go that far," Caroline said, shaking her head. "She was a little like Alice in that way, never letting people get too close. If *she* talks to us this morning, it will be the first conversation I've had with her that lasts more than a few sentences."

"So you really don't know her at all?" Riley asked. "You've lived within a few miles of each other for twenty years."

They closed Riley's front gate and turned the corner towards Lilac. And ran into a wall of humanity. There were people *every-where*. Summer tourist season seemed to be in full swing. Elderly women in matching T-shirts for the Northern Stars Ladies' Euchre League. Couples strolling hand in hand. Families with small children begging for midmorning ice cream. Two of the largest tandem bikes Riley had ever seen were parked in front of the Starfall Be-Spoke Tours office. She didn't even understand the physics of how a dozen people pedaling a bike would work, but they all looked *thrilled* to be doing it. She could barely see the other side of the street. Everything smelled of sunscreen, melted sugar, and sun-warmed concrete.

For a moment, Riley was struck with a wave of homesickness. "What in the hell?" she gasped. "Where did they all come from?"

"Forgot it was Saturday, huh?" Caroline said, pursing her lips.

Riley searched her brain, trying to remember what day it was. She *had* forgotten what day it was. How long had she been on the island? With the ghosts and Edison and everything she was learning, she was losing track of time in a way that was more than a little frightening.

"This is nothing," Caroline told her as they passed the real estate office. "Wait until the high season starts, midsummer."

Riley nodded to the redheaded woman, once again at her post at the office window.

"So, you were saying about Alice?"

Caroline shrugged as they picked their way through the

crowd. "I mean, everybody on the island knows her story, so it's not exactly a secret. Her parents were in college when they met at a party and...well, her dad basically knocked her mom up, and they got married just a few months later."

"I'm assuming they didn't live happily ever after?" Riley said, wincing.

Caroline looked pained for a moment. "They did well for a while. And then Alice's mom developed some sort of clotting disorder and died of a stroke at twenty-five, of all things. Her dad tried to raise Alice on his own, but then there was some story about a fire. Her grandparents, the Proctors, never really let people talk to Alice about it. She lost everybody but them over the course of just a few years. By the time she was nine, she was living here with them. I felt so bad for her. Her grandparents are just hard people. Hard-hearted. Hardheaded. They always made her feel in debt to them for raising her, something that most grandparents would do out of love or just kindness. They just don't have that in them. I mean, my family are a bunch of loud, rowdy, loud—"

"You said loud twice," Riley noted.

"Yes, I know. My point is that they would never do anything to hurt me, not *on purpose*. And if they realized they'd hurt me, they'd apologize. They wouldn't be graceful about it, but they'd tell me they were sorry, and they'd mean it. Alice's grandparents? Never let her forget that it was her fault that her mother 'had' to get married, that her father hadn't been good enough. I didn't want to say anything in front of Petra because her in-laws and the Proctors are distantly related, but I get the feeling that part of the reason they homeschooled Alice was because they didn't want her to have anybody but them. Easier to control her that way, keep her in the shop working for free."

"So…you don't like them…" Riley said, intentionally squinting at her.

"I'm the town bartender. People tell me everything," she said. "I ingest it, assemble it, and decide where my grudges land. If people don't want me to hold those grudges, they shouldn't unload their secrets on me."

Riley nodded. "Seems reasonable."

They paused in front of Superior Antiques of Starfall Point. It was not exactly an inviting building. It was stiff and formal with its overdone silver lettering on the window, steel gray paint, and heavy ironwork, decorative curlicues that didn't seem to go with the look of the other buildings on the block. The visitors seemed to be avoiding it actively, like trout dividing their swimming stream around a rock.

Riley supposed that, if she had her druthers, she'd prefer buying fudge over an armoire.

"Are you sure we're going to be welcome?" Riley asked.

"Well, Alice's grandparents aren't in town, so more than likely, yes."

Riley gave her a pointed look. "Are you caffeinated enough to restrain yourself from snippy comments about Alice's grandparents?"

Caroline shook her head solemnly. "I make no promises."

"Always nice to be walking into a potential social minefield." As soon as Riley stepped into the shop, she realized that something was…building. She could feel a sensation of completeness settling into her chest. It was like a series of tumblers clicking into place, a lock closing. She was walking towards something important, which was odd because the shop was no more welcoming inside than it was outside.

She blinked at her surroundings, breathing through the discomfort of *anticipation*. It was hard to find a focal point with so much furniture against the broad charcoal-and-silver-striped wallpaper. Heavy-handed piano played over the speaker system, reminding Riley of a funeral parlor. The Proctors had obviously put a lot of effort into arranging the furniture into what might have been considered suites in a showroom. All the pieces were highly polished and seemed to be in good condition. The Proctors didn't seem to favor a particular style or period, but it was obvious that each piece was of high quality. But the smell—Riley had apparently become accustomed to the light smells of lemon and vinegar for cleaning. Whoever maintained the furniture here used some sort of highly floral wax paste that made Riley want to gag. It smelled like something a randy octogenarian would wear to Swinging Singles' Bingo.

Riley scanned the shop. There were some smaller items displayed in the back of the store, antique sewing machines, enamelware, jewelry, and the like. After her time in Shaddow House, it was enough to make her nervous. "Do you think Alice is working today?"

As if summoned, Alice appeared from behind a heavy oak counter, wearing a beige gray suit cut in the same prim lines as the outfit she'd been wearing when Riley met her. Did the poor girl never wear a primary color? She was so lovely, and yet all her choices seemed designed to make her fade into the background—an especially odd choice given her vibrant red-gold hair. Riley didn't want to stereotype redheads, but Alice seemed especially lacking in zaniness and a fiery temper.

"Riley! Hello!" Alice called, beaming as she crossed the shop floor. "And Caroline, I don't think you've ever been in the shop before. Um...thanks for coming by."

"Hi," Caroline said, raising her coffee cup. And then she seemed to realize she was waving hot dark-brown liquid precariously around expensive, easily stained items and glued her arms to her sides. Riley glanced between the two of them, wondering why things were so awkward.

"So, your grandparents help you run this place?" Riley said.

"They're in Boca Raton now," she said. "They prefer to spend most of the year there but come back every summer so they can review the books."

"Because a visit just to see you would be too much," Caroline muttered.

Alice didn't look offended. "They're...difficult people to know and love."

"They're just difficult," Caroline countered.

"They mean well," Alice assured her, turning towards the heavy oak counter where a phone was ringing. She turned towards Riley and shook her head. "I'll just let the machine pick that up."

"OK, well, I'm going to go...closely examine that very fancy but uncomfortable-looking chair over there," Caroline said, handing her cup to Riley. "I'm just going to leave this with...a responsible adult."

"How am I the responsible adult here? Is there some sort of history at work here that I should know about?" Riley asked as Caroline pretended to inspect a throne-like settee covered in red-and-gold damask. She turned to Alice. "Am I violating some sort of boundary by bringing Caroline here?"

"No, there's no big traumatic bullying incident or anything," Alice insisted. "Caroline's always been sort of intimidating to me. Not in an intentional way. I'm just afraid she's going to tell me what she thinks of me."

Riley asked, "Totally unprompted?"

"Yes." Alice nodded, biting her lip. "She has no compunctions about telling people when they're annoying her, which I admire in way. I've seen her take people down a peg or two, and it's a sight to behold. But I have enough of that with my... I just try to avoid her, so I don't annoy her and get an earful of hurtfully accurate opinions."

Riley shrugged. "I can see why that would be a concern."

"So how can I help you?" Alice asked. "Are the Shaddows planning on selling their furnishings, because that's a conversation my grandparents would want to be party to. Oh, they would never forgive me if I talked to you without them."

Alice looked so genuinely distressed that Riley reached into her bag and pulled out the wooden puzzle box. "No, no. Caroline just mentioned that sometimes you end up fixing the furniture people bring in, and you might have a tool that could help me pry it open."

It was a relief, to see how Alice instantly relaxed. She returned to the counter and pulled a deep drawer open with a loud *squeak*.

Alice retrieved a bright magenta toolbox with *Alice* painted across the lid in gold paint in swirling curlicues. It was the most brightly colored object in the store. "Oh, sure! People always think their family heirlooms are in much better shape than they actually are, especially when they're trying to sell them. But if it's a good piece, it's no trouble to fix it up a bit. I enjoy it."

She opened the toolbox and grabbed a set of tiny tools wrapped in a soft pink cloth. It looked like the kind of thing a tiny handyman would use to renovate a dollhouse. "I just have to clean up my workshop before my grandparents get here for the summer."

"Why?"

"They think it's a poor reflection on them if they admit that they would buy anything that's in less than perfect condition," Alice said, pulling out a small pair of pliers. She squinted at the joints in the puzzle box, turning it over in her hands. Caroline drifted closer, watching Alice working the pliers into a tiny space between two slats and gently pulling out a blunt metal pin. "The problem is that, if we only accepted items in perfect condition, we wouldn't have anything to sell. So I have to employ a little bit of deception, set my workshop up every fall, take it down every summer. Just um, please don't tell anyone."

"Wow," Caroline marveled.

Alice turned to Caroline, her expression anxious. "What?"

"I just never thought you would do anything so..." Caroline paused to search for the right word.

"Duplicitous? Mendacious? Treacherous?" Alice suggested, as she easily moved the wooden slats around like she knew exactly what sequence was needed.

"I was going to say sneaky, but OK. You just seemed like such a goody-goody growing up," Caroline said. "What little we saw of you, with the homeschooling for the supersmart you were doing."

"I wasn't a prodigy or anything. I was just a little above average, and it would have been hard for the teachers to give me what I needed when they were already teaching so many different grade levels. And my grandparents...they're..."

"Weird as hell," Caroline supplied.

"Caroline!" Alice said, laughing despite herself.

"Well, they are!" Caroline shot back. "How can two people consider themselves 'pillars of the community'—which no one ever actually calls them, by the way—and hold themselves completely separate from that community? That's part of the reason everybody worried about you so much when we heard they were raising a child. They just weren't *kid* people. They used to chase children out of their shop with a broom. They only stopped when the Chamber of Commerce threatened to remove them. They were selfish, snotty, standoffish users who only had a kind word to say to somebody if it made them some sort of profit."

Caroline sagged against her seat, letting out a pent-up breath.

"Feel better?" Riley asked.

"Yes," Caroline said. "I'm sorry, Alice. I know that was a lot, but I just hate to see the way they treat you, and then you act like you owe them somehow."

Alice's voice went soft. "Well, to be fair, they did raise me when they didn't have to."

"Without one drop of the milk of human kindness," Caroline huffed.

"You get really eloquent when you're mad," Riley noted.

"Years of training, yelling at my family," Caroline replied.

"Wait, so everybody was worried about me being raised by them, but no one ever said anything to *me*? Because it would have been really nice to have someone to talk to about...everything." Alice muttered as she moved the wooden slats. Suddenly, the box popped open. "Oh, there we go."

"That would have taken me so much longer," Riley said. "Thank you."

Caroline grinned. "So, what's inside? Is it treasure?"

"Is it evidence?" Alice asked.

"That's definitely a less fun, more 'Riley's aunt could be a murderer' approach, but all right," Caroline said.

Riley dropped the contents of the box into her hand. "Um, it's a tiny marble penis."

"It's not a penis," Caroline scoffed, her gaze dropping to the two-inch white marble fragment in Riley's palm. "Holy hell, it looks just like a tiny marble penis. Your aunt Nora literally left you a dick in a box."

"I told you!" Riley cried. "And then this weird-looking brass key. Have you ever seen something like this before?"

"Not really. Your aunt was into some...um, interesting things," Alice said, turning the key over in her hand. It looked like an old fashioned skeleton key with the "business end" shaped like a brass X.

"Is anybody else wondering what the hell that key unlocks?" Caroline suggested. "But at the same time, really, really not wanting to know?"

Riley swiped a hand over her face. She couldn't help but

feel frustrated by this never-ending scavenger hunt her aunt was sending her on. Would it ever end? Would she ever feel like she had earned her place at Shaddow House? As Riley mulled this over, she felt a now-familiar tingle of awareness ripple up her spine. There was a haunted object somewhere nearby, in the shop.

She looked over the contents of Alice's counter. It contained the usual computer equipment, shipping tape, scissors, pens necessary to run a place like this. Through the gap of the deep desk drawer, Riley spotted a pair of long razor-sharp shears with ornately cast handles.

"What is that?" Riley asked.

"Oh." Alice grinned. "Aren't they pretty? They're a pair of tailoring shears, manufactured in the 1950s, but still in amazing shape. I know it's wrong to stash them away, but I just couldn't bear to sell them. They just felt...special, so I keep them in my desk."

They were special, all right—especially haunted. Riley turned the large shears in her hands, feeling them sing with energy between her palms. "Where did they come from?"

"I'm not sure." Alice woke up her computer, opened a file and frowned. "Oh, your aunt Nora sold them to us. There are notes on the sale. My grandmother says she pretended that she didn't have an interest in them, but she was so excited by the idea that your aunt would sell her anything that *might* be from Shaddow House, she jumped at it. And then, I guess I found them in our sewing notions cabinet and hid them in my desk. After my grandparents left for the season, of course. I probably shouldn't have kept them. I hated the idea of some customer's grandchild using them to make paper dolls."

"I'm not sure that kids still make paper—you know what, never mind," Caroline said, shaking her head.

Riley simply stared at the shears. First, Aunt Nora lent Caroline a book and then sold a haunted object to Alice's family? Nora didn't lend things to people. She hoarded Shaddow House's treasures like a dragon. She was starting to wonder whether her late aunt had intentionally used these items to lead Riley to Alice and Caroline.

Maybe Riley was supposed to share this burden with them? She'd shared with Edison and nothing horrible had happened. Plover *had* said that sometimes Dentons had shared the secrets of Shaddow House with a select few friends. But Alice and Caroline didn't seem close. Why would the Denton magic choose two people who were so different?

Further musings were interrupted by the shears being yanked out of Riley's hands by an invisible force, circling the room and then embedding themselves in the wall behind the counter.

"Oh, shit," Riley gasped.

"Riley, how did you do that?" Caroline asked. "Is this going to be a *Carrie* thing, because I haven't had enough coffee for a *Carrie* thing."

"Oh, my grandparents are not going to like that," Alice said, shaking her head.

Before Riley could apologize, a short man in a shiny blue-gray sharkskin suit materialized in front of them. His dark curly hair was impeccably trimmed, and he had the faintest bruise on his cheekbone. He looked so angry, dark eyes flaming as he wrapped his hands around the shear handles.

"Who the hell do you think you are, touching my shears, ya

dumb broad?" he roared, but his nasal Brooklyn accent sort of made him sound like a petulant child. "I ain't gonna have some witch working on my shears. You hear me? You got no right!"

"Everybody else sees that, right?" Caroline whispered. "Otherwise, I'm gonna have to tell Petra that Iggy supplied a batch of his special brownies to the coffee shop."

"I see it too," Alice whispered.

"It's a ghost," Riley told them as the ghost scowled and yanked ineffectively at the shears. Apparently, he'd thrown them so hard at the wall, they'd turned into some sort of ghostly Excalibur.

The ghost yelled, "Stupid witches, touching a man's shears. Don't you know any better?"

"Why is the little man so angry?" Alice whispered.

"Little?" the ghost shouted. He clutched at his zipper. "I'll show ya 'little.'"

All three women groaned. All fear seemed to have evaporated now, as the ghost was reduced to a catcaller. That was something they could deal with. Riley much preferred the subtle antics of Eloise, or even the disappearing yellow dress ghost.

"That's just in poor taste," Caroline said, frowning. "It's the 2020s, man."

"The hell you say, sugar-tits," the shears ghost said, leering at her.

"Hey, no, not OK," Riley barked while Alice sort of sidled behind her.

"My name is Bobby Carlucci!" the man roared in Caroline's face. "And I'll be damned if any woman is gonna tell me what I can say!"

Fortunately, Caroline had worked too long behind a bar to be intimidated. She marched right up to him to yell down into his ghostly face, "Yeah, well, I'm Caroline goddamn Wilton, and I will put your shears at the bottom of a urinal with a little sign that says, TARGET PRACTICE!"

Bobby shrank back. "You're crazy, sugar-tits."

"Don't ever doubt it," Caroline seethed.

"I think I like you," Bobby purred. "What are you doing later?"

"Alice, you got any salt?" Riley asked.

"Um, sure," Alice reached under the counter and pulled out a carefully organized bag of lunchtime takeout materials—plastic utensils, napkins, and tiny packets of salt and pepper. Riley pulled on the shears until they wiggled loose from the wall. Alice spilled the salt packets onto the counter.

"Rip the tops off, but don't pour them out yet," Riley told her, turning to Bobby. "Hey, creep, get back into the shears."

"You don't tell me what to do, ya dumb broad!" he hollered back at her.

When she raised her hand to make the "closing" gesture—she wasn't about to make the mistake of salt-binding a haunted object without the ghost being inside again—Caroline put her hand on Riley's arm.

"What are you doing?" Caroline asked as a surge of magical energy seemed to zip up Riley's arm. Even as Bobby protested that he wasn't going anywhere, he was pulled toward the shears, unable to resist.

"I think you're helping," Riley said, a giggling bursting from her chest. It just felt so good not to do this *alone*. She picked up the salt packets and sprinkled a sparse line of salt around the shears while making the "closing" gesture.

"Really?" Caroline whispered. "Alice, put your hand on Riley's arm."

"Why?" Alice asked as she ripped open salt packets.

"No!" Bobby yelled, bracing his hands against the counter, even as his head was pulled toward the shears. "I'm not going back in there. Come on, baby, don't you want a little more time with Bobby? I can make it worth your while. You like silk?"

"A world of no," Caroline retorted while copying Riley's hand gesture. Bobby's form seemed to be pulled toward the shears even more forcefully, especially when Alice put her hand on Riley's shoulders and copied the "closing" gesture. That feeling of being complete, of all the pieces of her magic coming together, seemed to crystallize, and Riley felt...powerful.

"Back into the shears, Bobby," she told him. "And be less creepy the next time I see you."

Bobby sneered at her, even as his face disappeared into the silver surface of the shears.

"What the hell was that?" Caroline demanded. "And how did you know what to do?"

"Um, the shears are Bobby's attachment object, something that meant a lot in life to a ghost. Me walking into the store probably provoked him. Picking them up was a step too far. I should have known better."

"Because you have a problem with haunted sewing equipment?" Caroline asked.

"Because I'm a witch who is capable of forcing ghosts like

him back into their objects," Riley replied. "Or removing them entirely, in theory."

"Sure," Caroline scoffed. "I mean, if I had a nickel for every time I've heard that. So, that was a spell?"

"Yeah," Riley rolled her eyes. "I can't light a candle with my mind or ride a broom across the full moon or anything, but I can boss ghosts around. And every once in a while, I can make haunted things move with my brain, but I can't quite control it yet. It's a bit of a letdown, to be honest."

"Your magic spell didn't rhyme. Shouldn't it rhyme? There weren't even any words," Caroline protested.

Riley shrugged. "Beats me."

"Seems a little lazy," Caroline noted. "In terms of witchcraft."

"Plover said that most of the responsibility would fall on me, because I'm a Denton, but that I could find helpmates," Riley said, trying to control the shaking of her hands. "Aunt Nora preferred to work alone, but I guess my magic reached out to choose people to help me. Maybe you're supposed to be my coven?"

"Who is Plover?" Caroline asked.

"I don't like the sound of that," Alice confessed. "The coven is usually the first to go when the angry mobs get all testy. My grandma Seastairs was into genealogy, traced our family lines going all the way back to the Salem trials. It was *not* a good time for us."

"But that makes sense, doesn't it?" Riley suggested. "That you could have magic in your lineage, which seems to be calling my magic to it."

"OK, well, what about me?" Caroline asked. "My incredibly

limited gene pool comes from right here on the island, and as far as I know, not one witch among us."

Riley guessed, "Maybe we're related somewhere a few generations back?"

"Th-that is horrifying," Caroline sputtered.

Riley blinked at her. "Hurtful."

"No, I mean that one of my relatives managed to reproduce without the rest of us finding out about it," Caroline cried. "That's the kind of thing we try to limit. Have you met my brothers?"

Riley chose to ignore that. "Alice, I need a small box and all of the salt you can get your hands on."

"You want to put the haunted shears in table condiments?" Alice asked, frowning at her.

"I need to take these back to my house for safekeeping," Riley told her as Alice poured random office supplies out of a bright orange shoebox she found under the counter. Riley poured the remaining salt over them, making hasty gestures to keep Bobby contained. "It's not safe for you to have them here at the store. And it's definitely not safe to sell them to some unsuspecting customer."

"I can't let you do that. My grandparents would be *furious*. It would be like I just traded them back to Shaddow House after Grandmother managed to get them from your aunt," Alice said, her face turning an ashy gray. Seeing an angry ghost stab her wall hadn't made her go pale like that, but somehow, the idea of giving away stock made her physically ill.

Riley felt terrible, just demanding the shears like she had a right to them. Running Shaddow House, if she could call it that, had given her an odd sense of entitlement. And it filled her with shame.

"I could buy them," Riley offered weakly, even as Alice seemed to hyperventilate.

"I think you should go," Alice said, shaking her head. "It's bad enough that there's a stab wound in the wall but—oh my goodness, my grandparents are going to be *so* angry with me! Both of you need to go."

Caroline wrapped a hand around Alice's. "It's going to be all right, hon. I can get—"

"Just go," Alice wheezed.

"OK, I can't force you," Riley said, scribbling on a scrap of paper. "But if you need me, here's my number. I am always available. Do not sell those shears. OK? Keep them in the salt box."

Riley reluctantly left the shop, flipping the CLOSED sign on the door to give Alice a few minutes to catch her breath. Caroline was close at her heels.

"Well, that was weird," Caroline said, raking her hands through her hair as they made their way down the street.

Riley wanted to run back to Alice, to tell her she was sorry. But she didn't think Alice would be able to hear it. The fact that she'd upset Alice so badly made her want to cry, and Caroline seemed to know that.

"Oh, honey," Caroline sighed, wrapping her arms around Riley. "It's going to be OK. Like I said, Alice's grandparents are just a touchy subject with her."

"What can I do?" Riley asked as Caroline slid her arm through Riley's.

"I honestly don't know," Caroline told her. "Just give her some time. Maybe she'll come around."

They walked down the street at a snail's pace, because frankly, Riley's legs felt like they might collapse under her. The magic she'd worked with Alice and Caroline had been stronger than what she'd worked on Charles and his silver service. Now that she'd tasted that power, Riley didn't want to go back to practicing alone—which probably didn't speak well of her.

As they passed the real estate office, she waved to the now-familiar redheaded woman in the blue dress.

Riley stopped, dragging Caroline to an abrupt halt. She turned slowly back toward the office building. Something had been nagging at Riley in the back of her mind since the last time Riley had spotted the woman at the Realtors' window.

She'd been wearing the same blue dress every time Riley had seen her.

Riley was so stupid. This woman didn't have injuries, like some of the ghosts at the house, but she was obviously stuck in that outdated dress. She didn't have that silvery appearance that Charles or Eloise had, but Riley had never seen either of them in natural light. Maybe that made a difference?

"You OK? Are you seeing another gho—squirrel right now?" Caroline asked, glancing around the people milling around the sidewalk.

Riley nodded.

"Oh, shit, the girl in the blue dress?"

Riley nodded again. "You see her too?"

"Do you think you did something to my brain in the shop?" Caroline demanded. "Will I be seeing...squirrels all the time now?"

"A hearty 'I don't know' to both questions," Riley told her. "What would you think of going to talk to her?"

Caroline's dark brows drew together. "I mean, will she fling scissors at us or sexually harass me in particular?"

"The shears and the harassment seem like a Bobby-specific thing," Riley said.

"What do we have to lose?" Caroline asked. "We're obviously seeing her for a reason."

"I'll wait until later to tell you that ghosts can injure people."

"Wait, what?" Caroline barked as Riley walked away.

Riley straightened her shoulders. Right. This was just another customer service gig. She could do this. She'd handled way worse than this before. She was ninety-percent certain. Surely, that stint in tech support for a dog-walking app had to count for something. As they moved closer to the ghost, Riley saw the way the woman's opaque feet floated over the ground. Riley swallowed heavily.

No, she hadn't handled worse than this. What the hell was she talking about? She was a complete idiot. And she was dragging Caroline into her idiocy.

Caroline and Riley froze as the ghost turned to them, pale eyes narrowed. All around them, tourists and locals alike walked past them, clearly unable to see the woman like they could. Caroline and Riley just looked like they were peering at the Martin & Martin Realtors listings.

After a few awkward seconds, Caroline whispered, "Well, she hasn't called me 'sugar-tits' yet, so that's an improvement." Riley snorted, making the ghost frown.

Riley cleared her throat. "Hi. Can we help you?"

The ghost's head tilted inquisitively. "So you can see me?"

"A few times now, yeah. I've smiled at you," Riley noted. "I even waved."

"Yes, but I always assume you breathers are looking at someone else. You get ignored for a few decades and see how it hurts your social skills. I'm Abigail."

Riley extended her hand as if she could shake Abigail's and immediately felt like an idiot. Caroline gave her a confused look. "What are you doing?"

Riley shrugged helplessly. "I'm Riley. So…how long have you been dead?"

Abigail frowned at her. Caroline's jaw dropped. Riley pursed her lips and added, "My social skills have also suffered, but for other reasons."

"I'm Caroline," she said. "I'm new to this, hence, the not talking as much."

"Talking doesn't seem to be doing me any favors," Riley observed, making Abigail chuckle. "So, how long have you been *here*?"

"You can't tell by the dress?" Abigail asked, gesturing towards her high collar and matching white headband. "I'm like an extra from *Clueless*, a look I never thought I would regret."

"Honestly, that look has come and gone a few times in the last few decades, so good for you for keeping an air of mystery about you," Caroline said. "So, I'm assuming you're hanging out here for a reason. Is there anything I can do to help you, I don't know, find peace?"

"I don't think we're ready for *that* conversation just yet," Riley protested.

Abigail rolled her eyes. "Are you one of those do-gooder psychics trying to help us cross over? Like the wingnuts on the ghost tours?"

"Sort of?" Caroline guessed.

"I think maybe we should start over," Riley said. "I don't think we're making a very good first impression. We would be happy to talk to you about anything you need from us. No matter what that is. If you have something you need—"

"I think I'm good," Abigail told her. "I don't have time for games."

"One would think that, as a ghost, all you have is time," Riley pointed out.

Abigail huffed out an unnecessary breath and disappeared from sight.

"That was the wrong thing to say," Riley said, nodding as she pressed her lips into an unhappy line.

"Well, I didn't help," Caroline said. "I'm going to blame toxic ghost-shock syndrome."

Riley frowned. "Bobby was definitely toxic."

Chapter 9
Edison

EDISON SAT AT HIS DESK, poring over a copy of *Ghost Hunting for Complete Morons*. He was hiding it in the dust jacket for *A Tale of Two Cities*, because he did not need to be seen reading a detailed manual on how to interact with dead people. That was how Margaret would end up with his job.

Ghost tours were encouraged on Starfall. Ghost stories were celebrated on Starfall. But people who held publicly funded positions spending their work time reading ghost books for morons? Not so much.

He'd wanted to visit Riley since he heard about the attempted break-in at Shaddow House, but he also didn't want to crowd her. On her latest visit to the library to drop off an armful of E. M. Forster titles, Caroline assured him that Riley was just fine, more indignant at being woken up in the middle of the night than anything else.

So, although his anxiety was screaming at Edison to run to her porch and demand to see for himself that she was safe and sound, he'd kept his distance. Riley didn't appreciate being treated like she was fragile, so instead, he read. He wanted to understand Riley's strange new reality. He wanted to help Riley with her "job," if he could. He wanted to hide this book from Riley, because she was walking through the nonfiction section towards his office, chatting with Kyle. His erstwhile volunteer was smiling at her, talking about something to do with the T-shirt he was wearing, depicting a retro sci-fi series set in the 1980s. He hadn't seen Kyle grin like that in months. Riley had that ability to coax the smiles out of people. Unless, of course, there was a ferry involved.

Edison shoved the ghost hunting book under a pile of papers.

"A lovely lady to see you, boss," Kyle announced, teasing him.

Edison could only stare and stack more papers on top of his embarrassing book.

"I'm sorry he's so socially awkward," Kyle told her. "If you want to keep talking about Upside Down theories, I will be in the fiction section."

Riley's smile was radiant. "Nice to meet you, Kyle."

"H-hi!" Edison finally sputtered. "What are you doing here?"

"I needed some books?" she suggested, her smile tilting at a teasing angle. "And a very helpful public official allowed me to manipulate the library card system to my advantage."

"Don't you have all the books?" Edison asked, tilting his fists under his chin with all the bright-eyed enthusiasm of a child being told a fairy tale. She threw her head back and cackled in the most charming way possible. He made it one of his life's goals to make her laugh like that as often as he could. "I've heard the stories about Shaddow House's library. Are they true?"

"That it's big, cavernous, full of possibly haunted books?" she suggested, leaning across his desk so only he could hear. "Yes, all true."

"You're leaning awfully close over my desk, ma'am," he noted. "Is this where you confess to your secret librarian fetish? I've run into that before. It never turns out well."

Riley's gray eyes went wide in shock, which made him think he'd greatly miscalculated the subjects they were allowing themselves to joke about. And then those same eyes narrowed and the quirk of her lips went almost filthy. "I'm gonna need you to take off your glasses and tell me my books are overdue, and you're going to get the fines out of me in spankings."

He swallowed heavily, then squeaked, "It's not the first time I've heard that, believe it or not."

"Well, now I kind of *want* you to say it," she insisted, grinning at him.

"As much as I'm enjoying this, I think we need to lower our voices, or the Nana Grapevine will report this flirtation and feel the need to defend the honor of the granddaughters they have aggressively attempted to set me up with."

"Ah, yes, Caroline explained the Nana Grapevine. How many granddaughters are we talking here?" she asked. "And how many Nanas are seeking your hand in matrimony?"

"I don't think they're looking for marriage; they just want to prove that the guy who hasn't dated since he arrived on the island would want to date *their* granddaughter. I would make a *Moby Dick* reference, but that seems wrong on a lot of levels."

Riley laughed. "OK, so when you're not avoiding being set up by aggressive elderly ladies, do you date?"

"Not since Erin," he said, shaking his head.

She stared at him expectantly, as if waiting for him to add more. But there wasn't much to tell. Until that morning on the ferry, when this gorgeous, green-faced girl was yelling at him, he just hadn't had the inclination. He dodged her expectations with a question of his own. "What about you? Is there a nice boy waiting back in Florida?"

She scoffed. "No."

"Is there a *not* particularly nice boy waiting for you back in Florida?" he asked.

"I don't think Ted's waiting on me. Things did not end on a positive note," she said, shaking her head.

"You dated a guy named Ted in Florida? Have you never watched a single Netflix documentary?" he asked, making her giggle. "Was his last name Bundy?"

"No," she grumbled. "And he was a really nice guy," she objected. "At least, I thought so at first."

"So, was it an amicable breakup? Because the name alone would make me tread carefully."

Riley winced, making him ask, "You didn't set fire to his car or anything, did you?"

"No, not his *car*," she scoffed. When he blanched, she laughed. "I'm kidding! No major household purchases were harmed during my exit."

"Well, this story I have to hear," he said.

"Not here, within earshot of your Nana Grapevine," she said, glancing into the library space as if there was recording equipment hidden in the walls. He couldn't blame her.

"Agreed," he said, leaning closer and lowering his voice. "Meet me back here at six. I would like to hear your tale of heartache and barely avoided car arson."

"Is that the sort of prose you pick up reading Charles Dickens?" she asked, flipping open the book that Edison obviously failed at hiding.

"No!" He hissed out a breath as a gleeful smile broke open on her face.

She bit her lip and gave him the sort of look someone might give a newborn St. Bernard puppy. "That's so cute!"

"When I want to understand something, I read about it," he grumbled.

"I'll try to find something a little less moron-oriented at the house," she told him. "Something that's not considered a priceless treasure with a ghost attached to it."

"I would appreciate that, thank you."

Riley walked back into the library at six, just after Judith closed down the post office for the night. Riley had changed clothes, Edison noted, to a breezy summer dress the color of violets. By some trick of light, it made her eyes look more purple than gray. Edison didn't want to be the kind of guy whose heartbeat could be affected by eye color–related optical illusions, but damned if it didn't do just that.

Erin had been a known quantity. She was calm and rational, even when she was angry. It was one of the many things that he had admired about her. It was what made her the great lawyer that he could never be. He'd loved her stability, the knowledge that he could predict how she would react in almost any given situation. But Riley was…something else. There were times when spending time with her was comforting, and others when he felt like he was just holding on for dear life. He never knew what she was going to say or do, or what they were going to face when they saw each other. That was a heady feeling, a roller coaster. He couldn't see when the drops and dips were coming. And he didn't know if that made her exciting or just dangerous.

"I just realized the post office is in the same building as the library," she said, chin-pointing at the closed grate over the postal entrance. "Another one of those '*because Starfall Point*' quirks?"

"You should see the jail," he told her, walking her out of the building. He stopped to lock the front door. "It's like something out of Mayberry. It's just one holding cell, but it's pretty rare for more than one person to get arrested at a time."

"That makes sense," she said, turning to him with her hands spread in an expectant gesture. "OK, so we are intentionally going out together, to enjoy an activity. Again, *together*."

He noted that she didn't call it a *date*. He wanted to change that. He was not a well man.

"So, what are we going to do?" she asked.

He burst out laughing. "You know, I hadn't really thought about it. So many of our encounters have been defined by terror or emergencies. We just sort of show up and things happen."

"Well, we live in a tourist destination," she prompted him, "where you have lived for a lot longer than I have. So…this is on you."

"Haunted tour?" he suggested.

"You're joking!"

Edison threw his head back and laughed. "I thought maybe it would be sort of fun, watching someone fake it when you've seen the real thing."

"Not every haunted tour on the island is fake," she told him. "Now that I know what to look for, I've seen several ghosts around the island. Not all those ghosts are willing to talk, but they're here. They definitely don't stick around for the tours, though. I don't think they like overhearing what people say about them."

"Can't blame them. So, no tours. How many fudge shops have you visited since you got to the island?" he asked.

She shrugged. "Never been a big fudge person."

"OK, your aunt said the same thing... Who hurt you? As a family, I mean."

"Genetics and the magical universe at large?" she guessed. "Maybe we can go out to dinner? It would have to be somewhere on the island."

"What, because of the house?" he replied. "I thought you could leave for short amounts of time."

"No, because of the boat thing," she said. "I don't think putting you in a state of terror is a good way to start."

He smiled at her, pleased that she'd thought of it.

"Well, not on the first date," he said. When she didn't vehemently object, he went on. "We could go to The Wilted Rose. Not that I've ever really hung out at the Rose, and given your friendship with Caroline, maybe that would be weird."

"It seems like a lot of pressure to put on Caroline. And us," she observed.

"OK, do you like ice cream, or are you some sort of robot sent from the future to torture me with your wrongness?"

She snickered. "The non-robot-torture option."

They walked through town enjoying the late summer evening. The sky was still a perfect robin's-egg blue, tinged ever so slightly with creeping peach. The crowds had dispersed for the season, and while they still had to survive Labor Day weekend in a few weeks, it was starting to feel like the island belonged to them again.

"I haven't survived a winter here, I'm aware, but there is something to be said for living in a place that has all four seasons," she said. "In Florida, are only two—'sweaty' and 'still sweaty, but not quite as sweaty.'"

"Winter's not so bad," he assured her as they walked down the sidewalk.

"I'm picturing something out of *The Shining*," she said, wrinkling her nose. "Or *The Thing*. Or any number of winter-based horror movies. Why are there so many of those?"

"It can be scary, especially if you're not used to snow," he admitted, taking her hand. She didn't shrink away from the gesture. The cute nose-wrinkling smile shifted to one of amusement, just as she squeezed his fingers lightly. "It helps that you don't have to drive anywhere. It's the boredom that can get you. You need to find a way to keep yourself entertained. A hobby, crafts, reading, cooking. Whatever keeps you from focusing on the fact that the sun is setting before five."

"I will probably make use of the library card that local official has so thoughtfully provided for me," she noted.

Edison grinned. "The cool thing is that a lot of people make things when they're winter-bored. They brew beer. They bake. They knit scarves. And they'll share it with you because nobody needs fourteen scarves at their house."

"So how many scarves are at your house?" she asked.

"Fourteen," he mumbled. "Because they were awful early attempts with cheap yarn that I don't want to give to anyone. I can manage a pretty decent basket weave stitch now."

"That's very sweet. I will secretly inspect every scarf I see now, wondering if it's one of yours."

He vowed, then and there, he would make her the softest scarf possible in the exact shade of purple of her dress. He wanted to see it against her skin whenever possible.

"There seem to be an unusual number of locally owned businesses on the island," she noted as they approached Starfall Scoops.

"Well, the mayor and the city council work pretty hard to keep franchise licenses out of town," he said. "You don't come to a place like this to shout into a clown's mouth."

"What kind of franchises have you been going to?" she asked, shuddering.

"Prepare yourself for the best ice cream you've ever had," he told her, opening the door. "Hi, Regina."

Edison waved at the owner as they'd walked into a shop that looked straight out of the 1930s. Before moving to Starfall, he'd only seen a soda fountain counter like that in the movies, all polished steel and bubblegum-pink enamel. Chairs fashioned of wire-thin white wrought iron flanked high-seated tables, covered in pink and blue gingham.

"Hey, Edison! Oh, a newcomer! Welcome to Starfall Scoops!" a tall Black woman called from behind the counter. Her braids were arranged into an intricate crown that accentuated the angles of her high cheekbones. She wore no makeup, save for a plummy lipstick that made Edison think of the small-batch jam Regina mixed into the Strawberry Explosion ice cream.

"Regina, this is Riley," Edison said. "She's new to the island."

"New tastebuds to dazzle!" Regina cheered, sending a significant look at their joined hands. "Thank you, Edison. Riley, it's very nice to meet you. Sample with abandon."

"Oh, that is a dangerous precedent to set, ma'am." Riley giggled gleefully. "I love the store, by the way. You have a real eye for sophisticated coziness."

"Well, we're in pretty fierce competition with Mackinac Island, in terms of being quaint."

Riley gasped. "Wait, how did you say it?"

"Mack-in-Naw," Regina said again.

"I've been calling it Mack-in-Ack this whole time, and no one said anything to me?"

Regina patted Riley's free hand. "Most likely, no one wanted to hurt your feelings."

"Let's not tell her about how she pronounces 'Yip-silanti,'" Edison told Regina, making Riley gasp with indignation.

"Your usual? Single scoop of Superman?" Regina asked Edison.

Edison's cheeks went hot at the mention of his juvenile usual order. "Yes, please."

"I'm sorry, what?" Riley raised her hand.

Regina offered Riley a tiny sample spoonful of what tasted

faintly like sherbet of an indeterminate origin. Possibly bubble gum. She sniffed at it delicately and then tried it.

"I know, it's a kids' flavor," Edison said, rubbing at the back of his neck. "But it reminds me of when I was sick and my mother let me stay home from school. I would get chicken noodle soup and any kind of sherbet I wanted."

"That is also very sweet," she told him. "Very, very sweet. But why is it called that?"

"No one seems to know for sure, but most people think it's because the ice cream is all the colors of his costume," Regina said.

"Seems weirdly dismissive to call it a costume when he's flying so fast he's turning the Earth backwards," Riley said. When Edison's eyes went wide, she shrugged. "I used to work in a comic shop. Just don't make me argue the physics of it with you!"

"I like her." Regina snorted, as she scooped up Edison's order. "Anyway, if you run an ice cream parlor in Michigan, you better have Superman on the menu. Otherwise, chaos will follow."

Across the dining room, two kids at one of the tables got into a squabble over who had stolen a bite of whose ice cream, and suddenly chairs were being flipped over and a cone full of Mint Chip Mayhem had been flung at the window.

"Speaking of which," Regina sighed as the ice cream slid messily down the glass. "Excuse me. Shelley, can you finish up their order?"

Regina grabbed a roll of paper towels and speedily intervened on behalf of her windows. The kids were still crying and yelling over lost ice cream. Shelley, a teenage Starfall Scooper with long blond pigtails approached with a cheerful, "Anything else you want to try?"

"What is Petoskey Stone?" Riley asked, pointing at the tub containing a concoction in an almost lurid shade of purple with darker purple ribbons running through it. "What does that taste like?"

"Petoskey Stone," Shelley said, giving Riley a puckish grin. She wasn't trying to be rude to Riley. It was the staff's standard response to the question, which Edison heard nearly every time he visited the shop.

Riley blinked and nodded sharply. "Right."

"It's blackberry with black raspberry ripple and chunks of fudge cake batter," Edison told her. "It's the signature flavor, and Regina's family likes keeping a bit of mystery about it."

"I'll try that," Riley told Shelley. "No sample. It sounds delicious."

With their dessert secured, they took their ice cream to one of the pink tables situated on a tiny slate-stoned patio between Starfall Scoops and Waterstone's Wondrous Fudge.

They ate their delicious ice cream in silence for a few moments before Edison finally asked, "So this guy, Ted, whose car you definitely didn't set on fire."

She burst out laughing, which was exactly the reaction he was hoping for. "It was nothing remotely that dramatic. I packed my stuff from our shared condo and very quietly left him to explain to people that the wedding was cancelled because I caught him in bed with his parents' best friends' daughter. The meanest thing I did was leave him with a pile of opened wedding presents. But I took the list of who gave what, so he would end up having a hundred awkward conversations about his not sending thank-you notes."

"That's on him, not you. Not even her, really. He was the one who made promises to you. I mean, the thank-you note thing is a little on you."

"I agree," she said. "The worst part is—wait, no, that's not the worst part. The second-worst part was that I knew something was going on. I knew they weren't 'just like brother and sister.' It wasn't about jealousy. It wasn't about believing women and men couldn't be friends—which I do. But I let them tell me that I was suspicious, paranoid, crazy. I let them make me feel bad for saying I was uncomfortable with how often they went 'camping' without me or the fact that he deleted every text from her. I was so desperate for love that I let myself get talked out of what I saw with my own eyes."

"So what was the worst part?"

"The worst part was that I lost his family, which I know sounds weird. But I thought I was getting this big family, lots of siblings and cousins and aunts and uncles. I was looking forward to rolling my eyes at Uncle Lou's constant football talk and pretending to enjoy Aunt Dina's terrible dry ham. I was going to have a family, people who would care if I had a bad week or tell me when my haircut didn't quite turn out as flattering as I thought. I couldn't seem to connect with my parents. My siblings never accepted me. So finally experiencing that family closeness, thinking I mattered to those people and then having all of them drop me without a word within a week of the breakup? Yeah, that was the worst part."

"That seems all-around unfair."

Riley scoffed. "Who gave you the impression that families are fair? Or love, for that matter?"

"What gives you the impression that they're not?"

"I appreciate your optimism. And honestly, even though I haven't really dated anyone *seriously* since Ted, I don't think it scarred me so I can never love again or anything so Heathcliff-esque. Please note my classical literature reference because I do read."

He grinned at her.

"I mean, it has to be harder for you, losing someone that you were going to marry."

The grin slipped right off his face. "Well, I haven't been scarred into Heathcliff-level bitterness either, but I think I get what you're saying, about losing the family you thought you were getting. For me, one of the worst parts of Erin passing was losing the life we were going to have together. I didn't get to see what she was going to become, which was going to be amazing. I just wanted to see her happy and doing what she wanted with her life. The loss of her potential hurt almost as much as the loss of her."

"I think you're pretty brave to be able to talk about it so openly."

"I'm telling you because I want to be honest with you. Because I want to date you."

She nodded, taking his ice cream–free hand and squeezing it. "So you're going to make us Nana Grapevine–official?"

"It's either that or matching airbrushed T-shirts from the StarShirt Shack," he agreed.

"Maybe just mention it to Margaret at work tomorrow," she told him.

They ended the evening on Riley's front porch. She spared him the awkward internal goodnight kiss debate by standing up on her tippy-toes and kissing him. That kiss turned into two, and then a third, and several minutes later, he realized they'd been standing on one of the highest-profile front porches in town, making out like a couple of teenagers for an indecent amount of time.

He wasn't going to have to do anything to notify the Nana Grapevine. He was sure the word was already spreading.

Riley reluctantly pulled away from him, sighing against his mouth. "I think we need to slow down. I mean, as much as I would like to invite you in, I don't know if my ghost roommates would be cool with it."

"You never do what I think you're going to do," he said, shaking his head, grinning.

She bumped her nose against his. He glanced towards the glass of the front door and yelped.

Plover was standing on the other side of the glass, glaring at him. He turned towards the giant grandfather clock in the foyer and pointed at it. With one last narrowing of his eyes, Plover disappeared in a dramatic swirl of ghost smoke.

Riley giggled, practically collapsing against his chest. "Oh, I didn't count on the ghostly British father figure of it all."

"I don't think anyone else has ever counted on the ghostly British father figure of it all."

Chapter 10
Riley

THE GRIFFIN STATUE IN HER atrium was mocking her.

That was a sentence she never thought would float through her head. She never thought she would have a griffin statue. Or an atrium.

It had been about a week since "Sheargate" in Alice's shop. Riley sat in her favorite squashy chair near the atrium, reading Aunt Nora's journals, listening as Eloise splashed around in the fountain. Riley glanced up, her eye catching the way the sunlight illuminated the griffin's white-and-gray marble wings. The time she'd spent working for an art gallery as an intake assistant—certainly not trusted with appraisals, but trusted enough to take notes while experts did—made her search for lack of symmetry. It didn't take her long to find it.

Standing, Riley moved closer, looking at the back of the griffin's far wing. There was something wrong with the part of the wing structure between the griffin's body and the beginning of its outstretched feathers. It was like it was missing part of the tendon that supported the wing.

Riley jogged into the office and plucked the weird phallic marble bit from the puzzle box in her desk drawer. She placed the missing marble bit in the negative space and pushed it in with a "snap." She'd half expected the griffin's mouth to pop open and reveal the next clue in this messed-up treasure hunt. Instead, she heard the groan of mechanical works inside the statue and stone moving against stone. The griffin's tail lifted, and a small door dropped open, leaving the griffin to "deposit" an envelope and a leather-bound book onto the base. The blue leather looked worn and was stamped with the now-familiar Shaddow House logo. The lock on the sturdy curved metal bracket that kept it closed had a strangely shaped opening, like an X.

"I just pulled a book out of a mythological creature's butt," Riley said. "Weird."

Riley flopped back on the chair, exhausted. She took one step forward with this place and got sent three steps back. Plover materialized nearby and stood quietly at attention. He clearly knew things that he wasn't sharing with her, which usually triggered Riley into a self-destructive spiral, but she only felt good intentions from Plover. He had no reason to work against her. He wanted her to fulfill the purpose Nora left for her. Her interests were Plover's interests. He'd become, if not a friend, a sort of surrogate uncle-mentor-spiritual guide.

Everybody had one of those, right?

Riley retrieved the key with the weird X-shaped end from the puzzle box and unlocked the journal. She traced her fingers over the yellowed pages inscribed with iron ink so old it blurred purplish-blue. She let out a shaky breath. This was definitely the

Codex, a complete detailed list of items in the house with the entries starting in 1791.

Aunt Nora's neat handwriting graced the last ten or so pages. The weird thing was, Riley couldn't find any mention of Natalie's whiteboard or any of the entries that would most likely have come into the house during Aunt Nora's time as steward.

She turned around, looking around for Plover, who was mysteriously absent. She thought he'd want to be there to congratulate her for taking one of her first major steps as steward, unlocking the Codex.

Weird.

Riley locked the Codex in the least accessible drawer of her desk. She wanted to text Caroline and Alice about the non-penile nature of the marble bit and her progress with the Codex, but she didn't have the nerve. She texted with Caroline, but neither of them had heard from Alice. Riley and Edison had been on two more dates—a tour of various fudge shops (to make Edison happy) and a ride on Mitt Sherzinger's outrageous thirteen-person tandem bike on the last weekend he was open for the season.

She'd seen so much of the island from that rolling seat. There was so much open, quiet green space away from the busy foot traffic. It was nice experiencing that part of the island, feeling a thrum of energy that seemed to pulse from beneath their feet. Maybe this was what her family felt when they'd decided to establish their home here. Had they been happy when they realized the Wellings' trickery had trapped them here? It was lovely, but not having the option of leaving? Was more effective magic worth that price?

Plover said that it would be uncomfortable for a Denton to leave the island, to the point of being unbearable. How long had that lasted for her mother? Had Ellen been miserable her entire adult life because she'd chosen to move off-island? Was that why she was so reserved, because she was fighting off a magical migraine?

These were heavy things to ponder, but still, it was nice to experience these things *with Edison.* He made her laugh. He was considerate, giving her the more comfortable seat, the colder drink, the bigger piece of pizza—not because he didn't think she could handle the hardship but because he didn't want her to. He was fascinated by her work history, particularly her stories of working for a divemaster who specialized in finding jewelry people lost during watersports. (Edison insisted that made her "basically a pirate.")

That was what had been missing from her relationship with Ted. She'd been so worried about fitting into his family, keeping him happy, that she'd made herself smaller. She'd worked at the telemarketing job for far longer than she should have, because Ted thought her frequent job changes made her look "flaky." And that might have been true, but Riley had preferred to think of her professional life not as a series of failures, but *learning* experiences that provided her with a number of very strange and useful skills.

And yes, spending time with Edison meant they were setting the Nana Grapevine on fire. It also meant more of those soft, skilled, *intent* kisses from him, which were definitely leading somewhere.

But circumstances were keeping them from shared nudity, and those circumstances were ghosts.

When a knock sounded on her front door, Riley half expected to find Edison on her porch. Instead, she found Caroline, holding a six-pack of green bottles with a frankly haunted-looking tree on the label. Which was almost as good.

"Is it weird that I *felt* that you needed to talk to me?" Caroline asked. "I'm not sure how I feel about that. You could have just texted me."

"I know, I know," Riley muttered, closing the door behind her.

"So, I hear you and Edison went on that all-important third date the other night," Caroline teased as they perched on the steps, drinking cider and watching the sun set over leaves that were already starting to turn fiery yellows and reds.

"God-dang Nana Grapevine," Riley mumbled into her bottle. With all the apples grown in Michigan, locals took their niche alcoholic cider preference as seriously as their fudge. Riley's favorite tasted like Granny Smith apples and sunshine.

"So...postmortem?" Caroline asked, waggling her eyebrows.

"Should we really call it that, given my job as house manager to a bunch of ghosts? It seems rude, like talking loudly about sex when your dad is in the next room," Riley noted.

She glanced over her shoulder, through the front door—where Plover kept his vigil every time Riley went out with Edison. She realized she'd started to feel for Plover something akin to what she might have felt for a father who was deeply, deeply...deeply involved in her everyday life.

"Besides, it didn't really happen."

"What!" Caroline cried. "Are you holding out on me? I told you about the accountant from Iowa!"

"And I begged you not to," Riley countered. "And really, there's nothing to tell with Edison. The ghosts actually let him into the house long enough for us to enjoy a little over-the-shirt affection, and then, I realized that just because I couldn't see Plover didn't mean he wasn't there. And then Lilah, the little Victorian girl who's attached to the fancy brass match cloche on the mantel? She decided to try to make things 'romantical' by lighting a fire and scared the hell out of both of us."

"It is really not great that a ghost child can physically interact with matches," Caroline said, shaking her head. "So after that, I guess you couldn't follow through?"

"There was a ghost minor somewhere in the house! And who knows how many other ghosts I don't know about. I still haven't figured out who that ghost in the yellow dress is, but I have a theory it could be my aunt. Who moves really quick for a dead person in her seventies... Oh my god, I'm never going to be able to have sex in my own house."

"I thought your bedroom was some sort of safe zone?" Caroline asked.

"Well, so far, but I don't know that for sure!" Riley exclaimed. "And I'm not willing to take that chance!"

Caroline bit her lip and tried to look sympathetic. Riley sighed. "Go ahead and laugh."

Caroline burst out in raucous snickers. "I could bartend for fifty years and never hear dating problems like yours."

"True," she agreed, sipping her drink. "You know, you're taking this whole ghost thing really well. A lot better than I did."

Caroline jerked her shoulders. "Well, my family has a history of spiritual fuckery, shall we say."

"Is that stitched on a sampler somewhere? Maybe under the Wilton family crest?"

"I don't leave the island," Caroline confessed. "Not for more than a day."

Riley's bottle froze halfway to her mouth. "Like as a life philosophy?"

"As a health precaution," Caroline heaved a sigh. "Any Wilton who leaves the island for more than twenty-four hours dies in some awful, sometimes humiliating accident. So, I've had a few doctors' appointments off-island. I took the SATs before I'd accepted the situation and thought I could still go to college. But I've never tried to test it more than that."

"Like if you came back in twenty-*three* hours, you're fine?"

Caroline shot her a deadpan look. "I. Never. Tried. To. Test. It."

Riley made a series of "wha" sounds before settling on, "How?"

"There are a lot of family theories. Bad luck. Coincidence. A hereditary curse. The world being a dangerous nightmare-scape. I mean, the number of relatives I've lost to getting run down by a taxi seems damned unreasonable. At this point, all I know is that we're a dwindling family, and my parents and siblings never leave the island; it's making my parents a little crazy. They're scared for my brothers and me. They resent being trapped here."

Riley blinked at her, mouth agape.

"It's not that bad. I mean, you're basically going through the same thing, right? The Last Living Denton Unable to Leave Shaddow House."

"Well, hell," Riley mused. "I guess you're right."

"I wanted to go to nursing school," Caroline said quietly. "I made the appointment in Lansing to do an admissions interview, and it went really well. But when I was walking back to the car, I came *this* close to getting run down at a crosswalk by a campus bus. I mean, I felt the front bumper graze my jeans. And I remember thinking, *This is it. This is how the latest Wilton dies, and I'll never know how I did on that damn interview*. I stood there with my eyes closed for about two minutes, waiting to see St. Peter. Thought he'd look like Vince Vaughn with a beard. And then when he didn't show up, I threw up, got in the car, and went home. And I didn't leave the island again for more than three years, not even for lunch."

"How did you do on the interview?"

"I got in," Caroline said, her eyes suspiciously shiny. "With a pretty decent scholarship."

Riley put a hand on her shoulder. "Of course, you did."

"I've taken some online classes over the years, enough to be a very mature sophomore," Caroline said. "More to prove to myself that I'm smart enough than anything else."

Riley drained her bottle. She'd been so thoroughly swept into the havoc of life at Shaddow House, she hadn't truly considered what it meant for her long-term. What if Riley had children? Was she really OK with her potential offspring being saddled with a haunted house and a lifetime of servitude to ghosts, or would she make the choice her mother had made? What if she *didn't* have children? Who would inherit Shaddow House and its inhabitants? She hated to think of Plover being left all alone.

Pondering the burdens the Wiltons and the Dentons had left hanging on their daughters' shoulders, Riley spotted

Alice approaching with a familiar bright orange shoebox in hand. Speaking of undue burdens placed on daughters. (Or granddaughters.)

"Alice, you OK?" Caroline called.

Alice looked haggard, pale, and irritated. Instead of her usual crisp neutral-toned pantsuit, she was wearing a plain dark-blue T-shirt and khakis. There were shadows under her seafoam-green eyes. Her penny-bright hair was slicked back into a sloppy ponytail, and she wasn't wearing even her usual minimalist makeup.

"Very much not. Remember when I said I couldn't possibly let you have the shears with the degenerate potty-mouthed ghost attached?" she asked, thrusting the box toward Riley. "I was mistaken. Please take the degenerate potty-mouthed ghost back, far, far away from me."

"Why don't you come inside?" Riley offered, opening the door. Caroline and Alice walked in, and when Riley shut the door behind them, suddenly the Mueller clock gonged loudly. A rolling wave of energy seemed to ripple through the first floor of the house, rattling silverware, pottery, and everything else that wasn't nailed down.

Alice, her nerves already frayed, shrieked and dropped the shoebox, spilling the salt and shears onto the floor. Bobby burst out, a delighted grin contorting his face.

"Oh, no," Caroline groaned as Bobby made little kissing noises that made Riley's skin crawl.

"Plover, if they just entered into another blood contract without being aware, I'm going to be *so* ticked off," Riley called.

"I'm sorry, what now?" Alice asked.

Plover appeared to Riley's left. "It's only natural that the house celebrates the assembly of your coven within its walls, Miss."

"Well, sure," Alice said, shrugging. "That makes sense. Now please take this pervert ghost off my hands. He keeps figuring out how to slip loose of the salt and sexually harass me while I'm working."

"You liked it," Bobby countered. When he spotted Caroline, he licked his lips and purred. "Ohhh, I've been thinking about you, girlie. Did you miss Bobby? Because Bobby missed you. Well, parts of you."

Caroline's nose wrinkled. "Ew."

"Oh, come on, baby doll, don't be that way—" Suddenly, Bobby's face twisted in fear. Riley followed his line of sight to the black oily mass crawling along on her ceiling. The creepy ceiling ghost was back again.

"Oh, dear," was all Plover had to say about it.

Horrified, Bobby took a run at the door. The magical wards prevented him from leaving, making him bounce back on the floor.

"Forget this," he yelled, bolting back towards his shears. "No pair of knockers is worth you broads and your bullshit."

"I beg your pardon!" Plover thundered, planting his noncorporeal feet in a most un-Plover-like manner. "Apologize at once!"

"How does Bobby manage to be offensive *and* terrified at the same time?" Caroline asked as Bobby disappeared into his shears. The ceiling ghost oozed over their heads and through the cellar door, as if it was no longer interested in them.

"Well, that can't be good," Riley said. "Plover, what was that?"

"Honestly, Miss, I don't know," he said, frowning. "I've never seen such a spirit before."

"I saw it creeping around on the night of the attempted break-in," Riley noted.

"Does that mean the ceiling ghost is...new?" Caroline asked. "Also, hi, Plover. It's nice to meet you officially."

"It's possible," Plover said, bowing slightly to Caroline. "It's also possible that it's a ghost that has lurked in the house for years but only felt confident to emerge after Miss Nora passed."

"Ouch," Riley groused. She dropped the shears back into Alice's shoebox. With a sigh, Alice collapsed on the couch.

"Thank you." She let her head tilt back on the couch.

"If I may make a suggestion, Miss. With particularly aggressive cases, your aunt would occasionally lock them in the display cabinets over there. They've been protected with special runes and spells." He nodded to the glass-front cabinet that contained a few small items that didn't match in look or era—a pair of blue wooden knitting needles, a silver hand mirror with an ornate handle made of roses, a set of shot glasses with CANCUN printed on them. "And in exceptional cases, she would force the ghosts away from their cherished objects altogether."

"And what happens to them?" Alice asked.

"They go on to the next plane, wherever that may be for them," Plover said. "But that only happened in cases where the ghosts were exceptionally dangerous. Or annoying."

"Bobby covers the annoying part," Caroline noted.

"I don't know if being obnoxious and gross counts as dangerous," Riley said. "I don't know if I'm willing to send him to an unknown afterlife just because he's annoying."

"Well, what if we helped a spirit who *wants* to move on?"

Caroline asked. "It would be like working our way up to dealing with hostile, pervert ghosts."

"That sounds like a very specific segue," Alice noted.

"I went back to the Martins' office to talk to Abigail," Caroline said. "I realized that, instead of approaching it like an awkward job interview, I should just talk to her like one of my customers. I listened. I sympathized. And the story just spilled out."

"I talked to her yesterday too," Alice said. "Now that I've seen Bobby, it's like I'm seeing ghosts all over the island. I didn't have to use professional subterfuge, so she must be opening up socially. Did she tell you about the ring?"

"Well, I'm feeling a little left out," Riley said. "What about a ring?"

"Abigail was a receptionist for Martin & Martin Realtors back in the early nineties. She was young, happy, and engaged, and going out every day, being a working gal in an environment that was just a little more receptive to behavior like Bobby's," Caroline said.

"Another odd segue," Alice noted. "Abigail didn't mention that to me."

"I mention it because Mrs. Martin had this client, Mr. Carlson, who had what you might call an *interest* in Abigail. He'd hang around before and after his appointments, find reasons to hover over Abigail at her desk, dropped things so she had to pick them up. That sort of thing."

Riley grumbled something that made Plover take a step back. Caroline continued, "Anyway, her boss, Mrs. Martin—"

"Anna Martin? She must be seventy years old," Alice said.

"The same. Mrs. Martin didn't want Abigail to make Mr. Carlson think she was unavailable. She *really* wanted the listing. And then when she did get the listing and it took a while to sell, she was afraid that some other mainland real estate agent would convince Mr. Carlson that they could sell it faster. So to keep him coming around, Abigail was supposed to put her engagement ring in her desk drawer."

Alice shuddered. "That ring belonged to her fiancé's mother. Abigail said he apologized because he couldn't afford to give her a new one."

"Her fiancé sounds like a sweetheart," Riley said. "But I have a feeling this story is about to go sideways real hard."

"It took a few months, but Mrs. Martin finally sold the house," Alice said. "She wanted to open a bottle of champagne to celebrate. Afterwards, Abigail was carrying the tray of champagne flutes down from her office and tripped on the stairs."

"Normally, that wouldn't be too serious; it's only three stairs," Caroline added. "But the champagne flutes broke and one of the stems went right into Abigail's neck."

Riley gaped at her. "Oh, that is *awful*."

"Abigail bled out right there on the steps," Alice said. "She doesn't want to haunt the office because she doesn't want to spend any more time there. But she does want to give the engagement ring back to her fiancé, who apparently still lives on the island."

"OK, any idea where it is?" Riley asked.

"When she died, the new secretary didn't want to touch her desk. Neither did her replacement or *her* replacement," Alice said. "It was as if they felt the desk was cursed or something, the legend of the dead secretary of Martin & Martin Realtors."

Riley's brow lifted. "It's still in her desk...almost thirty years later?"

"In a special hiding place at the back of the top-right drawer," Alice noted.

"She's been watching it this whole time," Caroline said. "She doesn't have anything else to do. The Martin family bought all new office furniture, and they just sort of shoved her desk in the corner of the filing and storage room, and piled a bunch of junk on top of it."

"Abigail's one regret is that she couldn't get the ring back to Laurence, her fiancé," Alice said. "Because it belonged to his mother, and she hates the idea that Laurence might think she was careless with it, all these years later."

"So we need find a way into the real estate office, and then into the probably locked filing room, and find a way to search an abandoned desk covered in junk, and then steal it," Riley said. "How am I going to do that?"

"No idea!" Caroline chirped. "Aren't you glad you're not alone in this anymore?"

"Very glad," Riley assured her.

In the end, Riley decided to exploit Mrs. Martin's Achilles heel— her salesmanship. Riley called Mrs. Martin and pretended that the Shaddows *might* be interesting in selling Shaddow House. The very possibility of the listing had Mrs. Martin salivating to the point that Riley was pretty sure she could have just demanded a tour of the filing room and she would have gotten it.

"Are you sure we shouldn't go with you?" Caroline asked, as Riley stood outside the real estate office with Abigail, Alice, and Caroline, steeling her nerves. She had broken out one of her office work outfits for the occasion, a knee-length dark-blue skirt, a prim white blouse, and a jaunty-navy-and-aqua silk scarf. Alice had tied it in a very complicated knot at her throat.

"How is it going to look if all three of us approach Mrs. Martin about selling a house, when neither of you are really connected to it in any way?" Riley said.

"Weird," Caroline agreed. "It's just, I feel bad sending you to do the hard stuff."

"I've got this," Riley promised.

As she approached the front door of the office, she knew she didn't have this. But who would?

The problem with knowing a little bit about sales is that Riley felt really insulted by Mrs. Martin's unsubtle, hard-pressed sales tactics. For a half hour, the woman relentlessly pushed for Riley to help her secure a contract on Shaddow House. She seemed desperate for it. Riley might have felt bad for deceiving the woman, but Mrs. Martin had subjected Abigail to pretty awful treatment.

Riley carefully slipped off her scarf mid-meeting and slid it into her purse. She took some brochures and promised Mrs. Martin she would ask the Shaddows to consider the listing. As she very carefully walked with Mrs. Martin down the three stairs to the main office door, Riley huffed, "Oh, shoot. I think I left my scarf in your office."

"Oh! I'll go get it for you," Mrs. Martin said. "You just wait right here."

It took Mrs. Martin, who was indeed bumping seventy, a little longer to climb those steps. Riley dashed towards the unmanned front desk, where Abigail was pointing to a key, hanging from a hook under the printer station. She snatched the key and hustled over to the door marked STORAGE.

"Are you sure you left it in here, dear?" Mrs. Martin called from her office. "I don't see it."

"I'm sure!" Riley yelled back, wincing as she popped the door open. "Maybe by the sofa? It could have slipped under it."

"You put your scarf in your purse," Abigail said, nodding to it.

"Yeah, so it's going to take her a while to find it," Riley whispered back.

"Wow." Abigail blinked and for the first time, looking at Riley with something akin to respect. "The desk is right over there. Top right drawer. In the back."

Riley slipped between several filing cabinets to get to the old, scarred maple desk. The drawer slid open with a loud creak, making her wince.

"Any luck?" Riley called to Mrs. Martin.

"Not yet, dear! I'll keep looking!"

"OK!" Riley patted around the back of the drawer, praying she wasn't about to stick her hand in thirty-year-old desk snack cakes. Her fingers slipped over stacks of papers and bumped against a wall in the back of the drawer.

"That's a false back to the drawer. I made it myself. If I was going to have to hide my ring in my desk, it was going to be safe," Abigail told her. "Pull on the peg on the right, and it will pop free."

Riley followed the instructions and the back wall indeed popped free. Her searching fingers closed around a small velvet-covered ring box.

"Oh my gosh." She pulled the small respectable diamond solitaire out of the desk drawer. Abigail wavered there, lips parted with some emotion Riley couldn't name, while Riley closed the drawer and scrambled toward the front desk. She locked the door and managed to hang the key back on the hook just as Mrs. Martin came out of her office.

Mrs. Martin was sighing, "No luck, dear. Maybe I'll come across it later. All the more reason for you to come back so we can discuss getting that albatross off the Shaddows' hands."

Riley smiled brightly. "Sure, thanks for looking for it."

Riley hurried out of the building, making it almost a block down the street with Alice and Caroline none-too-subtly following. She pulled the ring box from her pocket.

"You got it!" Caroline crowed, raising her hand for a high five. Riley absently met her hand while studying the ring. It was a little dusty but still in good condition.

"A very nice setting," Alice assured Abigail, who had appeared at their sides. "Oh, and it's inscribed."

"*To Abby, Love, Dutch.* That's sweet," Caroline cooed. "Wait, I thought you said his name was Laurence."

"He was a junior," Abigail said. "He didn't much like it, so I gave him a nickname. Dutch. He was afraid of windmills."

"That is weirdly specific, in terms of phobias," Riley noted.

"I've been picturing a Laurence grieving romantically this entire time," Caroline said.

"So do I just mail this to your fiancée?" Riley asked. "Anonymously? That's not going to freak him out?"

"I told you, he still lives on the island." Abigail frowned at her. "You know, if you're going to make a go of this do-gooder thing, you're going to have to be a little braver. More creative."

"Well, there can't be that many *Dutch*es on the island," Alice said.

"I can only think of one. Dutch Hastings," Caroline said. "He's a regular at the Rose. Good tipper. Hates IPAs and windmills, apparently. Lives on Seddamore."

"That's my sweetheart," Abigail said, smiling sadly.

"But how do I explain how I found this ring and knew it was his? A total stranger?" Riley said. "I'm afraid if we wait, I'm going to lose my nerve."

"I think I might be able to help there," Alice said. "Let's go."

They trooped over to Seddamore, with Riley's feet feeling heavier with every step. Was she really about to do this, interrupt some stranger's day with a gut punch of heartache? Maybe she should back out. But it wouldn't be fair to leave Alice and Caroline to deal with this alone. They'd already been left with enough uncomfortable duties by their families. They arrived at a comfortable-looking one-story house with bright red petunias planted along the walk. Abigail smiled fondly at them. "Those are my favorites."

"You ready?" Riley asked.

She shook her head. "I don't want him to see me. He's so much older now. He could have a heart attack. I don't want him to join me that way. Tell him I still love him. And I'll see him again soon. If I learned anything from all this, it's that there's an after."

Abigail stepped back and disappeared from sight. Caroline, ever more confident than Riley, knocked hard on the door.

"Dutch is a wee bit hard of hearing on his left," she whispered.

When he opened the door, Dutch had a face that had obviously been rugged and handsome in his prime, but now he was settled into late middle age gracefully, apart from the thick salt-and-pepper beard scruff and unkempt hair. The house was immaculate behind him though, all plastic-covered furniture and vacuum tracks in the carpet.

"Can I help you, ladies?" he asked, squinting at them in the bright sunshine.

"It's sort of a funny story, Dutch," Caroline said, leaning towards Dutch's right. "Riley and—have you met Riley? She's Nora's niece from the mainland. Anyway, we were over at Alice's antique place, having a bit of a shop, and I saw this in the jewelry case. When I saw the inscription, I thought of you. Didn't you say your fiancée's name was Abby?"

Dutch's brown eyes went filmy with tears, and his hands shook as he took the ring from Caroline's hand. Riley bit her lip, feeling very guilty for letting Caroline carry the weight of this task. How were they going to deliver Abigail's message without sounding completely deluded?

Alice cleared her throat. "I don't know how it ended up there. I believe someone must have found it and sold it to my grandparents as part of a parcel."

With shaking hands, Dutch turned the ring over and over, examining it.

"I'm sure whomever you gave that to, she must have loved

you very much. Obviously, you loved her very much to give her a ring like that," Alice added, frowning.

"I did. She passed real sudden," Dutch croaked. "Years ago. I haven't thought about her ring since...oh, since it happened. I always thought she'd been buried with it. I was in a bit of a fog at the funeral."

"I'm sure she's out there somewhere, waiting for you," Riley said. "We don't ever really lose the people we love. They're just in a different place."

"That's a real nice thought," Dutch told her. "Thanks for bringing this back to me, you girls. Not everybody would have bothered. Do I owe you anything for storing it for me? I know your grandparents are real particular about their stock."

"Oh, no, I just couldn't stand the idea of you not having it," Alice assured him.

"Well, I didn't know your aunt Nora very well, but I'm sure she'd be real pleased with how you've turned out," Dutch told Riley.

"Thanks," she told him.

Suddenly, Dutch threw his arms around them in the most awkward group hug imaginable and dashed back inside his house. On the other side of the door, they could hear soft weeping.

"Aw, man," Caroline sighed. "I hope he's going to be all right."

"He always felt better after he cried it out," Abigail said, appearing behind them.

They turned to Abigail, who looked less haunted, if that was possible.

"Do you feel better now?" Riley asked.

Abigail bit her lip. "I think I do. I think I can move on now. I don't want to hang around anymore, watching the breathers. I want to see what's next. Thank you, do-gooders."

Riley made a hand gesture she'd learned from Nora's journals, which, coincidentally, looked like opening a book. It was supposed to help the ghosts move on to wherever they destined to go. A warm pleasant light appeared behind Abigail, and she stepped toward it. As Abigail faded from sight, the three of them murmured goodbyes. Riley sagged against Caroline, suddenly exhausted.

"How do you feel?" Caroline asked.

"Kind of sad and empty," Riley said. "I mean we really didn't do *much*, magically speaking. Abigail made the decision to move along on her own. We just kind of nudged her."

"You did risk breaking-and-entering charges," Alice reminded her.

"Oh right," Riley said, pursing her lips. "But overall, I am content. I feel a lot. And I'm very grateful that the two of you are here to help me."

"I think that's normal," Caroline said. "As normal as you can get in this situation. Maybe now, we can talk about banishing the creeper trapped in your lovely china cabinet."

"Or we could spend more time helping ghosts *inside* the house who want to move on, stabilizing the whole ghost-based leaky-nuclear reactor situation building there," Riley said.

"Also a valid use of our time," Alice agreed.

Caroline stretched her arms over her head. "Anybody else need a drink?"

Alice and Riley spoke together: "YES."

Chapter 11
Edison

EDISON DIDN'T KNOW IF HE would ever get used to his "special lady friend whose company he enjoyed" (*thank you, Kyle*) having dozens of dead roommates. He wasn't sure that was something he was *supposed* to get used to.

But somehow, nights spent on Riley's couch became more attractive than holing up in his house, if for no other reason than he got very confused around her friends when he missed out on important ghost conversations.

His life was becoming very strange.

He found that he liked Alice and Caroline quite a bit. He felt foolish for not spending more time with them over the years, considering they were two of his best customers at the library. He was happy they'd been drawn into this...endeavor with Riley. The idea of her trying to manage Shaddow House alone made his chest hurt. It was just too much.

Riley had taken a page from Natalie, as the Codex had proven to be largely unhelpful. She started a whiteboard list of known ghosts, their objects (as vaguely described as possible to deter thieves), and what their potential issue could be. Riley figured they could remove the item from the house once they'd determined that issue and help the ghost move on. Edison didn't like it. It seemed cavalier to treat this like casework. But as he had not been gifted with magical abilities, he decided to keep his mouth shut.

There were times when he was disappointed that he wasn't chosen to be part of Riley's coven, but he supposed there was only so much closeness a couple could take. Riley always referred to her relationship with the ladies as "sharing magic." Maybe sharing magic with him, on top of everything else, would be too much?

It was possible he was overthinking this. But the work she was doing sounded so *dangerous*. He definitely didn't like the sound of this Bobby ghost Riley and Plover were discussing while Riley lounged in the parlor with a cup of tea. Edison hadn't quite reached that level of comfort with the ghostly butler, so he was sitting up very straight and was careful not to lounge—as not to provoke Plover's fatherly protectiveness.

Again, a very weird mental sentence.

"I'm just glad Bobby can't get into my room, even if the salt protection fails," Riley said. "How long has he been here, anyway?"

"For two years, at least, and then Miss Nora transferred him to the antique shop, so to speak," Plover replied, standing poker-straight beside the fireplace. "She hated to move him, but she felt it was an important test of Miss Alice's potential. He'd never proven himself to be dangerous."

"And did he, I don't know how else to put this, but did he treat Aunt Nora the way he was treating Caroline the other night?"

Plover's whole presence took on a darker energy. "Much to my chagrin, yes."

Riley had voiced a suspicion that her late aunt had been *something* with the ghostly butler, and now Edison wondered if she was right. He didn't know how that was possible, emotionally or physically. And he didn't really want to know.

"But you said Nora *could* banish spirits, right?"

"It took much effort for her as a solo magical practitioner, and she only did it in extreme cases," Plover said.

"And now I'm facing the exact same problems, only without her training or experience," Riley sighed.

"But you're on the right track, Miss, gathering your friends about you. And I believe your intentions to help the more benevolent spirits move along are noble. But I would encourage you to focus on the goals your aunt has laid out in her journals. Meeting those goals will help you in all your other efforts."

Edison tried not to frown. It hurt his feelings, ever so slightly, that Plover didn't trust him enough to discuss all of Riley's "efforts" in front of him. It only proved to Edison that what Riley was doing was not entirely safe. It wasn't insult that made his chest ache with anxiety. He couldn't lose her. He knew that. He just wasn't sure what to do about it.

Riley tilted her head against the back of the couch, smiling warmly at Plover. "Are you sure you don't want to move along yourself? I know it can't be satisfying for you to hang around here babysitting me."

Plover sniffed. "If there is anything you should know about me, Miss Riley, it's that I don't shy away from work. And there is much work to be done here. Miss Nora would have wanted me to stay the course, to help you fulfill your purpose."

"Thanks, Plover, even if I do think you're just trying to get out of telling me what your attachment object is," she said, yawning. She'd been spending so much time reading Nora's journals, making herbed salts, and practicing her magic gestures in sync with Caroline and Alice, that she was exhausted. Edison dared to reach across the couch to stroke her bare ankle. Plover's lip curled in distaste, which again, Edison tried not to take personally.

"I'll give you two a few moments to say *good night.*" Plover disappeared, something that Edison still found unnerving. He leaned across the couch and brushed his mouth across Riley's. "I believe your ghost dad just kicked me out."

"We still have a few minutes," she told him, kissing him back. "You OK over there? You've been awful quiet."

Edison shrugged, unsure if this was an unfair thing to lay on Riley's overtaxed shoulders.

"You can tell me. I deal with super scary shit every day," she said.

There was a displeased noise somewhere near the foyer. She rolled her eyes. "Plover, if you're gonna eavesdrop, you can't get mad when you hear things you don't like."

Edison laughed, which made it easier to ask, "It's Erin. Do you think there's a reason she didn't stick around? To haunt me? What if she's out there somewhere and I don't realize it?"

She took his hand. "There's no way of knowing that. She could be attached to anything, anywhere. She could be back in California, at her parents' house. You could drive yourself crazy, trying to figure it out. I think it's a good sign that I haven't seen her nearby. I hope that means she found peace and she was able to move on."

Edison kissed her knuckles. "Me too."

"If you're not ready for this whole dating thing, I understand," she told him. "We can pull back, think about it a little more."

"No!" he said quickly. "I don't want that. It's just something I didn't have to think about before I knew about ghosts, you know?"

"It is a perspective-altering experience." She grinned at him.

"I was actually hoping that we would move our relationship to another level," Edison said. "Spending time together *after* our dates."

Riley immediately understood the word's emphasis. Her smile grew—somehow—brighter. "I would be open to that."

Another displeased snort sounded from the foyer.

"OK, honestly, Plover!" Riley called. "I am an *adult!* And I've never judged your unconventional relationship with my aunt!"

The foyer remained silent.

"We might have to go to the hotel or something," Riley said. "Yup."

They didn't make it to the hotel.

Days later, they were standing outside The Wilted Rose, fully intending to go in to join Caroline for a drink, but instead, they chose to make out on the sidewalk. This was getting out of hand.

Riley pulled away from him, her little hands twisted into

the front of his blue dress shirt. "I think we should retire for the evening."

Edison blinked at her, confused. "Oh, OK. Um...did I do something to—"

She shot him an amused look. "I mean, together."

"Are you sure you're ready for this?"

"Yes, but it has to be at your house," she said, breathing heavily into his mouth. How did she always taste so sweet? It was some sort of life skill. "Because of all the ghosts. Not just Plover. Some of the ghosts just don't make themselves visible as a habit."

"Wait, all of them? They've been watching us this whole time?"

She exclaimed, "You told me you didn't want to know!"

"We can never have sex at your house," he said, shaking his head.

"That's what I said!" she laughed. "What about your house?"

"But my house is halfway across the island," he said. "And I have a bit of a situation here. That will get people talking."

"I mean, I admire your confidence. What about the hotel?"

"And we're back at the *people talking* scenario. Your backyard?"

"That is not how I want to go to jail," she told him.

He nodded, breathing deep through his nose. "The library is just down the street. Just walk in front of me."

"I thought you said that librarian fetishes are degrading," she giggled as they scampered down the street.

"Well, then don't fetishize me, just sexually objectify me in a regular, normal way."

Losing all sense of trying *not to* look like they were running off to have sex, they ran down the street at a full tilt, studiously avoiding eye contact with anyone they knew. Edison already had his key out as they ran up the stairs. The huge darkened building was quiet.

"Wait, what if there are ghosts here?" he asked as she climbed his body and wrapped her legs around his waist. "I never thought to check."

"They're just going to have to live with it," she panted. "Do we need to worry about security cameras?"

He shook his head, trying not to focus on the way she was squirming on him.

"Well, what section should we go to?" she asked. "Also, I can't do this in front of the children's section!"

"What about biographies?" he suggested.

She looked aghast. "With famous people looking down on us?"

"Science fiction?"

Riley scoffed. "So I can get impregnated with an evil alien spider baby?"

"My office!" he yelled, throwing her over his shoulder. She laughed, her face buried in the small of his back. She pressed both hands against his ass, he supposed, so she could lever herself into a more dignified position. She shimmied at the hips, and he took that as a hint to pull at her pants, tugging them off her ankles.

His office was tiny, but he did have a rather large chair, which he lowered himself into carefully so it wouldn't roll out from under them. He was grateful she could kneel over his lap without the chair arms causing a problem.

"OK?" he asked, grinning up at her, sliding his palm along her jawline. She tugged his shirt out of his pants, tossing it aside. She nodded, grinding down on him, applying just enough pressure to his growing...*dilemma* to make his eyes roll back. He cupped his hands around the rounded globes of her ass cheeks and rolled his hips. She felt so good against him, and her hair was falling around his face again, smelling of flowers and the sea.

He pulled her shirt over her head, throwing it over her shoulder to join his on the floor.

"There are no ghosts," she murmured into his mouth, flicking her tongue just under his top lip. He slid his hand between her thighs, finding her wet and wanting, running his thumb over the hard little nub he hoped would make her feel as good as she was making him feel. The light coming in through the stained glass window made her skin glow an ethereal blue. He didn't think he'd ever seen her look so beautiful—naked, perfect, *his*.

"No poltergeists." She tugged open his fly and pulled his erection free, encircling the length of him in her warm little hand. He groaned, barely restraining himself from pumping up into her grasp. It had been so long since he'd been touched this way, and if she kept doing that, he was going to finish before they got started.

"No phantoms of any kind," she giggled, squeezing him tight enough to make him moan. She pulled a small foil packet—from where, her shoe?—and rolled a condom down the length of him. He was so glad she had the mental power to think of that because right now, he had two operative brain cells and they were fighting each, shouting, *Sex now!* and *Sex now, PLEASE!* on a loop.

Moving her hips, she guided him inside her. He shuddered as her warmth surrounded him, and he gripped the chair arms to keep himself still, to put off the climax building at the base of his spine.

He would not have an orgasm now. He would not embarrass himself and climax without even moving.

Oh, no, now she was moving. He groaned as she rolled her hips, forcing himself to focus on kissing her, on communicating how desperately he wanted her. She gasped against his mouth, gripping his shoulders as she moved in a primal rhythm as old as her magic. He took her hand and pressed it against his chest, so she could feel his racing heart. And only when she smiled down at him could he move under her. He planted his feet, pulling her hips down as he thrust up, which turned out to be a mistake. He put too much weight on the back of the chair and flipped them backwards like some awkward sex turtle.

She yelped as they landed, then burst out laughing against his shoulder. He covered his face with his hands, his cheeks burning.

She kissed his flaming face, and they moved together. She was there with him in every touch and gesture. He reached between them and rubbed at her, making her gasp and her back arch. He concentrated on firm, tight circles, even as his eyelids fluttered and he wanted to just lose himself in her heat. He could feel her fluttering around him, drawing him in. He felt that climax threatening again, tingling at his center and spreading up his spine until he was crying out so loud that his voice echoed in the old halls.

He emptied himself into her, and he felt it in every sense of the word. He was hollowed out, lost in her. She collapsed in a damp heap on top of him, and he buried his face against her neck. He stroked his hand down the silky skin of her back. He could feel her heart against his, and there was so much contentment there that it scared him.

"Finally, we got it together," she sighed, laughing against his cheek.

He just wanted to hold her close and lay like that forever. But that would probably get him fired.

"We'll get it together again soon," he promised. "Just give me a few minutes to recover. Eventually, we can go to my house and use an actual bed."

She nuzzled his neck. "I thought this was pretty nice."

"Me, too."

A week later, he sat in his home office, staring at his phone. It felt weird, having his usual scheduled phone call with his parents. He considered telling them about Riley. He wasn't sure if she was ready to meet his parents, even over the phone, but he needed to at least introduce the *concept* of Riley so it didn't feel like it came out of the blue when he talked about her place in his life.

How had that happened so quickly, he wondered. It had only been five months or so since she moved to the island. She'd survived her first Halloween in the mother of all haunted houses with relatively few issues, other than aggressive trick-or-treaters trying to get past her spot near the gate. Snow was starting to fall on occasion. The year was flying by, and all he could think of was what the next year would bring, what it would bring with Riley.

He probably should have known better than to casually drop

Riley's name into his description of his week. His mother fell on it like a carrion bird on a battlefield.

"Wait!" Catherine cried. "You're dating someone else now? Is it serious?"

Though Edison could very well be on the way to loving Riley, he wasn't ready to say it aloud, and his parents weren't ready to hear it. "It could be on the way to being serious."

He heard his father sigh, and he could imagine Amherst rolling his eyes. "I'm sorry, I just can't keep up with your love life. First, you're mourning Erin, and now you have this new woman. I can't help but feel you're being rash, son, making imprudent choices."

"And what sort of stock could she really come from if she's from that little fishing shanty town? Really, darling—" His mother sounded so disappointed in him. It was almost as bad as the day she'd found out Edison had no interest in being a lawyer. And he was done with it.

For the first time in his life, he interrupted his mother. "OK, we need to talk about a few of those points. First of all, Starfall isn't a *fishing shanty town*—your disdain for which is inappropriate on a couple of levels. You would know that, if you ever bothered to come to visit me over the last few years. It's a charming little tourist destination. People actually pay quite a bit of money to visit here every year. It's a comfortable place to live, and I've really come to love it here."

As the words came out of his mouth, he realized it was true. Starfall wasn't just a stopping point where he could heal before returning to his life. It had become his life. Even if his parents weren't ready to accept it, maybe they needed to hear that. He didn't want to end up like Riley, with a parent he couldn't talk to anymore and a mouthful of things he wished he'd said.

His father started, "But, son, the opportunities available—"

"It's not about opportunities, Dad. It's about the life that I want. The fact that you can't extend yourself enough to understand that? It makes me sad for you, but it's not my problem. Secondly, I'm not making imprudent choices. I needed time to mourn Erin."

"And you had to do that away from us?" his mother cried.

"Yes, I did, because you tried to dictate how I should feel and on what timeline, exactly like you're doing now. And I've had that time now, and I'm ready to move on to a relationship with someone else."

"Well, how are we supposed to respond to that?" his father demanded.

"I don't know; maybe take a genuine interest in my life and how I live it before you decide it's a disappointment?"

"I never *explicitly* said it was a disappointment," his father hedged just as his mother said, "That's a wonderful idea. We should visit after Christmas."

"What?" Edison said just as his father echoed the sentiment.

"Well, you know how many social commitments we have over the holiday season, darling. And we've already sent positive RSVPs to so many people. I couldn't take them back now," his mother insisted. "You're right; before we can tell you that you should move, we should see your conditions for ourselves. And then maybe we can help you arrange for packing! Your father will make all the arrangements. Talk to you soon!"

His mother ended the call.

His parents were coming to visit him. Maybe. They never followed through when they said they might come to Starfall, but there hadn't been the temptation of meeting someone he was dating. How had this happened? How? He should have known better than to speak openly to his parents. That was a *terrible idea.*

Edison turned around in circles, as if his silent house was going to somehow provide him with a solution. "Oh, no."

Chapter 12
Riley

IT WAS A LITTLE HUMILIATING to have her friends arrive at Shaddow House to find Riley perched in front of their ghost board, wrapped in Edison's fleece blanket, drinking hot tea, with a hot water bottle duct-taped to her chest. But Riley didn't know how else to handle the four inches of snow piled up in her yard. And people were just out on the street, walking around, like this was a totally normal thing to happen in November!

"Oh, no," Caroline sighed. "Baby's first subfreezing temperature drop has hit you a little harder than expected, huh?"

"I have made a huge mistake moving here," Riley told them, teeth chattering. "I'll never survive the whole winter. I thought I had a lot more time to get a winter coat!"

"You can borrow one of mine," Caroline told her. "It's pretty rare to have just one coat up here because we have several *grades* of coat weather. Early fall cold. Wet cold. Windy cold. January cold."

"I don't think you're helping," Alice whispered as Riley's face went several shades of pale. "So how goes the work with the ghost board?"

Since the Codex was basically useless the three of them had focused on the ghost board, working through their known ghosts who seemed open to the idea of resolving their issues. It became an everyday occurrence, solving a case. It took all of Caroline's notable communication skills some days, to tease the ghosts' stories out, but she was so good at it—at listening to people and getting them to share their cares and woes. In most cases, she was able to get the ghosts to tell the ladies what they needed most in order to feel comfortable leaving this world.

Some of the tasks were pretty simple. One woman who wanted to see the Acropolis was satisfied with an internet image search, which was unavailable to the ghost when she'd been alive. Others involved anonymous calls via burner phones to police agencies, insurance agencies, and prosecutor's offices, and once, a family in Iowa so an elderly lady ghost could hear her former schnauzer bark and determine that he was happy with his new adoptive family. Riley's much maligned skills as a telemarketer came in handy there, putting the call on speakerphone so she could stall with a fake pitch for aluminum siding until the dog spoke up.

They couldn't guarantee that the cases related to the ghosts' calamities were resolved, but they were giving the ghosts a voice, allowing them to make the gesture that gave them closure. And in return, Alice would take their haunted objects outside the restrictions of the ghost locks, and Riley and Caroline would offer her magical support as they opened the door to the next world.

The reward for this strange work was the look of contentment on the ghosts' faces before they brightened into a concentrated spot of light and faded away into the other side of...whatever dimension they were currently occupying. But none of the items that they worked with were listed in the Codex. They only seemed to find ghosts willing to cross over as they searched around the house.

More and more ghosts came out of the woodwork, so to speak. The piano was haunted by a virtuoso who only spoke Italian and didn't particularly like Riley's requests for Elton John classics. "Rocket Man" was particularly offensive to his sensibilities, it seemed. With a formal introduction and apology mutually arranged by Plover, she met the silverware ghost. Charles Mulworth turned out to be a very nice, if easily excitable Regency-era gentleman attached to silverware belonging to his lost lady wife, Edith. Unfortunately, he lost Edith because she poisoned him so his brother could inherit Charles's title—*and her*—which Charles could not accept. While cradling her favorite soupspoon, Charles wept long and eloquently about her devotion, her attention to his smallest comfort—after all, hadn't she brought him cocoa every night before bed because she knew he enjoyed it so much? And if it tasted of bitter almonds, well, she was a genteel lady and didn't know much about the kitchen.

Lilah, a little girl who spent the 1910s helping her father deliver firewood, had died when she tumbled headlong into a coal shuttle while admiring a fancy brass match cloche a customer kept on her mantel. She was attached to the cloche now...and could set fires whenever she wanted. Riley found that a little unnerving, but Lilah was a sweet, lonely child. She just needed somebody. Riley had never been that somebody for someone before.

Riley enjoyed recording their stories, talking to them. It was like living with a large extended family under one roof. And yes, the ceiling ghost sucked, and Charles's weeping got to be a little much sometimes, but it was nice knowing that there would be people waiting for her as she walked down the stairs in the morning. People who knew her and would ask about her day and be happy when she returned. It was what she had been missing growing up, and it broke her heart a little that it took a bunch of dead people to make her feel like she had a home.

And somehow, the coven managed to carry on everyday lives. Caroline ran the Rose and poured drinks. Alice sold (non-haunted) treasures and avoided calls from her grandparents. Riley searched for the locks and tried to hold the house together.

Riley wrapped the blanket tighter around her neck. "Well, the ceiling ghost is really creeping me out. It doesn't talk. It doesn't seem to have an attachment object. It just oozes along the ceiling like some nightmare," Riley said. "But I don't know how we could banish it, without knowing its object."

Alice protested, "It seems sort of cruel to pick a ghost at random to banish in the afterlife. We don't know what's waiting for them on the other side."

"I'm not saying we pick an object at random," Caroline said, giving the shears a very intentional look.

Alice's mouth twisted into an unhappy line. "Bobby? Really?"

"The guy who calls me 'sugar tits' on a regular basis? Yes," Caroline shot back.

"I concede your point," Alice replied. "It just feels extreme."

"I heard somebody mention my name!" Bobby's voice boomed across the parlor.

"How does he keep doing that?" Riley huffed.

"Admit it, sugar tits, ya missed me," Bobby said, grinning at Caroline.

"How do you *expect* me to respond to that?" Caroline demanded.

Bobby shrugged. "Well, where I come from it's a compliment. It was a different time. Girls were less uptight."

Caroline shook her head sharply. "Nope. Try again."

"I don't know; the guys I grew up with, you had to put on a strong face."

"Meaning...*the family*?" Riley asked.

Bobby looked incensed. "Are you calling me a gangster? You're only saying that because I'm Italian!"

"I'm saying that because you look like something out of Scorsese central casting!" Riley told him.

"I was respectable!" Bobby shouted. "I worked in a tailor shop. I was the youngest guy there. It was my job to wear the latest, flashiest stuff so our younger customers could see what was possible. I liked the shop. It was where I belonged. I'm alone here. And none of the other ghosts are like the guys back home. The best times of my life were there. It was the only place where I felt like I had a family, sitting on the stoop, watching the girls go by. And sometimes, yeah, I maybe overcompensated because the neighborhood guys expected it."

"Oh, please, don't try to make me feel sorry for you," Alice sighed, rolling her eyes.

Bobby rolled his eyes. "I'm not asking for much, just a little naked stroll down the hall every once in a while. Maybe do a little dance. Show Daddy a little jiggle."

"OK, that's it," Riley told him. With her blanket still clutched around her like a cape, Riley crossed to the display cabinet, where Bobby had managed to ease aside enough salt grains to sneak out of his containment. She didn't know how he did it. But that skill alone was enough to banish him, in her opinion. As Riley carried the shears outside, they seemed to shudder in her hands. It didn't seem to be a response to the numbing cold, but leaving the protections of Shaddow House. Caroline and Alice followed her, tugging on their coats.

"*No!*" Bobby screamed. For the first time, he sounded genuinely angry, instead of his usual state of agitation. His shears lurched out of Riley's hand, singing over her shoulder, slashing a shallow line just shy of her jugular. She gasped, turning to watch the shears fly across the darkened backyard and embed themselves in a slim willow tree just behind Alice. The blades had damn near planted themselves in Alice's ear.

The next few moments were chaos. Alice cried out. Caroline screamed for her and pulled her away from the embedded shears. And Plover was barking orders at Bobby from the kitchen doorway, demanding that Caroline fetch the first aid kit from inside the house.

"You can't make me leave!" Bobby howled. "There's a voice in the house telling me I can stay there!"

Clutching her bleeding neck, Riley looked to Plover, who shook his head. "I hear nothing, Miss."

"That's it," Alice said, stepping in front of Bobby, her lips pulled back in a snarl. She looked angrier than Riley had ever seen her. "You're a danger we can no longer afford."

Alice made the "banish" gesture, shoving her hands towards Bobby's trembling form. Caroline and Riley scrambled to make the gesture that would push Bobby along, whether he was interested or not. In the shadowed yard, a wide bright light opened, as if ready and willing to pull Bobby in. Bobby screamed curse words Riley didn't know existed as Alice growled. She flexed her arms forward and pushed him through.

The silence that followed made Riley's ears feel like they were ringing. Alice caught her before Riley could fall to her knees in the snow. She practically carried Riley through the kitchen into the parlor and helped her sit. More than ever, Riley felt the magic of Shaddow House close around her like an embrace. An ancient metal first aid kit that was dented and partially rusted, landed next to her with a rattle.

"Is my first aid kit haunted, too?" Riley asked, feeling a little woozy from the blood loss and the magical effort.

"By the ghost of a paramedic who died in 1969," Plover told her. "See to her wounds please, ladies."

"Aw, that's nice. Thanks, paramedic ghost," Riley said, blowing out a breath. The supplies in the first aid kit were brand new, thank goodness. Alice and Caroline were able to clean and bandage the wound quickly, all things considered.

"That's going to sting when you take it off. There's a lot of tiny hairs in the way," Alice tsked, applying a large bandage to her neck. She turned toward the front door. "Oh, no, Edison's walking up the front steps."

"Can we not tell Edison about the whole 'injured by flying shears during a ghost tantrum' thing?" Riley suggested. "Might make him nervous."

"Honey, you have a giant bandage on your neck, he's going to notice," Caroline told her, offering her a bottle of water.

"We can always change the subject to that enormous puffy orange sleeping bag he's wearing," Riley said, wincing as she craned her injured neck to take in the sight of Edison's winter regalia.

"Oh, no, the coat," Caroline said, cringing.

"Bo Stinson had that coat in stock at the general store for three years," Alice said. "Edison forgot to buy a winter coat before he moved here, and it got cold in October, way before he expected and…"

Riley gasped. "He tricked Edison into buying an ugly sleeping bag coat? That's so mean."

"No one had the heart to tell him how silly it looks," Alice said, shaking her head.

"Well, I'm not going to tell him!" Riley cried.

"Still pretty sure he's gonna be focused on your neck," Caroline pointed out.

Chapter 13
Edison

THE SHEARS INCIDENT SCARED EDISON more than he was willing to admit, and he was willing to admit a lot.

Riley could have *died*. And while she seemed to grasp that it wasn't safe to have giant sharp scissors flying about the house, Edison didn't think she understood how close she'd come to being fatally injured. And yes, Edison realized that he treated her like she was made of glass for weeks afterwards. He didn't touch her again, his eyes always falling on the thin healing wound left on her neck and making his hands retract. The thought of losing her so easily paralyzed him, and he just couldn't let himself make contact.

Any time the women discussed another possible banishment target, Edison brought up a more benevolent case that might need them more. It felt like they were going round and round, unable to land on the right course of action. And Riley seemed no closer to finding any of the Wellings' locks or an explanation for why she couldn't find any of the items listed in Nora's precious Codex. And there was no evidence that Nora had helped any of the ghosts listed resolve anything. It was like watching someone he loved running on a hamster wheel, if that hamster wheel was made of fire.

On top of that, he would probably have to introduce her to his parents soon, and that felt like the worst indignity of all.

"Why don't we take a break?" Caroline asked one December night as they sprawled on the Shaddow House library furniture, poring over books, papers, anything that could help them find a direction. "I think we're pushing our brains a little too far here."

"Eventually, one of us is going to wear out and snap like a rubber band," Alice agreed.

Riley didn't respond. She was still flipping through the Codex.

"I don't get it. None of the objects listed in the Codex are here," she told them. "Did Aunt Nora clear them and not update the record?"

Plover's face was transparent and silver, but somehow, Edison thought he saw him blanch a little.

"What? Is this about my butchery of the English language again?" she asked.

"Your aunt Nora predicted this might happen," Plover said vaguely.

"She predicted I would be unable to make sense of the most valuable object in a house full of priceless supernatural relics," Riley snorted. "That's reassuring, thanks."

"I can't keep letting you do this to yourself," Plover sighed. "I know she said it was an important step, but this sort of distraction can't be good for you or your mission. And the mission is the point."

Caroline's brow wrinkled, staring at the ghostly butler. "What are you talking about, Plover?"

Alice tilted her head, looking at the desk. "Hey, Riley, have you ever noticed that your desk has six legs? That's not typical for the style."

"No, but now that you bring it up, I feel foolish for not questioning it." Riley set the Codex aside and crossed the room.

"Um, girls, Plover was just speaking," Edison noted. "Seemed important."

Caroline and Riley knelt next to the desk, examining the underside. The legs weren't attached like the rest of the body, with braces and screws. They almost looked tacked on with glue. The first popped off easily enough, but it was just a solid wooden leg.

"How many secret hiding spaces are there in this freaking house?!" Caroline yelled.

"I have also asked that question, several times." Riley muttered, as she unscrewed another leg from under the desk and found the hollow leg stopped up with cork.

Caroline pulled a corkscrew attached to a keychain out of her pocket and handed it to Riley.

"You are both so handy to have around," Riley told her. Caroline preened. Riley popped the cork out of the desk leg. She found a letter rolled up inside, written on her aunt Nora's stationery. Dread crawled, cold and slimy, up Edison's gut. This was going to be some new clue, something that sent Riley on some dangerous new adventure that was sure to get her hurt.

Riley read aloud.

Dearest Riley, I congratulate you on your diligence. By now, you have probably determined that the Codex is not genuine.

Caroline shouted, "Wait, *what!*"

Edison's mouth fell open and the cold dread was filled with the white-hot sear of rage that crawled up his neck. All of this had been for nothing? They'd been sent on a wild goose chase by a dead senior citizen?

"I had *not* determined that," Riley sputtered. "Fuck!"

Plover blanched fully this time.

"Plover, don't start with me," she told him.

"That can't be right," Edison insisted. "Nora wouldn't do that to you."

Riley continued to read.

It seemed unwise to keep a genuine record of the many acquisitions of the house all in one place. The point of this exercise was for you to become familiar with the island, the house, the people I thought might have the potential to support you, and to earn the ghosts' trust through interacting with them. It was vital that they accept you as the new steward. I'm sorry to have led you on a merry chase, but believe me when I say my own initiation was quite similar. My mother had me searching for a nonexistent book on invisible charms for more than a month. Please devote the skills you have acquired to locate the Welling locks. It may seem an insurmountable task given that no Denton has managed it in more than two hundred years, but the time of confrontation with the Wellings is drawing near. We can't delay any longer.

"It's a fake?" Alice marveled.

Caroline's head shook back and forth. "I know she's your family and all, but damn, your aunt is *mean*."

"I don't feel that is fair," Plover objected.

"I can't believe it." Riley sat on the couch with a thump. "I just thought at the end, there would be this conversation with Aunt Nora, where she explained everything to me. And it would all make sense. Instead, I get *this*." She tossed the letter to the floor.

Edison felt sorry for her. Riley had worked so hard and put so much of herself into this and yet…he couldn't help but feel relieved.

"Plover, is there anything important in here that Riley might regret, you know, exploding?" Caroline whispered out of the side of her mouth.

"You OK, Riley?" Alice asked, putting her hand on Riley's shoulder.

"No, I'm not OK. I'm mad as hell! All the time I've wasted on these bullshit treasure hunts! I had a *life*! It wasn't much of one, but it was mine, and I don't appreciate being manipulated and put through all this horseshit!"

"And there is the rubber band snap," Caroline muttered.

"She had her reasons," Plover told Riley. "She said it was important that you work your way through it, to build yourself up. That blades that aren't tempered properly, break."

"I'm not a blade," Riley ground out. "I'm a person."

"Well, maybe it's not so bad," Edison suggested gently. "Maybe you take a step back from the house. Put your energy into something else. Find another job. Focus on your life instead of the dead. Something that won't put you in danger."

"What's that supposed to mean?" Riley asked, her eyes blazing.

"I just mean that you don't *have* to devote all of your time to the house, to the ghosts," he cried. "Finding the locks can just be something you do in your spare time."

"Oh…no," Caroline said, shaking her head at him.

"Oh, Edison," Alice whispered. "No."

But Edison had already jumped out of the plane, so he might as well embrace the parachute.

"You worked through these like they were on some sort of murder board, like you're running some sort of investigation on ghosts," he told her. "But these are *people*. Their lives, their stories. They're just not just numbers for you to clear from your board."

"That's not entirely fair," Alice countered.

But Riley was already talking, clearly oblivious to the people around them as the rage colored her cheeks. "You don't know how I feel about them! You don't see what we go through to connect with them."

"It's not something we would do just for fun," Caroline agreed softly. "It's not like we're in this for money. Or glory. We're just trying to help."

"If you saw what we saw, you wouldn't question why we're doing this," Riley said.

"Oh, I don't have magic, so I don't have a voice?" Edison countered.

Riley's brows drew together. All around them, decorative bits began to rattle on the shelves. "No, that's not it. You have a voice but you don't have a *vote*. You're not the one whose ass is on the line."

"You say that like it doesn't affect me, but trust me, it affects me!" Edison cried.

"We should let calmer heads prevail, ladies, sir," Plover protested.

"What point are you trying to make here, Edison?" Riley demanded. "Because I'm not getting it."

"I'm saying maybe you shouldn't interfere so much and just let the ghosts work through their issues at their own pace," he insisted. "For the most part, that's what your aunt Nora did, and she seemed to avoid getting impaled in the throat with a pair of scissors."

"But even if they do that, they won't be able to leave the house," Riley replied. "The locks keep them trapped here."

"So focus on the locks so you can release them," he said. "Why do you feel you have to reinvent everything while you learn?"

"I don't try to," she began to object and then stopped. She shook her head. "I'm trying to fulfill my purpose here, Edison—"

"Like you've done with all your other jobs? Because from an outside perspective, it seems like you have a pattern of diving in too fast, burning yourself out, and then moving on. You can't do that here, and you know it. You can't just float along to the next shiny object that catches your attention when the commitment scares you."

"Whoa, Edison, that was a little too close to the bone," Caroline intoned.

"I agree," Alice said. "You need to fight fairly."

To his shock, Riley didn't yell or cry or even make the dishware explode. She laughed. It wasn't her normal sweet silvery laugh. It was almost scary, like nails scraping across a broken slate. Even Alice and Caroline looked frightened.

"I'm the one who's scared?" she giggled, wiping at her eyes. "Fine. I might be scared, but at least I admit it when I am. I don't weaponize my trauma like it's some sort of universal excuse. I can't leave this place, but at least I own my part of the choice and try to improve the situation. I'm not the one who squirreled himself away on this island just to avoid awkward conversations. Because guess what, Edison? Those conversations are part of *connecting with people*. You don't get that, because it doesn't suit you to get it. It's easier to hide. But I'm not going to just throw my hands up in the air and stop trying to fix this mess. You might be fine with running away and playing it safe, but I'm not."

He wasn't sure what hurt worse, that she'd said those things, or that she was right. He was scared. All the time. He was hiding—from the past, from his parents, from life. He hadn't even made real friends—friends who knew him on more than a surface level—before she'd moved here, before she'd forced him out of his tidy little shell. But it hurt too much for her to have laid it all out like that, in front of their friends, for him to admit that she was right.

He was afraid, and it was his fear of what could happen to her, of what he could lose all over again, that had him lashing out at her. "If I'm such a coward, I guess you'd be just fine if I left, hmm? I'm just in the way here."

Her gaze dropped to the floor as she breathed deeply.

"Remember, you tell anybody what happens here in Shaddow House, there are consequences," Riley said, her voice far flatter than the emotion in her glittering gray eyes conveyed. Alice's eyes darted towards her, clearly shocked. Even Caroline seemed uncomfortable with the idea of threatening him.

Hurt somehow overrode the fear. She thought he would betray her, after everything they'd seen. And she was threatening him, like he was some jerk off the street. She was acting like they were already over.

"Well, it won't be too hard for you to get along without me," he spat. "We're probably going to run into each other. We can just pretend we don't know each other. 'Cause I'm not sure I really knew you in the first place."

He walked out into the cold November wind, pulling his collar up over his ears. He wanted to run back. He wanted to apologize, to find a way to take it all back. But maybe it was for the better. He wasn't up to the task of helping Riley with the house or the ghosts or any of it. She was so far beyond him. Maybe she was better off with Alice and Caroline and people who understood her. His fears would probably just get in the way, put her in danger.

Edison was going to lose her either way, he supposed. It was better if he wasn't the one who got her hurt.

As he made his way towards home, he saw that Kyle was standing outside The Wilted Rose. He was pale, with dark purple shadows under his eyes, like he hadn't been sleeping well. Edison supposed that was normal, with the holidays approaching without his mom. His smile was thin as he spotted Edison.

"Hey, Kyle," he said, his voice hoarse.

"I guess Caroline won't serve me, either, huh?" Kyle chuckled bitterly.

"I don't think she's working tonight anyway," Edison said.

"You got time to talk?" Kyle asked.

He should say no. He wasn't any use to anyone right now. He was too emotionally drained. But he couldn't turn Kyle away when he was clearly in pain. He knew what it was like to hurt and have no one to turn to. At least he'd left Riley with people who would listen.

Edison nodded. "Sure."

Chapter 14
Riley

RILEY COULDN'T MOVE FOR A long time after Edison left.

She just sat on the floor in the parlor staring into the atrium. She felt as listless as Eloise the fountain ghost, forever left behind, doomed.

The things she'd *said.* She felt the burn of shame, remembering for days the look on his face when she brought up his reason for coming to the island.

Alice and Caroline stayed with her as long as they could, but they had lives to return to. Riley was ashamed to admit it, but she fell apart in ways she never had after she and Ted split. She couldn't sleep. She didn't eat, despite Plover's many suggested delicacies in Aunt Nora's treasure trove of international goodies. She just wandered the house, encountering ghosts she had no interest in talking to, which was a problem, given her vocation.

She understood why Edison was upset with her. The things that she said to him were awful. They'd both suffered loss, but they'd handled it in different ways. Their losses were different. And she'd been so cruel.

Late one night, she was wandering the hall near her room and caught sight of the yellow dress ghost's skirt. She barely had the energy to track the movement with her eyes. She wanted to just let the ghost go. But what if she was hurting? What if the reason she was always running away was that she was in pain? Riley sighed, following in the direction that the ghost had run. She walked up a staircase that led directly into the ceiling. "Right. I don't want to push, but if you want to talk, I'm here, OK?"

No response.

"It's not like having a toddler, it's like having a teenager," she muttered, walking down the stairs.

If the yellow dress ghost was her aunt Nora, secretly evaluating Riley's performance as steward, Riley couldn't be impressing her too much.

Walking by her room, she passed a number of paintings on the way to the library, a weird mix of mismatched styles—portraiture, landscapes, abstracts. She'd developed a bad habit of running her fingertips over the frames as she passed, which was probably a good way of accidentally poking a ghost.

But this time, as she passed an eerie landscape painting, her sensitive fingertips recognized the rippling bumps of a...seashell on its frame. Riley paused, turning to the frame. The painted night sky featured a large full moon shining down on a ring of standing stones, not unlike Stonehenge. The tiny brass title plaque read, MOONLIGHT ON MONOLITHS.

She'd passed this painting so many times since she'd moved into the house. How had she never noticed the name plate before? Mouth agape, Riley ran for Caroline's returned Wilkie Collins book, *The Moonstone*, which she'd placed on her nightstand. She compared the book cover with the painting's frame. The pattern on the book's linen wasn't magical runes. It was an exact copy of the seashells carved in a repeating pattern into the frame of this painting—a painting of the *moon* shining on *stones*.

"Well, I just *super* overthought this," she muttered. "Which is so unlike me."

Riley took a step back to reexamine this painted storm. What was so special about this painting, among all the others? Why would Aunt Nora take the time to recover the book with these shells? Riley examined the painting. It didn't feel haunted. Aunt Nora had been right about that sensitivity eventually developing. She could sense at least four haunted objects within ten feet of her, and nothing at all from this paint-covered canvas. But there was something behind the painting. A different kind of magic, in the wall.

She pulled on the frame, wondering if she could take it off the wood paneling. It wouldn't lift, like one would expect a frame hung from a wire. It swung out, like it was on a hinge, from the left side of the frame. Behind it lay a tiny raised square, about the size of a Rubik's Cube. It might have looked like a cabinet drawer, except there was no hinge and no pull. How was she supposed to open it, and how important could something be if it was hidden in a cabinet that small?

She pulled at the knob, but it wouldn't move. There was no lock, no mechanism for her to spill blood on—for which Riley was grateful. The blood sacrifice required to start her job still creeped her out a little bit.

And yet, she could still feel the magic emanating from the wall. It was a different energy than what she felt from the ghosts. It felt...alive, and not necessarily in a good way. Whatever was behind that wall *wanted* something, and Riley didn't think it was anything positive. It was that feeling you had when you walked down the hall at your high school and just *knew* the mean girl was about to insult your outfit. Whatever was inside her wall had plans, and Riley wanted it out of her house.

She'd accidentally struck out with magic to move things before. Maybe she should try to do it on purpose now? She could feel her magic connecting with whatever was behind the wall. It certainly wasn't Denton magic, and it wasn't a ghostly presence either. It *tasted* different, something dark and acrid, like salt and ash. Riley imagined her magic wrapping around that darker flavor, as if she could protect herself from it, while pulling it towards her. But whatever it was, it didn't want to cooperate. She heard something rattle behind the wall. Grinning, she pulled harder and heard a metallic thumping against the wood.

It was like having a conversation with the object, asking it very politely to move through space on its own. It wasn't an easy conversation, but she felt like she was making some progress in the negotiation. She took a deep breath from her gut and *flexed*. The wood buckled and the square popped loose from the wall a bit, like the timer on a particularly evil turkey. Riley huffed out a breath. "One more time."

She screamed as she focused all her energy on that crack that surrounded the cube-shaped drawer and imagined whatever it was busting through and landing in her hands. The hallway echoed with a thunderous *thunk*. The cube popped loose, and dust exploded into her face, making her cough as a cold metal object stung her palms. She waved her hand to ward off the still-floating debris.

"You know, maybe a direct set of instructions next time, Aunt Nora?" she called in the direction of where the yellow dress ghost had run. "Because I am clearly not good at this scavenger hunt thing!"

She hissed as the cold metal seemed to bite at her skin. She was holding a tarnished copper object that looked like three loops welded together, forming that now-familiar nuclear shape. Nora's drawing had not done the lock justice. Save for tiny sinister-looking runes etched in the center of each loop, they were perfectly smooth. The runes on the loops looked entirely different than the runes designed by the Dentons. There was a sharper aggression to the shapes that made Riley's skin crawl. Honestly, it looked like the sort of thing you would find in a pretentious home décor catalogue.

"Of all the weird things I have found in this house, this is the ugliest," Riley muttered, flinching when the copper somehow got even colder. The lock didn't like being called ugly. The hideous ritual object was sentient. Great.

Tossing the lock back and forth between her hands, Riley spotted a piece of paper in the back of the drawer. It was a piece of stationery from Aunt Nora's desk, embossed with the Shaddow House symbol and her name.

"I hope it's a vague and unhelpful note," she huffed, scanning Aunt Nora's neat script. "Oh, good!"

Dearest Riley,

I know you are probably still upset over the Codex, but I congratulate you on your success! This is the only ghost lock our family has ever managed to locate, in all our years at Shaddow House. Make no mistake. These are dedicated ceremonial objects created with one purpose, the enthrallment of spirits. That purpose is against everything our family stands for. We do not allow the dead to hurt the living, even if they don't intend it. There are at least eight more of these locks, which we never managed to locate. I wish you luck in carrying on our search for them and finding a way to successfully destroy them, which we were also unable to do. Secure this lock in the place you think best. Trust it to no one.

With much pride,
Your aunt Nora

Riley dropped to the floor, letting the lock roll to the carpet.

She should be thrilled. She'd made progress. She'd pulled a lock through a freaking *wall*. And yet, it just all felt so pointless. Caroline and Alice weren't there. Edison was furious with her. And she just didn't know if she had the strength to look for eight more of these things. She scooted back against the wall, burying her face against her knees.

Eight more. Where was she going to find eight more? Where would she even look? How was she going to find eight copper knickknacks when the entirety of her family had spent centuries looking for them and found nothing? She'd never finished a job in her *life*, and the stakes were certainly lower at the telemarketing company.

And where was she going to keep this one? Did she try to hide it somewhere new in the house? If she'd found it, anyone could. Or maybe she needed to move it outside of the house, even off the island. Surely, she could get a safety deposit box on the mainland…but then she would probably just create some sort of haunted bank situation, and that would definitely go against the magical precept of *Do no harm*.

She had no idea what to do.

She heard footsteps on the carpet to her left, coming up the stairs. She recognized Caroline's boots and Alice's sensible flats. The girls dropped to the floor on either side of her.

"What are you doing here?" Riley asked without lifting her face.

"We felt you," Alice said. "We could feel that you needed us, that you were doing some sort of big magic without a safety net."

"That's pretty neat, huh? I guess it is better than texting," Caroline said, attempting to sound cheerful. It had to be pretty bad for Caroline to try to sound cheerful.

"How did you get in?" Riley whispered.

"Um, the door was locked, but then it just let us in," Caroline said, tucking her chin over Riley's shoulder. "It felt like the house recognized us, which is good news."

"I found the ghost lock," Riley nodding toward the copper sphere. "Yaaay."

"Well, that's good," Alice chirped.

"There are eight more to find," Riley added. "We also have to find a way to destroy them, something that generations of my family never figured out. Oh, and then we have to figure out how to safely clear a house full of increasingly dangerous ghosts, just to increase the challenge level."

"Well, dammit," Alice huffed.

Riley snickered at the rare profanity from Alice. "Exactly."

Caroline and Alice wrapped their arms around her and she relaxed into them, breathed with them.

"I'm just so tired," Riley whispered. "I can't do this without you two."

"You don't have to," Caroline promised.

A dandelion-colored skirt glided into Riley's line of sight, floating over a narrow pair of bare feet. Riley let her eyes follow that skirt up to a loose, faded cotton dress. The ghost's hair was swept back from her face in a prim bun, the sort of thing that used to emphasize the silver at her temples. But now it only seemed to highlight how large and liquid her gray eyes were. Riley's eyes.

Riley's lip trembled as her eyes seemed to burn. "Mom?"

"Hello, sweetheart."

Riley inhaled sharply, desperately blinking to keep the tears at bay. Alice's hand slipped into hers, squeezing it tight. She could feel Caroline's hand on her other arm, stabilizing her, keeping her from flying apart.

"What are you doing here?" Riley asked. "I've been here for months and I've seen you... Have you been here this whole time, watching me? Why? Why didn't you say anything? Was it really so awful to have to talk to me?"

Riley's scant emotional reserves seemed to dry up all at once. Even after all she'd seen, with the ghost of her mother standing in front of her, Riley could not handle another surface conversation where she found out her mother didn't want to spend time with her, even after death. She just didn't have it in her.

Ellen frowned. "What? No, Riley. I had my own reasons for being here, and they didn't line up with yours. I was going to be a distraction to you, so I stayed out of sight. You needed to do this without me. You needed to find your coven, harness your magic. And if I was around, you wouldn't have done that. You wouldn't have performed the remarkable things you've all accomplished."

"So it's not because we're basically strangers?"

"No. Riley, do you know why I wear this dress, even in the afterlife?"

Riley examined the dress. Years before she'd moved out, Riley bought the dress as a Mother's Day gift, making another bad guess at Ellen's favored style and color. Ellen had worn it on hot summer days at home when the family didn't have plans. Riley always assumed it was because Ellen didn't like it enough to wear it out. "It's comfortable?"

"Because you gave it to me," Ellen told her. "Because this shade of yellow was my sister's favorite, and wearing it around the house reminded me of her. You gave me a little piece of home that I didn't even know I needed, even when I was trying to run from it. That's what you're good at, Riley—giving people what they need, even if they don't know what it is. It's a talent, and you're using it now, giving ghosts what they need to move on to the next world.

I'm so proud of you… And now, it's time for me to move on. I just wanted to say goodbye before I left."

"Wait, what? Mom, you can't just leave. I have questions. I have *so many* questions. I need—" All of the air seemed to rush out of Riley's lungs. Her mother had only seen her for a few seconds and now she wanted to leave? "I just need you, Mom. We lost you so quickly and I wasn't ready and then all of this happened. And I'm a *witch*. And occasionally, I throw things across the room with my mind, and that would have been handy information for you to leave on like a Post-it or something for me to find."

Riley paused to wave her hand at the house. "Why didn't you tell me? I know I didn't give you a lot of reason to trust me or my judgment—"

"No, no, no. That has nothing to do with it. I was trying to protect you," Ellen said. "I wanted some sort of normal life for you, away from all this."

"Well, as you can see, that worked out just *great*," Riley muttered.

"It was inevitable. I should have seen that." Ellen reached for Riley's face, leaving it with that odd pins-and-needles feeling rippling down her neck. Beside her, the girls shuddered. "I kept you far away from me emotionally, so I couldn't hurt you any worse than I was already. I know that. I never let myself relax into our relationship, because deep down, I think I knew that one day, you would know about all of this. I was afraid that you would hate me. I felt such awful guilt about what our gifts would bring you. I knew that you would never forgive me. That episode with the 'shower curtain lady' only drove home to me the curse I'd laid at your feet and the terror it would bring to your life."

"Mom, I feel more fulfilled here than I ever have. I have a purpose. There's something I can do that almost no one else can do. And the people who can do it are my *best friends*—the only true friends I've ever made in my life."

"Aw," Alice sighed. Caroline simply rubbed her thumb up Riley's bicep, which was going to be as squishy and sentimental as she got in that moment.

"That's what you gave me," Riley said "And yeah, some issues that I've had to spend a lot of time in therapy working out. But in terms of pros and cons, it all balances."

"Yes, and that is *why* I can leave now," Ellen said. "I would stay here if I thought it was the right thing for you. But I don't want to keep you from growing, from coming into your full power. That's the best gift I can give you, letting you figure this out on your own. I see you now, thriving as you never did in life, and I'm at peace. That's all I need."

"Well, that's not all I need. Holy shit, Mom!" Riley exclaimed.

"Oh, Riley, language, please," her mother sighed.

"Have you ever thought, for just one second, this might not be about you?" Riley cried.

"I'm dead, Riley, we're not exactly known for prioritizing other beings' feelings," her mother said, shrugging.

"It wasn't a priority for you when you were alive either." Riley pinched the bridge of her nose. "So I guess I shouldn't even ask about Dad?"

Ellen's transparent brow creased. "What about your father?"

"Does he know?" Riley asked, gesturing around the room. "About any of this?"

Her mother burst out laughing, then stifled it when Riley glared at her. "Of course not. That was one of the reasons I chose your father. He's a man of science. He was as far away from what I grew up with as was possible. The reason our marriage worked was that he gave me my space, and I gave him the distance he required. It was the best sort of love I could hope for. And we were fond of each other in our own way."

"Actually, he's mourning you pretty hard, Mom. I can't even talk about you with him. It just breaks him."

"Really?" Her mother's expression was somehow simultaneously shocked and secretly pleased. Riley nodded.

"Well, that resolves the need for a lot of awkward conversations for you," Caroline noted. Riley nodded, but could only focus on the fact that her dad would never be able to visit her at Shaddow House. If he met her roommates, he might have an actual cardiac event.

"It's time for me to go," Ellen said. "I'm ready."

"But what if I don't want you to leave?" Riley protested. "I'm still not ready. There are a lot of things I need to say."

"You can still say them. I'll be out there somewhere, listening. I don't know exactly how it works, but I know enough to trust that." Ellen kissed her forehead, leaving a cold, concentrated spot on her forehead. "Tell your father... Well, I suppose you can't really tell him anything, but keep encouraging him to talk about me, at least every once in a while. It will help."

Riley smiled, trying to memorize the curves of her mother's

face, knowing this was the last time she would lay eyes on her for some time.

"Do you need any help from us?" Alice asked.

Ellen shook her head. "I'm a little different from the other ghosts, and not just because of our magic. I don't have an object that binds me here. I had resentments that I needed to work through with the house itself, with our history. And now, those resentments are resolved. I can move to the next world on my own."

Her mother wanted to leave on her own terms, and as much as it might hurt Riley, she had to respect that. All Riley could do was accept it and move on in her own way. "I love you, Mom."

"I love you too. I always did, even when I wasn't good at showing it. Goodbye, sweetheart."

Slowly, Ellen faded from sight, her transition gentler than the other departures they'd seen. And for Riley, there was a certain logical beauty in that.

Alice wrapped her arms around Riley's shoulders, warming her, even as Riley shivered. "Do you feel better?"

"Well, I don't feel that I resolved all of my issues with my mother in one conversation," Riley replied. "That would be too much to ask for. But yes, I do feel better."

As the three of them sank onto the couch, Riley's mind traveled to Edison, or rather the Edison-shaped hole that ached in her heart. The fact that her mother seemed shocked that she was mourned by her husband... Suddenly, she was sad for both of her parents, for what they'd lost, the opportunity to love each other fully and deeply. They'd built what most would consider a successful relationship, with the fondness her mother spoke of, but neither had found deep connection or true fulfillment in it—all because they were afraid of what the other person would find in them. She didn't want to repeat their mistakes.

After the initial peace, knowing her mother passed over and wasn't hurting or haunted, Riley was lost. She missed Edison with a visceral ache that hurt from the moment she woke up to the last moment of awareness before her brain gave up and let her go to sleep.

After a few days of checking on her, the girls were good enough to give her space to mope. They seemed to know that she needed it. Plover was disappointed in her, for letting her heartbreak beat her. He made a comment or two about picking up her work again, but one morning she found that if she muttered about trash compactors at an above-average volume, he left her alone.

She needed to get out of the house.

She put on Caroline's spare coat and braved the walk down Waterfront Street. An arctic wind blew across the sunlit frozen water to smack her directly in her face. Margaret Flanders, however, was walking down the sidewalk with a box marked EDDIE'S OFFICE THINGS, wearing a light cardigan as if it was a pleasant fall day. The woman had to have actual ice in her veins.

"Oh, you!" Margaret growled. "I have a bone to pick with you, missy."

"I'm sorry?"

"Eddie quit. He did one of those video interviews for a job at some college in Boston, and now he's supposed to go out there for some on-campus interview. Kyle says he asked me to pack up his desk and drop it off at his place. He's moving out next week. I assume we have you to thank for that."

Riley froze. Edison was leaving? Without even saying anything? Yes, they had a fight—a fight with higher stakes than most relationship tiffs—but she'd thought that eventually, they'd at least *talk* again, even if they never got back together. Her stomach rolled and it was all she could do not to throw up on *Margaret's* shoes.

"Well, I guess that's good for you then," Riley offered lamely. "You get the librarian job, just like you always wanted."

"It's not how I wanted it!" Margaret yelled. "I may have given Eddie some guff, but that boy, odd as he is, was like a son to me. And I don't appreciate you coming in here and chasing him off."

"I didn't... OK, maybe I did," Riley sighed. "But there's nothing I can do about it now."

"Well, not with that attitude," Margaret sniped. "But if you can find the energy to do something about it, he's staying on the mainland at a motel near the airport. He couldn't get a flight until tomorrow morning."

With that, Margaret huffed on down the sidewalk. Riley rolled her eyes and continued toward the bar.

The Wilted Rose definitely looked like a bar that had been open for more than a hundred years. The unpainted wooden exterior was so old and weathered that the whole building looked like it had been scoured by time. The newest thing about it was a sign that looked like it had been painted in the 1970s, all dull gold lettering and overtly curled script looping around a drooping white rose.

Inside, Riley found a sparse crowd of people watching a college basketball game and sipping lunchtime beers. The wood-paneled room was practically papered with neon beer signs and lined with taps from all the beers served over the years, with particular attention paid to classic Guinness ads.

Caroline stood behind the bar, chatting quietly to Alice. She dried pint glasses with lightning speed while Alice was drinking something bright blue with a tiny pink umbrella and looked very glum.

"I'm just saying, if she doesn't start leaving the house soon, we're gonna have to force her," Caroline was saying.

"I'm worried about her too," Alice replied, stirring her drink absently. "But I don't think forcing her to do anything is a good idea. She has to work through it in her own time."

"That's the sort of thoughtful, loving advice that applies to situations when you're not dealing with a houseful of unpredictable...squirrels," Caroline hiss-whispered.

Riley took a deep breath. Her friends were concerned for her. And while it warmed her heart that there were people in the world that took the time to overanalyze her feelings, she also felt a lot of guilt that they were spending a pleasant afternoon worrying about Riley over beverages involving blue curacao. Riley shuddered. No good conversation happened over blue curacao.

Determined to pretend she hadn't heard them talking about her, Riley just waved and grinned. "Alice?" she said, with a laugh. "What are you doing here?"

"Oh, uh, hey Riles," Caroline said, her cheeks flushed.

"New friends call for new hangout spots," Alice said, shrugging. Behind her, Caroline offered Riley a pained smile, then slid Riley's favorite cider across the bar with a wink.

"What are *you* doing here?" Alice asked gently. "It's not that we're unhappy to see you out and about…"

"No time like the present to take up day-drinking," she mumbled. "I just experienced Margaret's less grandmotherly side. She's so mad that I'm *making* Edison leave the island, she's probably going to add hundreds in spiteful late fees to my library account."

Caroline dried her hands on the towel. "Edison's leaving?"

"Got some sort of job offer pending in Boston," Riley said, sipping her drink.

"So you're just going to let him move because you two had a little fight?" Caroline asked.

"Is your memory broken?" Riley asked. "Because I believe *savage, below-the-belt verbal slugfest* would be a more accurate description."

A guy at the end of the bar shot her a quizzical look.

"Mind your business," Caroline told him, making him turn back to his drink.

"If that's how he really feels about me, then maybe it's better that he's leaving. I can't be with someone who…" Riley paused. "Maybe I just can't be with someone. Maybe that's not the life I'm supposed to have with this job. My aunt never did. She was apparently in love with her unavailable *roommate* for years. My mom ran away so she could have a life of her own. Maybe I'm a fool to try."

Caroline snorted. "Bullshit."

"Hey!"

"I mean it. Bullshit, Riley. You don't believe that. You're just saying that because this is hard. And it sucks. And fixing it is going to take some work. Tell her, Alice."

Alice cleared her throat and patted Riley's hand. "Riley, is it possibly you rejected Edison before he could reject you, because that happens to be a core issue for you?"

"I don't know what you're talking about." Riley said, shaking her head. The head kept shaking for several moments before she dropped it to the bar. "Fuck."

She felt Caroline patting her hair. "There we go."

"I'm gonna have to get on the ferry, aren't I?" Riley asked, afraid to look up.

"Riley, it's winter." Alice reminded her. "The ferries don't run when the lake is frozen over."

"Oh." Riley hadn't even thought about leaving the island in so long, she'd completely forgotten about the lake freezing. "Right."

"Don't worry. I got this," Caroline told her and pulled her cell out of her pocket.

"What are you doing?" Riley asked.

"Activating the Nana Grapevine," Caroline said as the phone rang.

"Oh, no," Alice said. "I don't think you're ready to wield that kind of power, Caroline."

"She communicates with 'squirrels' on a regular basis," Riley reminded her in a quiet voice.

"I'm aware," Alice scoffed.

———————

Within thirty minutes, a dozen men in parkas were crowded into the bar, unaware of exactly why they were there.

"Mom said you needed me to come by immediately," Jeff Flanders said. "You all right?"

"Same here. But both my grandmas called to tell me to get my butt over here. Is there some sort of emergency?" Iggy Gilinsky asked, his brow furrowed in concern. "Am I going to need my tools?"

"Not that kind of emergency," Caroline assured them. "Guys, one of our own is in need. Who wants to give Riley a ride to the mainland?"

A wave of a mild grumblings was her only answer, except for Iggy who winced and said, "I've had two beers. Is that a problem?"

"A hundred bucks off the tab of anybody who gives Riley a ride to the mainland!" Caroline yelled. Suddenly, a dozen hands shot up.

"That's what I thought," Caroline said dryly.

"You're going to go broke if you keep offering people money off their tabs to help me," Riley said.

"I'll be fine," Caroline assured her.

Dutch Hastings lumbered up to the bar, his silvery beard creasing around a friendly smile. He hadn't been one of the men summoned by the Nana Grapevine, but Riley found she was more comfortable with him. "I'll take you across, Riley. It's the least I can do."

Riley smiled back. "That's great, Dutch, thanks."

"Can you be ready in twenty minutes?" Dutch asked.

Riley nodded. She hopped off her barstool and tilted her head quizzically. "Wait, if the ferry's shut down, how exactly is this ride being offered?"

Alice grimaced. "You're going to need a hat, maybe a ski mask."

"What?"

"You're gonna want to finish that drink," Caroline told her.

Chapter 15
Riley

EVEN CLINGING TO DUTCH HASTINGS for dear life, with her face pressed into the cigarette-scented and Old Spice–soaked fabric of his coat, the frigid wind slapping at every inch of skin it could reach—it was still a more pleasant ride across the lake than her trip on the ferry.

"Having fun?" Dutch yelled over his shoulder.

Riley was too cold to do anything but shake her head up and down in a semblance of a nod. Yes, technically, this was more fun than say, getting poked in the eye repeatedly by Freddy Krueger. But she wasn't about to hurt Dutch's feelings when he was doing her a favor. In all sincerity, Dutch appeared to be having the time of his life, whipping the snowmobile along the ice at breakneck speed. Riley forced her brain to focus on the task ahead—an apology. The mother of all apologies.

As soon as her feet touched non-Starfall soil, she felt...wrong. It was manageable, like a low-grade headache buzzing at the base of her skull. But she didn't feel balanced in the way she did at Starfall. It was like she wasn't fully in touch with her magic, half-charged. And it was right that she felt like that. This wasn't home, this strange place with too much land and too many lights and too much noise. She'd never realized how *noisy* cars could be.

The quiet of Starfall, however eerie, was home now.

True to her word, Alice had a cab waiting for Riley at the landing. Dutch waved her off, promising that he could entertain himself at one of the many bars open nearby. Riley gave the driver the name of Edison's motel and enjoyed the first car ride she'd taken in months. It was weirdly disorienting, but again, still preferable to boat travel.

She hadn't considered how she was going to find Edison, once she got to the motel.

A ghost was hanging around in the parking lot in a bellman's uniform. Riley imagined he was a leftover from the 1950s when the motel was newer and more glamorous.

"You didn't see a tall handsome guy in a hideous orange coat come through here, did you?"

"Dumbest-looking coat I've ever seen," the bellman said, nodding.

Riley bit her lip. "That's the one."

"He's in room 112. Can't miss him."

"Thanks," she called over her shoulder, running away. "If you have unfinished ghost business you want resolved so you can move onto the next plane of existence, I'll be right back!"

It felt wrong, but every once in a while, she was going to have to put her own needs first.

She knocked on Edison's door, and for just a moment, she wondered if she was doing the right thing. Maybe he was better off without her. Maybe he could make a life away from her and her ghosts and her craziness. But then he opened the door and she realized she couldn't leave things the way they were. The look on his face, the hurt. She couldn't leave that hurt there.

"I can't believe I have to ask this, but did you send ghosts to find me?" he asked, frowning at her.

"Not technically. Margaret told me where you were staying. But the bellhop ghost in the parking lot did remember your coat," she replied.

"I've got to get rid of that thing," he sighed. "What can I do for you?"

"I'm here to offer you another one of our dramatic, big-gesture apologies. I shouldn't have said what I did. It was cruel and mean," she told him. "I'm sorry. I really am. You hurt me, but that doesn't mean it was OK for me to talk to you that way. I wish I'd never said those things or hurt you the way I did. All I seem to do is hurt you. Maybe you're better off somewhere else, away from me. You know what? Never mind, I'm just gonna slink back to my haunted house in shame."

"I'm not going to be better off without you. Nothing you said was wrong," he said, taking her arm before she could bolt. "I am afraid, not of life or going back out into the world, but every minute of every day, I'm afraid that I'm going to lose you. I'm so scared that your work is going to put you in danger. And I said those things because…I'm an idiot."

"The multiple PhDs would suggest otherwise, but OK," she told him.

"I said those things because I was trying to push you away,

to hold you at a distance—even if I didn't realize it." He pulled her close, shivering as the snow from her coat fell against his skin. "I lost Erin, and I survived it, just barely. I don't know if I could survive losing you too. So I let you go before it could happen."

"I don't know if I can promise you nothing bad is going to happen," Riley said, pressing her hand to his cheek. "I'm constantly surrounded by reminders of how short, harsh, and unpredictable life can be. I'm just as scared as you are, but I'm not alone. Not anymore. And neither are you. I just wish you could see that. There are people who love you, who want to be there for you."

"Are you included in those people?" he asked.

Eyes burning, she nodded and let him press his lips to hers. She'd never said these words to anybody and *known* that she meant it, that it was forever. It felt like extending some part of herself, a vulnerability that could be slapped away, hurt, used against her. But she did love him. Of all the people on the planet, he was one of a few she could see herself spending a lot of time with and not regretting it.

"I love you, Edison Held, you highly intelligent, annoying, sweet, infuriating, curious, opinionated, adorable man."

"I can't tell if that was a compliment or not."

She wrinkled her nose. "Mostly, it was."

"I love you too, Riley Denton-Everett. I would like to spend a lot more time with you, in your nightmare house."

Her eyes narrowed as she smiled. "You're just trying to get inside my doors, aren't you?"

He held up his fingers to measure a tiny space. "A little bit."

"So I don't want to hold you back professionally, so if you

feel the need to go to Boston for that job, I will support that. From a distance, because I'm magically bound to a house full of ghosts who need me."

"What are you talking about?" Edison scoffed.

"Kyle told Margaret you're flying to Boston for a job interview," Riley said. "She blamed me. Loudly. On the sidewalk with a box of your desk debris."

Edison laughed. "I'm going to a Midwest Librarians Association quarterly meeting. It's in Green Bay, not Boston. But I usually go to the winter session so I don't have to ride on a boat."

Riley laughed. "What?"

"I'm not leaving. I was trying to work up the nerve to apologize. There were going to be flowers involved. And probably Petoskey Stone ice cream."

Had Kyle really told Margaret about the job interview? Or had Margaret made the whole thing up as some sort of weird *Parent Trap* manipulation? She would have to yell at them or thank them later. She wasn't sure which.

"Let's go home."

Dutch rented a sort of sidecar sled for Edison to ride on the way home—as Edison had decided that the conference could wait. It was highly uncomfortable, but Dutch argued that he didn't know if Edison wanted to spend a whole hour with his arms thrown around Dutch's waist. Edison conceded.

"Thank you, Dutch," Edison said as they beached the snowmobile near the docks. He handed the older man a magenta helmet he'd borrowed from a fellow sledder at the bar. "That wasn't emasculating at all."

"You'll be all right, kid," Dutch told him. "Just do what she tells you."

"I'm not sure that's the best policy," Riley conceded. "Thanks, Dutch. You're a peach."

"Good night," Dutch called as they made their way up the hill towards Shaddow House. Something was off about the outline of the house against the falling snow. Riley couldn't put her finger on it. It wasn't just that Mimi the Destructodog was sitting outside the gate, staring up at the house.

"Mimi, go on home, you'll freeze!" Riley called. The dog just stared at her, like she was a doofus. Mimi was probably right.

Could Mimi see the ghosts? Was that why she frequently stared up at Shaddow House with a slightly befuddled and yet judgmental look on her canine face?

"You left an awful lot of lights on," Edison noted.

That was what was wrong with the house. The upstairs bedrooms, the parlor, the atrium, even the obscured cellar windows, were all lit up like she was throwing a holiday party. Riley never left that many lights on, even at night.

Noting the way Riley was frowning up at the house, Edison asked, "Did you leave them on?"

"No, but it could be..."

Riley tried to imagine which one of her friends would venture into the house unaccompanied. Alice wouldn't go into the house on her own. Caroline might, but she wouldn't go into the basement, given her whole "not dying in a horror movie scenario" policy. Also, Alice and Caroline were racing up from the direction of the Rose, waving and smiling, which definitely eliminated both of them from the list.

"You got him back!" Alice cried, beaming.

"I guess I have to pay my late fines after all," Caroline teased.

"You should really do that anyway," Edison said as Alice threw her arm around his shoulders.

"Any idea who could be in the house right now, if we're not in the house?" Riley asked.

"Could one of the ghosts have turned the lights on?" Edison asked.

"It could be possible, but they haven't done that in all the time I've been here," Riley said, frowning.

They approached the rear of the house slowly, peering through the windows. A figure in a black hoodie was crouched in the parlor, as if he was looking for something in the back of the fireplace. The figure was wearing latex gloves.

"Son of a bitch," Riley spat.

The figure froze and looked up. The four of them dived away from the window so they wouldn't be seen. After a few seconds, Riley slowly peeked back through the windowpane. The figure was still knocking on the floorboards. Riley looked past the office, near the parlor. On the floor, in front of the fireplace, were two of the Welling ghost locks, exact replicas of the copper object Riley found behind the *Moonstone* painting.

"Son of a *bitch*!" Riley whispered. "They've got *two* of the Welling locks on the floor. I only found one!"

"Well, we better get in there and grab them," Caroline said, rolling her neck to crack it.

"We could also call the police," Alice noted quietly.

"And tell them what?" Riley asked. "Please come into my haunted house to stop the bad man from stealing the magical objects from my floorboards, which I definitely can't let you take into evidence because they're concentrated evil?"

"A little rephrasing might be necessary," Edison conceded.

"What if we use the ghosts against him?" Alice asked.

"I haven't quite mastered the 'sic the ghosts on people like dogs spells'," Riley shot back.

"No, but you could maybe hand him something that could attract a ghost that could rough him up," Alice said, shrugging.

When Riley gave Alice a surprised look, Caroline shrugged. "You're the one who wanted her to be more confident."

Riley shook her head. "I have made a mistake."

Hoping to sneak into the house without being seen, the four of them crept around to the kitchen door. Riley only hoped that Hoodie Guy wouldn't look outside and see their tracks in the snow. Riley noted that one of the panels to the atrium was smashed, the opening big enough for most adults to just walk through. They tiptoed up the snowy steps, clinging to the railing for dear life. Edison made to follow them in.

"Where are you going?" Riley asked Edison.

"I can't do magic, but don't leave me out there to just watch you run into danger. I can't do that, Riley. I won't lose you."

She nodded, kissing him deeply.

Riley used her key to quietly pop the door open. Plover met

her at the kitchen door, and it was the closest Riley had ever seen him to panic.

"Miss, I've tried to stop him—"

"Shh," Riley pressed her finger to her lips.

Plover shook his head. "I've hidden myself from him. He cannot hear me. Given the way he's behaving, I believe he's searching for the Welling locks. He has repeatedly looked at a piece of paper in his pocket, but he seems to be...sensitive. He can't see me, but he can sense when I am near. He becomes agitated, shoves the paper in his pocket, and begins yelling for his mother. I can't look at it long enough to read it."

Removing her shoes and coat, Riley crossed to Natalie's whiteboard. She wrote, SORRY, NAT on the board. Somehow, the marker hardly made any noise as it glided across the surface of the board. She couldn't help but think Natalie had something to do with that. She wrote, P-HAVE YOU SEEN LIST?

Plover shook his head.

NEED ALL HELP WE CAN GET, Riley wrote. RECRUIT FRIENDLIES.

Plover nodded sharply and disappeared.

Riley walked into the pantry and grabbed a spare laundry bag. It was something Aunt Nora kept handy for kitchen linens. She handed the bag to Edison and mouthed the word, "Catch. Don't touch."

Edison frowned at her, confused. But Riley didn't have the time or the verbal capacity to explain what she was about to do. She turned to Caroline and Alice, reaching for their hands. She mouthed, "Ready?" They nodded.

Shoeless, they walked into the parlor. Hoodie Guy was shoulders-deep in the fireplace, loosening the ironwork seal at the back of the flue. In his search of the first floor, he'd knocked holes in the walls and ripped up floorboards.

Oh, no.

Aunt Nora's ashes. The ceramic urn the funeral home sent the ashes home in was shattered on the floor in the foyer. Her ashes were spread across the floor in a dirty gray smear.

An unanticipated rage spread up Riley's spine, making her face flame. This person had come into her house and hurt the people she cared about. Aunt Nora's remains had been tossed aside like garbage. She was supposed to protect this place and its inhabitants. Un-fucking-acceptable.

Riley concentrated on the two ghost locks, the cold hostile energy radiating off them. Drawing a deep breath that stretched to the bottom of her lungs, she pictured the locks flying across the room and landing safely in her hands. They skittered across the table. Riley reached for her sisters' hands and felt their joined magic surging through her. The locks flew off the table with a speed that scared Riley a little.

Her eyes tracked their progress across the room. She willed them to land in the laundry bag Edison was holding.

"Run, lock yourself in the pantry. Don't open it, no matter what you hear," she told Edison as the Hoodie Guy whirled towards them.

All the youthful sweetness was gone from Kyle's features. He looked...haunted in every sense of the word. Tired and worn, shadowed. "I don't want to hurt you, Riley. It's nothing personal. But I've worked really hard to get into your house, to get what they're asking."

"I don't know what you've been promised, Kyle," Riley said. "But this isn't worth it."

"If I find them, if I bring them to him—I just want to talk to my mom again. I just want to see her face," Kyle cried. He hadn't gotten up from his position in the fireplace. Despite the fact that he'd broken into her house and basically terrorized her, she felt sorry for him. He was a boy who missed his mother, and he was lost. She knew how that felt.

"The Wellings can make that happen! And they'll only do it if I get the locks to them. I don't want to hurt you, Riley, but I will. You gotta get out of my way."

Riley's brain wanted to latch on to the first real-life mention of the Wellings and fixate on it. The Wellings were real and they were here on the island, at least by proxy. She didn't know what would happen if Kyle found the locks and gave them to "him." But she knew it wasn't good. An army of ghost assassins at the disposal of a bunch of misanthropes? Not good.

Plover appeared in front of Kyle, his hands folded at the small of his back. Kyle yelped, stumbling back into the mantel.

"I have a message from the spirits of Shaddow House," Plover intoned rather grandly.

"Wh-wh-wh—" Kyle stuttered, skittering back on the floor, into the fireplace.

Plover looked fiercer than Riley had ever seen him as his face contorted at unnatural angles and shadows. His jaw seemed to dislocate as his mouth opened to bellow, "GET OOOOOOOUT."

Kyle screamed. Plover turned toward the women and bowed. Suddenly, Lilah the match girl appeared at Kyle's side. She reached up into her brass match cloche and waved her hand over the matches, setting them ablaze. She smiled and tilted the box, dumping the flaming contents onto Kyle's head.

"Oh, shit," Caroline said, blinking at Kyle as he rolled around in the carpet, shucking his hoodie and throwing it into the fireplace. It blazed merrily there, on a stack of logs Riley had planned on using later.

Kyle pushed to his feet, beating at the embers still floating from his hair. Lilah disappeared with an echoing giggle, waving at Alice. Behind them, through the opening dining room door, the silver service box Charles spent so much time weeping over sprung open, and two of the heaviest service pieces came careening across the hall, beating Kyle about the head.

"Villain! Rapscallion! Reprobate!" Charles bellowed as he smacked Kyle around with a gravy ladle and a soupspoon so big it could be used to row a canoe. "To threaten my ladies with violence! Shame on you!"

"Charles realizes he has a box of knives, right?" Caroline asked.

"They're not very sharp," Alice replied, pursing her lips. "Even for butter knives."

Just then, the largest of the pie servers came hurtling out of the box and sank into the toe of Kyle's left shoe. Alice nodded. "That will do it."

"Enough!" Kyle roared, yanking the pie server out of his shoe. Riley had to imagine it had missed his toes, giving his lack of pained shrieking. Well, Charles was new to this. "I know where they are. If you stay out of my way, I can just take them and leave. But if you don't, I'm going to hurt you."

The sweet dorky guy who wanted to talk about *Stranger Things* was gone and replaced by an angry, desperate soul who was pulling a very large knife from his pants pocket.

"You don't really want to do that," Alice said, shaking her head. "You're a good person."

"No, I'm *not*," Kyle seethed, his voice shaking. "You don't think I would break that pantry door down and slit Edison's throat to get those locks back? To get to my own mother? Because I would, without even thinking about it, and he's my *best friend.* You, I don't even know."

Riley instinctively moved between Kyle and the door leading to the kitchen. Alice and Caroline moved with her, like a formation. "Look, the Wellings don't help people. It's easy to want to believe that. Hell, they fooled my ancestors with that story too. But they want to use what's in this house to hurt people. I can't let you do that."

"I'm not going to let you stop me, not when I'm *this close!*" Kyle yelled. He swiped the knife out towards them, the tip of it nearly catching Alice's shoulder. Caroline yanked her back just in time. Riley picked up a bronze figurine from the nearby coffee table and swung it up, catching the side of Kyle's head. He collapsed to the floor, dazed, the knife still in hand.

"What do we do with him now?" Caroline asked. "We can call Celia. We can just say that he broke in. We don't have to say anything about the ghost stuff."

Riley attempted to kick the knife out of Kyle's hands, but even half-concussed, Kyle was still swiping the blade at her ankles. Out of the corner of her eye, she saw another ghost, the dark slithering spirit that scared Riley the most, come creeping along the ceiling.

"What is that?" Alice whispered.

"We're fine," Riley told it, still dodging ankle-high swipes from Kyle. "We don't need any more help."

But the oily shape ignored her, the light from the fireplace reflecting in its eerie, shapeless form. It oozed toward the chandelier, wrapping itself around the fixture. Riley could hear squeaking as the screws silently untwisted themselves from the ceiling.

"What's it doing?" Caroline asked.

"Kyle, move. You've got to get up." Riley said. "I think we need to get out of here."

"What?" Kyle pushed to his feet, swaying. "I'll kill you. I'll do it."

Kyle stumbled directly under the chandelier, glaring at them. The chandelier started to sway, as if it could drop at any moment. It seemed much more sinister now. Riley held up her hands, trying to move it away from Kyle, away from them. But nothing she did had any effect, not even when Alice and Caroline supported her. The chandelier simply wouldn't respond to her magic. Nothing about the ceiling ghost obeyed the rules she'd learned.

"Kyle!" Riley yelled. But the chandelier dropped from the ceiling like a rotten tooth. The weight dropped on his head fully, sending him collapsing to the floor. He'd been hit so many times over the head that night, but the chandelier seemed like the final straw. His eyes were unfocused as he stared at the ceiling, watching the ceiling ghost creep back into the wall.

Alice and Riley moved the fixture off him. Caroline ran to get Edison, beating on the pantry door. Kyle was fumbling for something in his jean pocket as a halo of blood spread under him on the floor.

"Kyle!" Edison yelled. "Call Doctor Toller!"

Caroline was already on the phone.

"I'm sorry," Kyle whispered, holding up a folded piece of paper. "I just wanted to see my mom."

With his last bit of strength, Kyle threw the paper into the fire. In the chaos, Riley had forgotten that he had a possible list of lock locations in his pocket. It seemed unimportant now. Kyle's hand fell limp to the floor.

"I guess that was the list you were talking about," Riley told Plover, chin-pointing to the fire. Plover nodded.

They watched a misty gray vapor rise from Kyle's body, swaying toward a silver cigarette lighter that had fallen out of his hoodie pocket.

"We can't have him in the house, finding ways to let the Wellings in," Riley said. "Alice, your magic is best at banishing."

"If we don't let him stay, he might never find peace," Alice said, frowning.

"If he stays here, he could hurt a lot of people," Riley said gently. "Like us."

Nodding, Alice lifted her hands, making the "depart" gesture. Taking deep breaths, Caroline and Riley joined her. The gray haze shifted dramatically away from the lighter, moving towards the door like it had an agenda. They followed the haze outside and opened the necessary portal for Kyle to move on. It took all of Alice's strength to push him through, even with Riley and Caroline's support. When the gray mist disappeared from sight, Riley relaxed against Edison, who looked crushed on multiple levels.

"I'm sorry," she whispered, hugging him tightly.

"I hope he finds his mother on the other side," Alice sighed.

"You're too soft," Caroline told her, putting her arm around Alice's shoulders. "But I hope you never change."

Fortunately, the ghosts knew to make themselves scarce with new people in the house—those people being police officers. Riley supposed she had Plover to thank for that. Her ability to lie smoothly to people she liked was becoming a little disturbing to her. Edison stood at her side, his arm around her, silent as she spun a story about coming home with her friends to find Kyle ransacking her parlor.

"Any idea why Kyle would break in?" Trooper Celia Tyree asked. She'd allowed them to cover Kyle's body with a sheet. Riley was very intentionally not looking at him, or else her carefully composed emotion would fall into total upheaval.

"He said something about selling some of the antiques," Riley said. "I think he was having money problems."

Celia shook her head. "It's just so unlike Kyle."

"I never thought he would do something like this," Edison said hoarsely, squeezing Riley to his side.

The truth of that made her throat burn. Kyle had been a sweet kid, who did a wrong thing because he wanted to see his mother. This new life of hers was complicated and messy and dangerous. And she didn't know whether she could survive it without the people beside her—both living and dead. She pocketed the silver lighter, with every intention of dropping it in the lake when it thawed. Just in case.

Celia glanced at the ceiling, where a dark, dusty stain showed the fixture's former site. "And the chandelier just fell from the ceiling?"

"I've been meaning to get it fixed," Riley said, forcing her face to remain still, impassive. They'd debated setting up some sort of bizarre story, making it look like Kyle had been standing on a step ladder, attempting to unscrew the chandelier from the ceiling. But Alice said that forensically, there was no way that would stand up to inquiry. It was better just to tell a *version* of what happened instead of being caught in lie after lie. What was Celia going to do? Accuse them of using a light fixture as a murder weapon?

"A freak occurrence," Alice said, dabbing at her eyes with a handkerchief. She'd been precariously balanced on the edge of tears since forcing Kyle's spirit haze from the house.

"Weirdest thing I've ever seen," Caroline agreed.

"Edison, you saw this happen?" Celia asked.

Edison nodded.

"All right then, I'm just glad none of you were hurt."

It took hours for Dr. Toller to arrive, declare Kyle officially dead, and take his body to the island's lone funeral home. Edison finally broke down and cried when he realized there was no family to claim Kyle's body or make funeral arrangements.

"I think I'm going to have to do it," Edison told Riley. "I know that probably hurts you, after what he did, but I just can't leave him alone like that."

"He was your friend for a lot longer than he was a villain," Riley told him. "I understand."

He wrapped his arms around her and held her tight against him. "I'm sorry he used me to hurt you."

When Celia and Dr. Toller were gone, Caroline and Riley fetched tools from the basement and pried the iron seal from the back of the fireplace. In a hollowed space the size of a car battery, they found another ghost lock. Riley didn't know where the other two had come from. The remains from Kyle's list were still smoldering in the ash can.

Edison was keeping busy in the kitchen, making tea and sandwiches with Plover's supervision. He needed time alone to process, and Riley understood that. He'd lost a friend, the first significant friend he'd had since Erin's death. She honestly believed that Kyle didn't mean to hurt them. He was just desperate. She didn't want this to cause problems between them.

"So now, we have four," Caroline said, staring down at the assembled locks on the coffee table. "That's progress from the one you found behind the wall."

"It's sort of embarrassing that he was able to find two in one night when I've spent months looking for one more," Riley grumbled.

"He did have a list written by the people who hid them," Caroline reminded her. "Also, what was that thing on the ceiling?"

"It made my head hurt," Alice shuddered, as she stared down at an ashy smudge on her hand. "I don't know if I want to see it again."

Riley shrugged. "It just shows up sometimes. Even Plover

doesn't know who it is. We don't know what he's attached to—thanks, fake Codex—but I don't think it's the chandelier. Which means the rules don't apply to him. And that is scary."

"What use are the rules if the ghosts don't even pay attention?" Caroline grumbled into her mug of tea.

Riley turned to Alice, who was still staring at the tiny gray scrap in her palm. "You OK? It looks like you're trying to divine the future from Post-it leavings."

"I found it in the fireplace," Alice said, carefully dropping the silver of paper on the table. Caroline and Riley leaned close to examine the strange arched gold line with hashmarks against the lineless white paper. Something about it was very familiar. Riley had seen it before, but she just couldn't place it.

"What could that be?" Alice asked. "Is it a flower?"

"A lion's claw?" Caroline guessed.

"Wait." Riley jumped up from the floor and ran to her office. She rifled through her aunt Nora's files until she found the estate-planning folder. She jogged back to the parlor and showed them the letter she'd retrieved. She pointed to the watermark above the firm's address.

"It's not a claw," she said. "It's the curve of a griffin's beak."

"That's letterhead from Clark's law office," Alice said. "Why would Kyle have letterhead from Clark's office in his pocket?"

"What if Clark is the one that hired him to break into the house?" Riley said. "My aunt Nora was so zealous about not letting him in the house. Maybe she had some idea that he could be the heir to the Welling family?"

"That's not possible," Alice said absently.

"Why not?" Riley asked.

"I know his parents; they're both from Nevada. They've never lived on the island," Alice said, frowning. "They seemed nice."

"So maybe he works for the family, but he's not part of it?" Caroline suggested.

Riley chewed her lip, thinking of all the signs she'd followed to reach this point. Aunt Nora had left clues for her everywhere—the wooden box that led her to Alice, the book that led Caroline to Riley's front door, the marble bit that led her to the truth about the fake Codex. A marble bit that completed a *griffin* statue, holding false hope but also essential training. Riley wondered if somehow, deep down, her aunt hadn't trusted Clark and was trying to point Riley to a physical representation of her lawyer. Or maybe Aunt Nora only had one statue with a trapdoor in its butt, and it was a total coincidence.

"Maybe she was trying to keep an eye on Clark while holding him at a distance?" Caroline said.

"Are you sure you're not just reading too much into this?" Alice asked.

"Absolutely not. So what do I do? Just pretend I don't know anything until Clark rips off his mask Scooby Doo villain—style and confesses?" Riley said, flopping into one of the chairs by the fireplace. "This is bad."

"There are bright spots," Alice insisted from her own chair.

Over Caroline's shoulder, Riley spotted Plover picking something up from the mess of foyer debris on the floor. Her jaw dropped and she rose quickly and silently, motioning for the girls to follow her.

"*That's* your attachment object?" she gasped. "The mail tray?"

"See? Bright spots!" Alice cried.

Plover's eyes grew wide as he whipped the silver tray behind his back.

"We can still see it," Caroline noted. "Because you're, you know, mostly transparent."

"Come to think of it, you did bring up the mail tray on my first day here, so I'm a little disappointed in myself for not picking up on it," Riley noted.

"It meant much to me during my living days," Plover said, gently setting the tray on the entry table. "I was the first line of, well, everything in the household. Every communication, good news and bad, every calling card, every visitor was announced through that tray. It gave me significance. I couldn't just *let go* of it, even in death."

"You were significant without it," Riley told him. "But I promise not to stuff it in the trash compactor. I want you sticking around for a long while."

Plover smiled at her. "That's good of you, Miss. I am pleased to...stick around."

"But the rest of you?" Caroline yelled. "The trash compactor rule still applies to any sort of toy that speaks a creepy nursery rhyme without its string being pulled!"

"And any music boxes that play off-key plinky-plunky music too slowly!" Alice called, giggling.

"This is not a laughing matter," Riley told them very solemnly, even as the corners of her mouth twitched. "I told you the trash compactor rules in confidence. I trusted you."

Plover cleared his throat before yelling out, "Any object that independently rolls down the hallway toward the mistress's bedroom door? Trash compactor!"

"Yes!" Riley's crowed as she raised her arms, making the others cheer.

"I'm only joking, Miss, I could never in good conscience destroy another ghost's cherished object."

"I know, but it was totally worth it," she assured him.

"The creepy bronze stork statue in the library?" Alice called. "Trash compactor."

"I don't think we can just call out the objects we don't like," Caroline told her.

"I know but it's terrifying," Alice grumbled back.

"It's just goofy. It's playing a saxophone," Caroline countered.

"Exactly. How can a stork play a saxophone? It doesn't even have lips!" Alice cried. "It's unnatural! And why would someone want to preserve that moment in bronze? Even more importantly, what sort of ghost would be attached to something like that?"

"She makes several valid points," Plover said.

"You're supposed to be the voice of reason here, Mr. Good Conscience," Riley laughed.

"I have lived with that hideous statue for decades," Plover said. "I don't deserve your judgement."

Caroline cackled. "Oh, this is going to be so much fun."

Chapter 16
Riley

RILEY SHUFFLED INTO THE KITCHEN in the winter morning gloom. She'd dreamed of her mother, sitting on the beach, eating Petoskey Stone ice cream and talking about the weather. It was such a normal, boring dream, and yet Riley was so sad to have woken up from it. She wondered if it was some sort of message from her mother, from the beyond, or if it was just her subconscious trying to throw her a psychological bone. She hadn't had enough coffee to think that one through.

Kyle's death had led more islanders to talk to Riley, but it wasn't always a positive thing. Some locals came to her to tell them how sorry they were that she'd gone through something so awful. Others assured her that Kyle had always made *them* uncomfortable and they'd been waiting for him to do something like this for years. The rest of the island just ignored her, as if she'd gone out of her way to hurt Kyle, and she supposed that was what she preferred. The idea that Kyle was developing some sort of postmortem reputation for creepiness made her really sad. Sometimes she thought she saw Kyle's thin tall shadow outside the gate, unable to make it past the magical property boundary.

She still hadn't decided what to do about Clark. It was possible she was misconstruing the watermark on the paper from Kyle's pocket. She could be reading into it because she'd never quite trusted Clark. But for now, she agreed with the others that it wouldn't do to confront him over a paper scrap. It was better to watch and wait and keep Clark far away from all of them.

As she stood at the kitchen counter pouring the coffee grounds, she paused and turned.

There was a lady ghost standing in her kitchen, wearing what could only be referred to as smart-casual attire: a flawlessly tailored white blouse, gray slacks, and a blue cardigan that matched her adorable office-appropriate flats. Her dark hair was piled on top of her head. She was wearing large dark-framed glasses, which only emphasized how large her blue eyes were. She was standing far too close to Natalie's whiteboard—which was covered in tight, neat notes.

"Excuse me, please don't touch that. That would really upset Natalie."

Because it was so early and Riley was so deeply un-caffeinated, somehow she thought some other ghost had managed to write on Natalie's board. And Riley was offended on her deceased friend's behalf. The well-dressed ghost looked pretty amused at Riley's irritation.

"Aw, thanks, Riley," she said, tilting her head and grinning. "Plover and I were just making some notes for Edison's move."

Riley blinked rapidly, her brain barely processing the fact that the "new girl" was holding the dry-erase marker. "Natalie?"

Plover bustled into the kitchen, sighing, "I only hope Mr. Held realizes I will not spend my time answering every question that pops into his head. I am not a research subject. I have my duties to attend to—oh, good morning, Miss."

"Morning. This is Natalie. And her face!" Riley exclaimed. "She's letting me see her face!"

"I just thought it was time to let my guard down," Natalie said, shrugging. "You and Caroline and Alice have proven we can trust you. So why not?"

"Aw, honey, I wish I could hug you, but you know, you're incorporeal." Riley said. "Thank you."

And suddenly, Riley processed what Natalie was writing on the whiteboard. There were lists labeled TO DO AND HOUSE RULES. She and Plover had come up with a meal prep schedule and areas of the house that Edison should avoid for his own safety. They'd even figured out how Edison and Riley set up bank accounts to split their expenses.

"OK, I appreciate that you're being thorough, but the bank thing feels like an overstep," Riley said, gesturing at the board. "When did we decide that Edison was moving in? I thought that was against the rules or something."

"Well, Natalie informs me that social norms are changing, and this is an entirely acceptable and practical next step in your relationship. Besides, the restrictions regarding partners moving into the house was meant to protect the secrecy of the Dentons' work, with which Mr. Held is already acquainted."

"Well, that makes sense," Riley conceded. "But I've never been remotely close to asking someone to move in with me, much less 'Hey, want to move in with me in my haunted mansion?' How am I supposed to even start that conversation?"

Behind her, Riley heard Edison's bare feet on the hardwood. She turned to find him a rumpled, adorable mess, squinting through his glasses at the whiteboard. His head tilted as his lightning-quick reading comprehension processed it.

"Am I moving in?" he asked, noting the part of the board where Natalie had printed COMPLETION DATE. He blinked. "Am I moving in on *Friday*?"

"See? The board saved you from the awkward conversation!" Natalie said cheekily.

"Could you two give us a minute?" Riley asked. The two of them faded from sight, though Riley was fairly certain that they were still hovering nearby listening.

"If you're freaked out, we can just table this for another time," Riley assured him. "I know this seems really fast."

Edison shrugged, shaking his head. "No, actually, this makes sense. I mean, we've been through the really scary stuff already. Living together shouldn't be a big deal."

"You say that because we've never shared a bathroom sink," she told him. "And I don't think you've considered all the precautions we'll need to take to have you live with all the ghosts here."

He chuckled, crossing the room to kiss her soundly. "I'll call Caroline. I'm sure she has plenty of boxes from the bar, which she'll share if I agree to let her into the special collections unsupervised. And maybe Alice would like to rent my place. I'm sure she'd like some space from the shop."

She melted against him, nuzzling her head under his chin. It was so lovely, being with someone who thought of her friends, who wanted to do nice things for them. Even if the box thing was a little self-serving. Hell, it was nice just to have friends to call and share this news with them...and to ask for help with the move.

Suddenly, she pulled away from him.

"Oh *no*, how do you help someone move when we're not allowed to drive near my house?"

Alice had the answers. Because Alice always had the answers. Between her knowledge, Natalie's logistical skills, and Caroline's connections, they had Edison's stuff packed in banker's boxes and stacked in seventeen wheelbarrows and Mitt Sherzinger's two-person bike-cart by the arbitrary deadline. A few kids mistook it for some sort of parade as the wheelbarrow train marched up the hill to Shaddow House. Riley supposed that made Caroline the unofficial grand marshal.

"How did Caroline know that many people with wheelbarrows?" Riley asked the train approached.

"Caroline knows everybody," Alice told her. "And when she asked the bar crowd for help, she offered everybody who volunteered twenty dollars off their bar tab."

Riley snorted. "There it is."

Tab concerns aside, Riley was oddly touched that this many people were willing to help her move Edison into the house. And because this struck her as a grand gesture, which Riley had been assured wasn't to be expected for a newbie, she wasn't sure if it was a gesture meant remotely for her, or if it was directed at Caroline and Alice, or even Edison. It didn't matter really. As a group, they'd needed help, and the people of Starfall had come through.

To prevent the locals from entering the house, the self-proclaimed "Friends of Ghosts" club created a sort of bucket brigade, running the boxes from the wheelbarrows to the door. To prevent hurt feelings, they explained their reluctance to let others through the door by claiming it saved the other "movers" from the stairs. Tired from the march up the hill, none of them argued.

"So basically, you're bringing nothing but books and impeccably pressed dress pants," Riley said as she hefted the banker's box marked GOTHIC ROMANTICISM.

"Well, I didn't need to bring furniture with me, because you have all the furniture," Edison said.

"And that means I don't have to move any furniture," Alice said, grinning as she passed with a box marked BLUE DRESS SHIRTS. "Or really, tell my grandparents that I'm moving out."

"Still don't think that's a good plan," Caroline told her.

"Yes, but your idea of a good plan involves me walking away in slo-mo with my hair blowing in the breeze created by an explosion," Alice reminded her.

"It doesn't *have* to be in slo-mo," Caroline said, shrugging. "But the explosion is a requirement."

"How have you not been charged with a crime?" Alice asked as Caroline retrieved a box from Mitt's cart.

It took far more time to unpack the boxes than it did to move them in. But with Edison's work clothes safely tucked away in the gentlemen's closet, they wandered hand in hand to the parlor, exhausted but content. Unfortunately, Riley forgot that Caroline and Alice were still in the house, so when they were greeted in the darkened parlor by a shower of confetti and the pop of a champagne cork, Riley shrieked and sent a volley of three small china bulldogs flying from the coffee table toward the source of the noise.

"No!" Plover cried. "Those are Spode!"

Realizing that they were not, in fact, under attack, Riley stopped the bulldogs midflight with her magic. The Belgian housewife who had treasured those bulldogs since before World War I gave Riley a harsh glare. Rolling her eyes, Caroline plucked them from midair and set them on the table.

"Still really cool that you can do that," Edison marveled.

"So, clearly, this was not a *good* surprise," Natalie said, biting her lip.

"Why would you surprise me after the last couple of months?"

"Yeah, that was a miscalculation," Caroline admitted.

"It's just that you survived your first year on the island," Alice said, cringing. "We wanted to celebrate. Plover thought it was a good idea, too."

"Before you started magically flinging the *objets d'art* around the room," Plover said.

"My first-year mark is still a few months away," Riley told them.

"Time moves differently here on the island," Caroline insisted, pouring Riley a flute of a very nice champagne. "And we need to celebrate the wins where we can."

"You're right," Riley said, as her friends and Edison circled around her. Those with corporeal hands lifted their glasses to clink them together.

"I know that saying this will probably come back to bite us later, but I'm proud of us," Caroline said. "Our record isn't perfect. We haven't found any more of the locks, but we also didn't *lose* any of the locks. We held our ground here."

"We're making progress," Alice added, after a healthy sip of her bubbly. "And I think with something like this, progress is all you can hope for."

"Well, here's to progress," Riley giggled, drinking.

Plover smiled patiently at her. "Yes, with the help of your compatriots, soon you'll have the strength to deal with the other storage areas."

Riley froze, her glass suspended in midair. "Other storage areas?"

"You were saying, about coming back to bite us?" Alice said, her tone *sotte voce* and desert dry.

"OK, but that was much quicker than I expected," Caroline said, pursing her lips.

Plover nodded. "Of course, you don't think this home could comfortably fit hundreds of years' worth of acquisitions sent from all over the world, did you?"

Riley frowned. "I *sort of* did."

"When you're ready, that coin will grant you access," Plover said, nodding to the chain around Riley's neck. "There are many additional levels to this house in the basement, but that's a conversation for another time."

"Well, dammit," Riley sighed, downing the rest of her champagne.

Epilogue
Clark

CLARK SAT AT HIS OFFICE, staring at the notepad where he'd scribbled the instructions for Kyle. He thought he'd been careful, writing the note so none of his handwriting touched the firm's logo, but looking at the pad, he saw that the tiniest bit of the griffin's beak had been torn away. If Riley or her little friends looked close enough, she might recognize it. Stupid of him, to leave such an obvious clue. He was just so used to working from his office, playing both sides of the coin. He just didn't think—well, this sort of thing was bound to happen. He could always say that Kyle had visited his office for something related to his mother's estate.

Riley was proving to be more of a challenge than he'd anticipated. She was supposed to stay in the house long enough to give him access, maybe provide him a few hours of physical distraction while allowing his client to get what they wanted.

He'd worked for the Welling family for so long, he couldn't remember when his mind wasn't completely occupied with Shaddow House, its contents, and how to get to them.

The burner phone in his desk drawer rang. Only two people had that number, and one of them was dead. He took a deep breath, steeling his nerves for what was certain to be a very unpleasant conversation.

"I know recent developments have been disappointing," he said, not bothering to wait for the greeting that wouldn't come. "But we're closer than we've ever been before."

"I don't want to hear your excuses," the voice rasped on the other end of the line. "I want to hear how you're going to *fix this.*"

Looking for more swoony romance and witchy shenanigans? Read on for a sneak peek at Caroline's story in

Big Witch Energy

Caroline

TRUDGING HOME THROUGH SNOW FROM her first felony, covered in a crust of fake blueberry pie filling was not the way that Caroline Wilton planned on spending her one night off. But life as one of Starfall Point's resident witch-slash-ghost-wranglers had a way of happening even when Caroline planned just to sit at home and read her freaking mystery stories.

Her crime spree had started off innocently enough. Early Friday, Caroline had been inhaling her usual absurdly large post-double-shift coffee at Starfall Grounds, when she heard Willard Tremont complaining that he'd been having pest problems at Tremont's Treasures. While not quite as grand as some of the other shops on the island, Willard's shop catered to tourists' thirst to take a little piece of the island's ambience home with them.

"I'm telling you. I've been open for thirty years and I've never had problems like this," Willard grumbled to Petra Gillinsky, the coffee shop's owner and operator. Starfall Grounds—just across the street from Tremont's—was a shiny modern spot in the middle of a row of Main Square shops, all bright copper and deep blue calm. A display case running the length of the store featured sumptuous cakes, cookies and other delicacies, all of them baked by Petra and her twin brother, Iggy.

"I keep hearing weird noises, like something scratching all along the floorboards," Willard continued. "I never can figure out where it's coming from, and it's all hours of the day, doesn't matter whether I've got someone in the shop or not. Sometimes, I swear, it sounds like whispers."

Caroline damn near choked at that. Faint whispers from all corners of a room? Scratching noises? From her experiences at Shaddow House, the island's haunted epicenter, Caroline knew those were classics sign of ghost activity.

"Sorry," Caroline said hoarsely, pounding on her chest, as Willard and Petra turned towards her. "Went down the wrong way. Good cinnamon roll, Petra."

Willard gave Caroline a confused look but continued, "It's gotta be mice or rats or something, but I'm not finding chew marks on any of the furniture. And I'm not finding droppings."

"Yes, please mention rats and droppings a little louder while leaning against my bakery counter, Willard," Petra deadpanned, waving airily at the empty coffee shop. "You're lucky it's a slow morning, or you'd lose your rugalach privileges."

"Sorry, Petra," Willard said, flushing red under his more-salt-than-pepper hair. Willard was approaching seventy and a creature of habit. Petra's cherry rugalach was a major component of his morning routine. "I've gone all distracted with this thing. I could lose customers if I don't get rid of...whatever this is before the summer season starts up."

"I told you not to buy that stuff from Sally Fairlight's niece-in-law," Petra snorted, shaking her head. "Lindsay was way too excited about clearing all of Sally's stuff out of her new 'summer home.' She didn't even wait a week before 'de-Sallying' the place. There's gotta be some bad karma that comes with that."

"It was just a few things," Willard huffed. "But Sally *was* awfully house-proud. Maybe I should have just turned her away, let Lindsay have a yard sale."

"Eh, Sally would have hated that," Petra conceded, topping off Willard's tall black coffee. "Strangers picking through her stuff and haggling down to the nickel."

"I only bought the lot because I thought her collection of old cake stands was perfect for the store," Willard sighed. "My own ma had one of them when I was a kid. Pressed glass. A wedding present from her family back in Raleigh. I even put some of those pie-shaped air freshener things from Nell Heslop's candle shop in them, like a demo? They smell like real blueberry. I thought it would give the customer an idea of what they could do with it."

Willard just looked so upset, so bewildered, that Caroline decided then and there that she and her coven would do what they could to get whatever was troubling Tremont's—even if it was just rats. But Caroline was pretty sure it wasn't rats. Also, the fake blueberry air freshener pies at Starfall Wicks were disgusting—small, thin wax pie-shaped molds filled with a loose, gelatinous air freshener goo that jiggled inside the shell when tilted back and forth.

And they smelled like Barbie's rejected Dream Home air freshener, so really, the coven would be doing Willard two favors.

Caroline wasn't sure exactly when they started thinking of themselves a coven, but that's what they were—a group of witches working magic together, depending on each other. They were family, a word that was particularly vital to three people who'd had a hard time finding that.

Plus, it was a better word than "trio." Trio made them sound like a jazz band that played at corporate events.

Getting into Willard's closed shop had been easy enough. It was well-known to locals that Willard kept the key to the backdoor under a plaster frog. It wasn't exactly a secure vault.

"I don't feel right about this," Alice Seastairs had whispered in the midnight darkness, holding the flashlight as Caroline unlocked the door. As always, Alice was dressed appropriately for a spot of light breaking and entering—black sweater, black jeans, black ski cap pulled over her shock of penny-bright copper hair. "Breaking and entering Mr. Tremont's shop. He's always been so kind to me, even if we are competitors."

"We're not breaking... We're just entering." Riley Denton-Everett had selected a "plausible deniability outfit" of jeans, snow boots and a periwinkle hoodie that made her gray eyes appear bluer. Her plan was, if they were caught, just to pretend she was taking a nighttime walk in northern Michigan's early spring snow.

Caroline supposed she and Alice would be running while Riley lied her ass off. She thought maybe Riley was depending on the general local curiosity about her—the newest local on the island—to carry her over the "potential criminal activity" conversational bumps. Riley was resourceful enough to make little annoyances like that work for her.

"It's not my fault that Willard's been hiding his shop key in the same place for twenty years," Caroline muttered. They all relaxed ever so slightly when the door popped open without a sound.

Tremont's was a homier alternative to Alice's shop, Superior Antiques, where her unfriendly grandparents reigned with an iron fist. Tremont's had the *smell* of a proper antique shop, all lemon furniture polish and dust and—Caroline guessed—long-forgotten dreams. Huge stained glass panels, harvested from old churches off-island, cast rainbow shafts of light from the front display windows. Old-school tricycles hung suspended from the ceiling by piano wire. Mismatched glass cabinets displayed silver candelabras, porcelain figurines, overblown costume jewelry, tin wind-up toys, anything and everything that might catch a shopper's attention if they could fight through the sensory overload long enough to focus on one item long enough.

Caroline didn't even want to think about how many items in this place were "attachment objects"—something that meant so much to the dead in life or its significance in the person's death, that their spirit stayed connected to that item. Riley lived in a house full of them, with more than a thousand ghostly roommates. Caroline didn't know *how* she did it.

"You know, I'm concerned that, from the outside, a bunch of flashlights bobbing around a darkened shop might attract unwanted attention," she said, glancing around at the charming chaos of the interior. "Somebody sees that through the window, it's a pretty wide hint that this place is being burgled."

"Actually, I was thinking we might use this as an opportunity to practice some of our more 'basic witch' skills, light a few of the candles in this place?" Riley grinned, gesturing to the displayed flammables. "If anybody sees candles glowing through the windows, they'll just think Willard is adding a little romantic ambience to the store."

Riley had seemed fixated on lighting candles with her mind, ever since she'd gained her magic. Caroline was a little concerned.

"Do we really have time for that?" Caroline asked. "Isn't time of the essence when you're committing a minor felony?"

"Is there such a thing as a minor felony?" Alice wondered aloud. "If it's a question of lighters, Riley, I think Willard keeps one under the register."

"Come on, I think it will be good for us, practicing a very basic magical skill under duress," Riley implored. "It's not like the more hostile ghosts give us 'try again' chances while we're working with them, and that's with skills that we're actually pretty good at."

"Does 'haven't gotten us seriously injured yet' qualify as 'pretty good?'" Alice asked.

"You are *grumpy* when you're asked to stay up past midnight," Riley marveled.

"I get up at five-thirty every morning to open the store," Alice countered.

Caroline frowned. "But you don't open until eleven."

"Yes, but my grandparents call the landline at six-thirty and if I'm not there, they pitch a fit that can be heard all the way from Boca Raton," Alice sighed. "It's easier just to get up early, even if it means keeping old lady hours."

"We have got to get you a new job, sweetie," Caroline told her.

"Maybe Willard is hiring," Alice snorted. "Meanwhile, we've spent more time talking about me than it probably would have taken to light the candles with magical means or otherwise."

"I already did one!" Riley said, doing a happy little dance as she gestured to the flickering flame of a nearby hurricane lamp. Her cap of dark blond Denton hair bounced around her elfin face as she enjoyed her moment of victory. Magic had come to them all late in life, and to Riley, every successful spell that did not result in loss of limb or eyebrow was a moment to be savored. "I did what Aunt Nora's books said, pictured the bright light of the candle, and I could feel it growing in my chest, like the flame started near my heart! And *boom*, fire! Well, not *boom*, fortunately, there was no *boom*, but still, I have made fire! With magic!"

"While we were talking? That's cheating!" Alice gasped, just a little too loudly.

"Could we not yell while committing the minor felony?" Caroline asked, glancing toward the front windows of the shop. It was supremely unhelpful that the stained glass kept her from being able to see people approaching from the outside. But she could *hear* something, scratching noises from the far corner of the room, near a particularly creepy display of ventriloquism dummies. It was like her brain couldn't quite catch up to the noise, but she suspected the horrors of unsecured puppets had something to do with that.

"Still not sure that's a thing," Riley said, still smirking. "And just think of how many candles we could light if we did it *together.*"

"We could burn down the entire shop, which is a *big* felony," Caroline noted.

"That's a good point," Riley admitted, chewing her lip. "But you still want to try it, don't you?"

"Well, yes, *clearly*, I do," Caroline shot back, laughing despite herself. She joined hands with Riley and Alice. The familiar sizzle of that unearthly force zipped up her arm, straight to her heart. It made it so much easier for Caroline to imagine the warm glow of a flame building inside of her, wanting to burn, wanting to *be*. They giggled together, nervous about trying one of the more practical areas of magic that seemed to elude them, for some reason. She closed her eyes and felt the warmth growing, just as Riley described. It spread to the air around them and when Caroline opened her eyes, the room was bathed in golden light from dozens of flames—in lanterns, in candles, even a little Marilyn Monroe-in-the-fluted-white-dress votive whose taste level Caroline found seriously lacking.

"Look at that!" Caroline laughed, clapping her hands over her mouth. Alice simply stared in wonder.

"You have to admit, that's pretty cool," Riley said, her gray eyes glowing in triumph.

Caroline heard it again, the scratching that wasn't quite scratching. It *did* sound like whispering, and not particularly happy whispering. It sounded irritable, like the mutterings of someone who didn't think they'd be heard.

"It is *very* cool and we don't appear to be in danger of committing arson, so let's get down to business, shall we?" Alice suggested brightly. She placed her hand on the nearest piece of furniture, a tall rough-hewn cabinet with long spindly legs.

The whispering got louder.

"OK, everybody else hears that, right?" Riley said quietly, glancing around the now well-lit room.

"It sounds like my grandmother after a couple of martinis," Alice said, tugging at her ear gently like she was trying to pop it.

"I'll have you know that I have never been drunk a day in my life!" a cranky voice rasped to their right.

Caroline should have known better. One of the weirder parts of Caroline's new magical gifts was being able to detect which objects were attached to a ghost. While several items in the antique shop gave her nerves a small ping, the half-dozen glass cake stands to her left were sending psychic shivers down her spine. As Willard had promised, each stand contained a wax replica blueberry pie air freshener. Caroline was very grateful the smell was contained under glass.

The cake stands weren't the prettiest thing in the shop, but they exuded a certain power. The stands had been significant to Sally Fairlight in life. Caroline could tell by the way Sally's hands rested right on top of the largest cake stand in the center of the counter...and the incredibly annoyed look Sally was giving Alice. Apparently, Alice's right pinky was just a little too close to the precious glass base.

"Don't touch that!" Sally's ghost yanked the glass stand back, away from Alice's hands. Sally had been a "forceful" woman in life. She certainly hadn't gotten *weaker* after death. The lid fell off its plinth in the struggle and rolled on its rounded side. A wave of synthetic fruit smell Caroline in the face, knocking her back a step.

Sally's translucent fingers wrapped around the round glass knob on top of the cake dome, pulling it back. The wax pie had fallen into the lid in the struggle. . Its weirdly fragile wax shell broke and the unnatural berry filling oozed out. The ghost peered down at the mess in her translucent hands. And then she grinned, a scary, grinch-ish grin, as if she'd just granted a gift and an idea all at once.

"Oh, no," Riley whispered.

A ghost could only physically interact with its own attachment object. And Sally had just figured out that she could use her cake stand lid to sling those horrendous-smelling blueberry bombs at the humans.

This was a problem.

"Mrs. Fairlight, you don't want to do that," Caroline said, holding her hands up and using her most soothing drunk-customer-voice as Sally swung the lid towards them, splattering the case behind them with fake fruit gel "You don't want to make a mess of Willard's nice clean shop."

"*She* called me a drunk," the old woman snarled, pointing a long, bony finger at Alice. And somehow, she was managing to use *several* of the stand lids to throw blueberry bombs at them. She was only supposed to have one attachment object. How was that possible?

"No, I didn't," said Alice. "I was talking about my own grandmother. I didn't mean anything by it, Mrs. Fairlight, I promise."

"Also, just how many of these stands are you attached to?" Riley cried. "You are *not* following the ghost rules!"

"This *whole collection* is mine!" Sally roared back. "And I don't want it here at Willard's! No one asked me!"

Sometimes, Caroline forgot how fast Alice was on her feet. When Sally picked up a stand to throw another wax pie, Alice managed to dance out of the way, dodging, while Riley's feet were doused in cobalt goo.

"Oh, come on!" Riley cried as her feet squelched through the mess. "These are my *good* snowboots!"

"Young people used to have more respect," Sally huffed.

"Well, really, we're not all that young!" Alice replied in an attempt to placate Sally, who was having none of it. How many of those air freshener things had Willard loaded into the cake stands, anyway?

Alice danced, left to right, as another wax pie vaulted off a stand and splattered against Caroline's stomach, covering her entire torso in cerulean glaze. All three of the living women froze.

"Aw, honey," Riley tsked, her tone sympathetic. "And that was your favorite early spring coat."

"Oh, Caroline, I'm so sorry!" Alice gasped as one more pie launched off a nearby stand and smacked Alice in the chest.

"All right, that is *enough*!" Alice hissed. "Ma'am, you will stop throwing these vile pie things at us *right now* and listen to what we have to say."

"So much for the whole, 'trying to stay quiet during the commission of a minor felony' thing," Caroline muttered.

"Still not a thing!" Alice cried, pointing at Caroline without looking at her, making Caroline snicker. Riley couldn't help but follow suit. And soon, as she always did, Alice was laughing, too, but she managed to hide it by biting her lips.

"Fine," Sally harrumphed. "I'm all out of pies anyway."

Caroline pursed her lips. "That's a shame."

Acknowledgments

I'm new to Michigan. There are a lot of nods to my new home state in this book, and I hope my new neighbors see it as the loving tribute it's intended to be. I would very much like to thank Terry and Andrea Nerbonne for their patience and help, explaining small-town island life to me. Thank you to the friendly, *patient* employees of various restaurants, state parks, historical locations, tourist spots, and bookstores throughout the state for answering my endless questions with grace and panache. Thank you, as always, to my weird, wonderful friends and family, who listened to endless ideas for Riley's jobs and potential haunted objects. Thank you to my wonder of an agent, Natanya Wheeler of Nancy Yost Literary Agency—without you, none of this would be possible. To Rose Hilliard, who writes the world's most life-affirming editorial notes, my eternal gratitude. And to Jocelyn Travis, thank you for your warm welcome to the Sourcebooks family!

About the Author

A lifelong romance reader, Molly Harper is the author of more than forty paranormal romance, contemporary romance, women's fiction, and young adult titles. She graduated with a Master of Fine Arts degree from Seton Hill University, focusing on writing popular fiction. She lived in Kentucky for most of her life before recently moving to Michigan with her family...and she's still figuring out how to choose outerwear and play complicated winter card games. For more information, go to mollyharper.com.